Detective Bench
The Miami Beach Murders

Written by William A. Duck

Contents

Chapter 1

The start of it all

Robert was sitting in his car across the street from the dance club, watching the front door and the side of the building in case his target came out either way. It was a big club with at least 700 people inside, with a long line still trying to get in. Robert Bench was a homicide detective with a gold shield he proudly wore and earned faster than anybody in the history of the Miami-Dade Police Department. He was single and had no wife or kids, and this allowed him to focus on his career through deeds, not politicking like others did.

Robert was 32 years old and had been in the department for over eight years. He joined the department after he got out of the Navy, where he served six years in the navy seals and earned a degree in criminal psychology when he was not doing missions or training. Robert was proud of getting his degree while still serving in the military.

When he got out, he applied, went through the process, and was selected for the Miami-Dade police department. He ended up placing second in his class by scoring a half point lesser than the top spot. He knew he could have been first if he had just studied a little harder in the area of regulation.

At least he was first in all the physical areas. Robert even put to sleep the self-defense instructor who challenged him on the mat when he found out he was a Navy Seal. It backfired on the self-defense instructor, and what happened went around the Academy and the Police Department in a blink of an eye.

While he remembered the past, he saw a white male about 6 feet and 170 pounds bribe the bouncer and enter the club. Robert smiled and said Bingo to himself about his target. He always called the criminals he was hunting for 'targets.' He received information from a reliable snitch who told him the person he was looking for goes there to sell his dope on the weekends.

Robert jumped out of his vehicle, dodged a few cars, and went up to the door bouncer and flashed his badge on his belt. The bouncer recognized who he was because he had seen the same officer on television a few times. The bouncer pulled back the rope, so Robert could go inside. When there, Robert looked around and headed inside the club.

After he entered the club, the head bouncer approached Robert and asked him, "Is there anything they could do to help him out?"

Robert smiled and answered, "I appreciate it," then asked, "How many entrances are there?"

The head bouncer replied, "Front and back only."

Robert looked at his watch and said, "In five minutes, put two guys at the back door and two at the front door." The head bouncer looked around, and Robert took it as a cue to continue, "Then secure the front door, and nobody leaves until you hear from me. I don't want this guy to get away." Robert knew this criminal had too many warrants, and if he got away because of some mistake made by some stupid person, it screwed up his agenda. He said, "So let's do this right and catch him."

The head bouncer answered back, "I understand. I will put our beef at the door."

Robert laughed, thanked the bouncer and then told him, "I do not want any of your people approaching this guy, and if he runs and has no weapon, then stop him." Robert said in a serious tone of voice, "If he pulls one, tell your people not to be heroes and let him go, okay?"

The head bouncer shook his head, responding, "He will tell his people."

Robert entered the club, went up to the second level, and watched for his target to see how the club was set up, including the exit points. After a few minutes, he saw him on the dance floor with a blonde woman. Robert returned to the first level and looked at his watch to see how much time had gone by. When his watch hit five minutes, he observed the big bouncers block all the entrances. Robert then walked down the aisle and worked his way down to the dance floor and to his target.

He came up behind his target, pulled out a small stun gun he was carrying, and zapped him once. His target collapsed, and the woman his target was dancing with yelled, "What happened?"

Robert smiled and said, "He will be fine. He just had the shock of his life." The woman shrugged her shoulders and walked away, unhappy about how the guy passed out on the dance floor. She figured he must be a loser in not being able to handle his booze or drugs. She went back to the table where her friends were and told them about the guy she was dancing with just passed out on the dance floor.

The head bouncer approached Robert and asked, "Can we go back to normal?"

Robert answered back, "Sounds good," as he put cuffs on his target, threw him over his shoulder, and carried him out the front door with the bouncers leading the way and clearing a path through the crowd. Robert was a big cop and lifted and ran almost daily to stay in shape. He knew out-of-shape cops hindered themselves and society, and there were too many of those due to lowered standards and no accountability.

Once they got outside, he tossed the target on the ground, pulled out his cell phone, and called for a patrol car with two officers. The head bouncer asked Robert, "Is there anything else they can do?" And Robert grinned, looked at him, and stated, "No, we are good and thanks as they shook hands." The head bouncer then went back inside the club. Robert, while waiting for the patrol car, called his supervisor and told him he got him.

His target's name was Vincent Mason, a lifetime criminal with a mile-long rap sheet. Mostly drugs. He had been selling heroin tainted with fentanyl, killing seven people they were aware of. This thug went to college but never finished. Robert figured that's when he either started using or selling, and the money was just too good, so he quit college to push his dope and try and make money the easy way.

Vincent Mason originally fled the area and state for a couple of months but worked his way back to the area, and two more people died from the drugs he was selling. Robert was given the case two months ago and spent extra time on this case. When a reliable snitch told him about a new dealer fitting the description, he knew this person was his target. Robert studied this guy's jacket front and backward, looking for hints on where he might go or be. Robert checked off all the areas and came to three clubs. He bounced around from each one knowing sooner or later that Vincent Mason would show up, and it worked. Now he got his man after hunting this piece of garbage.

The patrol car drove up, and both officers got out. One asked, "Well, Bench looks like you got your man, and was he any trouble?"

Robert responded back, "No, he got the shock of his life and fully cooperated." Vincent started to come around, and the officers helped him up. They walked him over to the back of the patrol car and patted Mason down. They pulled a knife out of Mason's boot and 12 heroin sachets — all in his jacket pockets. The senior officer laughed and said, "*Merry fucking Christmas.*"

Robert told them, "Process that and send it to the labs and take this piece of garbage to the jail guys. I will follow you guys down." He walked up to the senior officer and told him, "No matter what, those cuffs do not come off." Both cops smiled and said, "Sounds good." Robert did not want this guy breaking free and running.

Robert Bench arrived 30 minutes later at the station to start his paperwork. A few homicide detectives were working on their shift, and they stood up and clapped as Robert walked to his desk. Robert bowed and said, "Thank you, thank you. I will be signing autographs after the show." There were a couple of derogatory statements and laughing in the office.

Jason Johnson came over and said, "Good job, Robert. Where did you catch him?" Roberts told him, "A Miami club." Jason asked, "Where is your partner?" Robert responded, "He retired and left town with his family."

Frank Jamison was his partner for a couple of years until he retired a couple of months ago. He was a good man but was burnt out and was gone more than he was at work. Frank used a lot of his sick leaves, which caused Robert to carry the load, but he did not mind because he preferred to work alone without arguing with a partner.

Robert sat down and started working on his report and writing it up so the D.A. could get a good prosecution. He was happy with himself after getting this thug off the street. He personally felt, and he knew, it was a waste of time because until the feds got hard on the illegal dope trade coming into the country, the only ones the drug war helped were the lawyers, big drug dealers, politicians, and prosecutors.

He hated it, but he could live with it since nobody in power gave a shit. His bosses sarcastically thought Robert had a bad attitude in this area, but when he challenged them, they admitted it felt like they were spinning their wheels with one scum bag replacing the one they just locked up. It never ended.

Around 2:15 AM, he finished his paperwork, left the station, and went to the Townhouse he owned. Once he arrived home, he threw his keys on the table, pulled out his wallet, and took his belt off and his holster with his 1911 Colt 45. He then crashed on his couch and tried to sleep. He was exhausted from working long hours to solve his cases. Robert knew time and effort were important in getting the bad guys off the street. He just wished there was more to getting criminals off the street than fighting crime and the stupid politicians who were weak on the criminals who preyed on the law bidding.

Chapter 2

The Family

Duston Jackson was the 23-year-old son of the wealthy investor Thomas J. Jackson who owned three sports teams in Miami and made his fortune in the high-tech industry and other investments. Thomas J. Jackson was suspected to be the wealthiest man in Florida. His influence in all areas of politics was well known. He did not care what side you were on as long as they did not threaten him or his family or business. If they did, he would destroy them with his money and media. Thomas J. Jackson had no issues using the private detective agencies he owned to collect dirt on every politician, no matter who they were. His family was the most important thing he had.

Thomas married his wife Catalina Garcia, a second-generation Cuban American after they graduated college in Tallahassee and had two kids. The oldest was the daughter Veronica who was 25 and single, and the youngest was Dustin, born two years later. Ana died of breast cancer when both were in their early teens, and it greatly affected them both, especially Dustin, who was very close to his mom. Her death affected him in many ways, and psychological aid never was able to help him in dealing with it.

Thomas J. Jackson dated some after her death but never married again. He proposed a couple of times, but the women refused to sign the prenups, so he broke off the relationship. One was even in the church, but she refused to sign, so he walked away. He told his friends when they asked why? Thomas asked why he should give these women half his money when he worked hard for it, not them. Nobody could blame him. Thomas knew his kids were not mad at him for walking away. He always felt they were not compatible with those women.

Dustin began to act out after his mom's death and was constantly getting in trouble. Thomas tried to get Dustin all the attention he could, but nothing worked. He tried getting his son therapy, but it was only a band-aid for a short period of time. In high school, Thomas had his son go to a military academy which seemed to work. The strict discipline seemed to work and keep his mind focused.

Dustin graduated at the top of his class, and his grades turned around and were near perfect. Thomas tried to talk Dustin into going into the military, but Dustin refused, and they finally agreed on going to Thomases Almada in Tallahassee. The first three years at college, Dustin did well. Then something happened, and he started skipping classes, dropped out, and went back home. When Dustin returned home, he was pale, skinny, and his hygiene was bad. Thomas knew immediately that his son was using hard drugs. He put his son in several clinics over the next few years, but they did not work. Thomas tried to get his son psychological help, but nothing worked.

Dustin's older sister Veronica tried to help her brother, and he would stop using for a while and act like his old self, then fall off again. Dustin loved his sister and tried to get the monkey off his back, but it would always come back. Veronica seemed to be the only one he would listen to sometimes.

Thomas would have bodyguards always assigned around Dustin, but Dustin would find a way and disappear for days. Thomas used his private investigators to follow his son. They discovered who the drug dealer was supplying his son, and Thomas notified the Police, who began a case against the drug dealer. The Narcotics department gathered all the evidence, and it was discovered this person was responsible for several people overdosing.

Then one day, the drug dealer dropped off the planet and disappeared. The drug dealer's name was Vincent Mason. He was a fellow college student with Dustin, and they shared a dorm together.

Thomas now knew who, what and where it all began. He sent his Florida detectives all over the state of Florida and other states looking for this individual. His men were told to look under every rock and keep looking till they found him. Unfortunately, they could not find Vincent Mason.

Then after a couple of months, Vincent Mason popped back up in town. Thomas's information pipeline told him Mason was someplace in southern Florida, but they couldn't find him. Then one day, Thomas was working at his office when his assistant came in and brought in the local paper, and it showed that Vincent Mason was located and arrested by homicide Detective Robert Bench.

The Newspaper documented how Robert Bench hunted this suspect down and captured him. Thomas looked at his assistant and said that the guy looked familiar. The assistant said, "Sir, he handles the tough cases for the Police Department."

The press says once he gets on your trail, you are caught; you just don't know it. Thomas smiled and asked what they were charging him with. The paper said 7 cases of homicide and drug possession—tainted drugs, with people overdosing. Thomas told him that that was good. He then asked to get his car and call his boat. He was taking his son on a cruise to get fresh ocean air.

Thomas, with Veronica and Dustin, got on his yacht, and they headed for the Bahamas. He owned a beach house on Lyford Cay and wanted to take his family away from the pressures and influences that could harm Dustin. The family had a good time. Dustin seemed to be getting better, and they went fishing and snorkeling just like they used to do. He began pulling jokes like he used to do as a kid. Thomas was happy his kids seemed to be turning around. While they were in Nassau, Veronica kept a close eye on her brother and was glad when he did not want to go to the clubs and drink. Nobody did any drinking. Thomas made sure there was no alcohol on the boat or in the house.

Dustin was getting color back in his face and gaining weight back on. They would play cards and kids' games with all the water time on sea dues. Thomas had to go to a get-together with the Prime Minister of the Bahamas. Veronica and Dustin did a lot of talking. Veronica loved her little brother and, in some ways, had to act like a mom he could talk to. Thomas came back around 11:00 PM to the house and noticed his kids had fallen asleep on the couches. He covered them up in a blanket like he used to when they were little. Thomas then went to bed.

When they got back to Miami after a couple of weeks, Dustin went and began working with his dad. After a couple of months, there was some bad news at the jail. Vincent Mason switched tags and cells with an inmate and was released by accident. When Thomas found out, he slammed his phone down, breaking the telephone. He went and opened his office door and yelled for his assistant, who came running. He has never seen his boss ever this mad. When he entered, Thomas told him to get his detectives out, flipping this city upside down, looking for this scum bag. If they found him, he would not be able to walk.

Days passed, and Dustin did not come to work one day. Thomas called home and had Veronica check his room. She called back and said his bed was made, and it looked like he did not come home last night. Veronica got a chill up her spine and said, " Dad, I'm worried."

Thomas agreed that he was too, before he hung up. Thomas then told his assistant to find his son. The investigators looked all over town. One hundred men, including bodyguards, looking in every building, club, restaurant, and homeless area, none stop. This is not counting the police, who were also on the lookout.

Two hours later, Thomas received a telephone call from the police and was told we had found his son. Thomas asked, "Is he all right?"

The police stated, "He was found at the Holiday Inn in Miami." The Police Investigator continued by saying, "I am sorry, it looks like he died from a drug overdose, and could you come here and ID him." Thomas was shaking and quietly stated, "I am on my way."

Thomas slowly got up and walked out of his office, pale and shaking as he leaned on the wall. His secretary ran over and asked her boss whether or not he was okay. When he whispered, "No," he said, "My son is dead." She cried out, "Oh my god." She yelled for Thomas' assistant, who ran over and asked what was going on. Thomas said, "They found my son. He is dead. Jason Davis, who has worked for Thomas for 20 years, yelled out for a secretary to get the boss's car. Thomas gave Jason the address so he could go and ID his son. Once Thomas could compose himself, he stood up, got on the elevator with Jason, and they went down to the first floor and went to the limousine with two Vehicle escorts.

Thomas called Veronica from his limousine and told her the bad news. He heard Veronica scream as she fell to the floor crying. Thomas heard the maids trying to help her up to a chair as he hung up. Veronica was crying and got out of her chair, went to the nearest couch, and cried.

When his vehicle drove up to the hotel, he observed several police cars in the parking lot and other city cars. Once the limousine stopped, the door was opened, and he stepped out. He had gathered his composure in the limo and started walking to where the investigator directed him. The Chief of Police walked up to Thomas, shook his hand, and said, "My condolences." The Mayor also approached Thomas and said, "My thoughts and prayers," and he also shook Thomas' hand.

The investigator-led Thomas to the room where the body was. Two officers were standing by the door to the room with the door closed. The door was opened by one of the officers wearing gloves, allowing Thomas to step in. He saw his son on the bed dead.

There was no blood, and he appeared to only be sleeping. The detective stood next to Thomas and asked, "Is this your son, sir?"

Thomas began crying and said quietly, "Yes." Two forensic officers were also in the room, and Thomas realized he was standing on plastic.

Thomas looking at his son, asked if it was drugs, and the detective said, "He believed so." The Detective then pointed at the needle and other items on the other side of the bed. He saw a band wrapped around his right arm still on him. The Detective added, "An autopsy will say exactly what happened."

Tears flowed down Thomas' face, and then he wiped his face and leaned on the wall.

When Thomas gathered his composure, he asked, "Do we have a suspect on who sold him the drugs?"

The Detective stated, "Yes, sir." Thomas demanded to know who it was, and the Detective said, "Before I tell you, I want to make sure we have all the evidence first."

Thomas angrily said, "Who is the suspect?"

The detective stated in a low tone of voice, "Vincent Mason." Thomas closed his eyes, clenched his fist, and left the room.

Thomas walked past everyone and straight to his limo. Everyone could see how mad he looked, and the Mayor and Chief of Police stepped away. They knew this man could help their careers or destroy them, and now was not the time to talk with him. Thomas's vehicles then left the area.

The Mayor had the Chief of Police and the Chief of Detectives walk him to his car, and he told them to do what they must do to find this guy. "If we don't find this guy, things are going to get very uncomfortable for everyone. Especially me." He stepped into his car and before the door closed, said, "Find him now." The Mayor's vehicle then drove away. The Chief of Police turned to the

Chief of Detectives and his assistant to put everyone on this case you can. Where is Bench, and why is he not here? The Chief of Detectives responded, "He is on other cases, and his plate is full." The Chief of Police said, "Then put everyone you can on this."

Thomas walked into his home, and Veronica came running up crying and asked, "Was it him."

He hugged her and said, "Yes." She cried in his arms and said, "Daddy, I want my brother back."

Thomas whispered, "I know." They walked to a huge couch, and Veronica cried while her dad held on to her until she fell asleep. He signaled to a maid to get a blanket and pillow. The maid returned with both while he slid out, put Veronica's head on the pillow, and covered her up.

Thomas then went to his office and called all his assistants and people who worked for him and notified them that the person who found this guy would get a one-million-dollar check. Thomas also added, "I do not care if he is dead or alive, walking, crawling, I do not care." He pulled off a picture book from his shelf and went through it pictures of his family while sitting at his desk. He then began to cry and looked at the photo of his wife and said, "I failed. I am sorry." One of the maids walked by with tears in her eyes and said, "Sir, I am so sorry. Do you want me to close the door?"

He looked at her through his tears and said, "Thank you, and please close the door." She immediately complied.

The funeral crowd was large at the catholic church, with VIPs throughout the church. Thomas held on to Veronica, who was constantly crying and shaking during the whole process. Once it was over, a long line of people gave condolences to Thomas and Veronica. Both U.S Senators and other VIPs in politics were there, all shaking Thomas's hand. The sky was clear, but Thomas was full of rage, but he could not show how furious he was. This person, who was responsible for his son's life, would suffer for taking Dustin's life. He would show no mercy to this evil man. He had raised the award to all his detectives and workers and now offered it to the whole world for his capture. He knew Florida was filled with bounty hunters, private detectives, and law enforcement spending their off time looking all over South Florida for Vincent Mason.

Chapter 3

The Most Hunted

Vincent Mason saw himself wanted on television and smiled in his hotel room in Orlando, Florida. The reporter discussed how Bounty Hunters and everyone else were looking for him. The award Thomas J. Jackson was giving had people flying in from other countries looking for Vincent Mason.

When he escaped from the jail's poor security procedures, Vincent Mason had cut off his hair and grew a beard. He paid off another prisoner to do a switch, and it worked. He walked out the front door with hardly any issue. He knew when he met Dustin by accident at the restaurant, he could get some money one way or the other.

Six months went by, and nobody could find Vincent Mason. Thomas had raised the bounty to 25 million, and Vincent Mason was the most searched-for person in America. Thomas watched as the media constantly talked about the criminal and, as usual, very little about the victim, causing tips to be called in by the thousands. Thomas had enough of waiting and watching time go by. He was having a political fundraising at the Manson, and all the VPs would be there.

Robert Bench was at a club dancing with his date and having a good time when he received a phone call on his cell from the Chief of Detectives. He called back after he got off the dancing floor, and his boss told him who he needed to report to as soon as possible. Robert asked, "Are you serious?"And his boss responded back, "Yes, be there in one hour," and hung up.

Robert went up to his date and said, "I am sorry, I have to go to work."

His date looked at him and said, "Bye," and Robert, with a puzzled look on his face, told her again he had to leave for work. She said, "Bye. I guess your work is more important than me."

He responded by saying, "It pays the bills." She responded angrily, "Go and pick me up later." Robert laughed and said, "No, you either leave with me or you're on your own." She then waved bye. He turned around and headed to the door. She ran up to him, grabbed his arm, and said, "That's it?"

Roberts said, "I guess so." She tried to slap him, and he blocked it and said, "Bye, bye, bitch," as he waved his hand and shot her the middle finger before leaving the club.

Once he got in his truck, he put in the GPS address he needed to go to. He arrived about fifteen minutes early and was astonished at how big the mansion and property were. Robert laughed, thinking this spelled lots of money. He drove up in his black 2016 Dodge Ram in front and got out. A valet approached him, wrote out a receipt, and handed it to him. Robert handed over the key to the truck and walked up the stairs.

It opened when he knocked on the door, and a well-dressed older gentleman asked him for his pass. Robert told him, "I was told to be here," and he showed his badge. The butler said, "Please come in, and what is your name, sir?" Robert gave his name, and the butler said, "Follow me, please." Robert followed the butler through the well-dressed crowd, amazed at who he saw.

He saw politicians he saw in the news and other VIPs. He continued to follow the butler, and they approached a door. The butler knocked on it, and Robert and the butler heard come in. The door was opened, and Robert saw his boss, who said, "Come in, Robert." Robert walked into the huge room and looked around, where he observed the Mayor, the Police Chief, the Chief of detectives and a couple of other men in the room who he did not know.

Thomas Jackson stepped over to Robert, stuck his hand out, and said, "Welcome to my home, Detective." Robert knew this was the biggest and most powerful man in the state of Florida. He responded by saying, "Nice to meet you, sir." Thomas said, "Please take a seat, and would you like something to eat or drink?" Robert said, "No, thank you, sir." Thomas then asked Robert, "So what did we pull you away from?" Robert grinned and said, "Nothing really, she was a bitch". Everyone in the room got quiet. Thomas smiled and said to everyone, "That's ok. I like a man who speaks his mind."

Thomas looked at the Police Chief and told him, "How about you start it off, Chief."

The Police Chief handed Robert a thick folder and asked, "Do you remember this guy?" Robert opened the folder and recognized Vincent Mason when the Chief said, "I am sure you heard the news about the whole fiasco at the jail?" Robert shook his head and stated, "Stupid idiots." The Police Chief stated to Robert, "We have been searching for this guy for six months, and we still can't find him."

The Police Chief looked around the room and told Robert, "Mr. Jackson has even put a 25-million-dollar award for him up from one million dollars, and he still can't be found." Robert had been following the news and was aware Florida had been flooded with who knows how many bounty hunters from all over the world looking for Mason. The Chief looked at Robert and said, "We need you to find him." Robert stood up and tossed the folder on the chair when the door opened, and Veronica walked in.

Thomas stood up and introduced his daughter to everyone. He then identified everyone, including Detective Robert Bench to her. Robert turned around to Thomas and said to everyone, "This is bullshit." He paused and then asked, "Why is the richest man in Florida, the mayor and Police Chief and Chief of Detectives and two clowns? I have no clue who they are really wanting?" He stopped and looked around the room and then said, "Because somebody better fucking tell me why I am here, or I walk."

Thomas sat down, put his head in his hands, rubbed his thinning hair, and said, "Gentlemen, Mr. Bench wants the truth, so here it is." He looked around and continued talking. "This punk is responsible for my son's death, and I want him." Veronica jumped in and responded, "Is that not clear enough for you, hot shot." Robert turned around and looked at Veronica and smiled before he said, "Typical spoiled bitch?" Veronica stepped close to Robert and tried to slap him with her right hand. Robert caught her hand and said, "Lady, that's twice tonight a bratty woman tried to slap me. You better do more than that." Veronica spat at him and stormed out of the room. Thomas and everyone in the room were surprised on what they saw. Robert looked right at Thomas and said, "Mmmm, maybe it's that time of the month."

Thomas stood up and asked everyone to step out for a minute while talking to Mr. Bench. Once everyone had left the room, only Robert and Thomas were there. Thomas asked Robert, "Will you please take a seat," and Robert, seeing the expression of sincerity on his face, complied. Thomas pulled up a chair next to Robert and told him about his son and what happened. He described the loss and how it has affected his daughter and him. Robert responded, "Sir, that explains her attitude." Thomas explained how the State Police, local authorities and all the bounty hunters could not find this guy. Thomas said, "I told the Mayor, I want you to clear your plate and work on this case and find him Robert." Thomas paused and informed Robert, "I will give you 100 million dollars for you to bring him in dead or alive, but I prefer dead." Both men had serious looks on their faces when Thomas added, "Those men will give you a free get-out-of-jail card."

Thomas got up, went to his desk, pulled out a paper signed by the governor, and informed him, "The Governor and the Mayor are giving you carte blanch on this case. In other words, do what you have to find him." Robert said, "Preferably dead, right?" Thomas responded back, "You know what I want? Find him and put his body in the morgue or bring him in; again, I prefer dead."

Robert stood up and scratched his 3-day stubble on his face and laughed. He grinned and then got a serious look on his face and asked, "So basically, you want me to hunt this guy down and kill him for you for 100 million dollars." Mr. Jackson did not respond. Still scratching his face, Robert did mention, "That's a lot of money and tempting, but keep the money, old man." Robert looked at Mr. Jackson and asked, "How will he do what is needed to catch him? If he cooperates, then it goes the easy way." Robert sat back down, looked at Mr. Jackson again, and told him, "If dipshit does not, then it's doom on him." Mr. Jackson cut in and replied, "He understood." Robert stood up again and told Mr. Jackson, "I am not a murderer, old man. Yes, I have killed, not murdered. There is a difference, and Mr. Jackson, there is a big difference."

Mr. Jackson also stood when Robert said, "I will find him on one condition." Thomas asked Robert, "What is it, Detective?" Robert smiled and said, "Your daughter will have to take me out to the nicest restaurant in Miami, and she will pay the bill." Thomas smiled and notified him, "I will see what I can do." Robert said, "Sir, no dinner, no deal." Thomas laughed and stated, "I will make sure that happens."

Robert responded, "Tomorrow, she picks me up in a limo because I have never been in one or ridden in one." Thomas smiled and replied, "Deal."

Thomas then opened the door and stated, "Gentleman, please step back in."

Once everyone stepped back into the room, Thomas announced, "Robert will be glad to hunt Mason down. I mean, look for this guy on only one condition."

The mayor asked, "What is it?"

Thomas looked at his daughter and before he could say anything, Robert interrupted and said, "I have work to do in the morning, and I need all files and video on my desk by 10 am."

The Chief responded back, "You will have it all."

Then Robert walked by the door and looked at Veronica and smiled and whispered, "I will see you tomorrow, and wear something nice." Robert looked around the room and said, "Gentleman."

As he started to leave, he remarked, "Damn," and he walked back to the desk, grabbed the piece of paper with VIP signatures, folded it up, and placed it in his shirt pocket and walked out.

Thomas looked at his daughter when she looked back and asked, "What did he mean I will see you tomorrow and wear a nice dress?"

Thomas responded by saying, "You are taking him tomorrow evening to dinner at the nicest restaurant in Miami."

She yelled back, "Dad, hell no, he is rude and a pig." She then realized what she had said, and she looked around the room and said, "Sorry, gentlemen, I didn't mean it that way."

The Chief of Detectives smiled and said, "He is rude, and we will ignore the other word."

Veronica looked back at her dad and firmly stated, "No way." Thomas looked at his daughter with everyone watching and told her, "He will find the guy not for the money but only for dinner with you."

Veronica got quiet. She asked, "So he refused the money but wanted a date with me?"

Thomas answered back, "Yes."

Veronica then got quiet and answered back, "Okay, but no funny business."

Thomas told her, "Robert Bench did not even bring that up, just you taking him out to dinner and paying for it."

Veronica was shocked about a man turning down money to go out to dinner with her. She then looked at her father and told him, "Ok, I will do it, but he better not pull any crap."

Thomas smiled and responded back to her, "I doubt it." Veronica then exited the room and went back to being the hostess.

Thomas talked to the men in the room and told them, "Make sure that young man gets everything he needs."

They all commented, "No problem."

The two unknown men told Mr. Jackson, "The governor will give him whatever assistance is needed." Then they all went back to the fundraiser.

Chapter 4
The Search begins.

Robert got in his truck and headed home, thinking about what had just occurred. While driving, he laughed at the amount of money he had just passed up, and the dinner date he had tomorrow. Once he arrived home, he threw his clothes on the floor and turned on the television and started watching the original Highlander movie on his couch. He always enjoyed the movie and the television series. He checked his messages and saw his mom had called a few hours earlier. It was late, so he decided he would call her tomorrow as he lay out on the couch as sleep came his way.

Veronica played hostess throughout the rest of the evening, and when everyone left, she went to her dad's office and stepped in, closing the door behind her. She asked about this detective and what he knew about him. He showed her a copy of his jacket, and she was impressed by his service record in the military and Police department. Thomas told his daughter, "His bosses say he is the best in looking for bad guys, and he is a very focused individual. Never been married, has no kids and a bit of a loner." Both read about where his parents lived and his brother and sister. Robert Bench had 75 confirmed kills in the Middle East and 4 as a Police Officer. So, he had no problem squeezing the trigger when needed.

Thomas stopped talking for a moment and then explained, "This Detective told me he will not murder someone, but killing is another story if the person becomes a threat." Thomas laughed and added, "This Robert Bench actually cussed me out, so he is not afraid of anyone, including me." Veronica smiled and said, "That says something, but will he help us." Thomas told his daughter, "Detective James will, starting tomorrow." Veronica yawned, stating, "It's bedtime." She stood up and went over to her dad and kissed his forehead. Thomas said, "Good night." Thomas then turned his office light off and leaned back in his chair to think about what occurred during the evening. When the sun came up a few hours later, he finally went to bed.

Robert was up at 6:00 A.M and drove to the beach and ran a few miles, and then went to the gym to get a workout out of the way. He showered at the gym and went to a Denny' for breakfast. He read the newspaper and then arrived at his desk at about 9:30 A.M on a Saturday morning. There were several of his colleagues also working, and were not surprised to see him come in. They knew he had no home life and was a workaholic. Guy asked Robert, "How was your date last night?" Robert said, "She was an entitled bitch." He gathered the cases he was working on and took them and opened his boss's office, and placed them on his desk.

Robert went back to his computer and started reading the files that were placed on his desk during the night. He also looked at the 25-recording disk collected as evidence. After a few minutes of digging around his messy desk, he located the information folder he had on Vincent Mason, the one he had put together before he caught Mason. During the day, he would go through each disk, watching each one. He watched Mason from the time he exited the hotel room till he got 6 blocks down the street, and he disappeared. He also saw him go inside a business, but the video was too blurry to say what it was. He went through the paperwork and found out nobody checked to see what the businesses were. He turned off the computer, grabbed his key, and realized it was already 2:30 PM. He exited the building, jumped into his truck and went to the location of that store. He knew that area, so blurry video or not, he knew where to go.

While driving, he realized somebody was tailing him. He figured it was either old man Jackson people or other cops seeing what he does. He pulled up to the businesses and parked. He got out and checked both businesses out. One was a small Cuban store, and next to it was a small barbershop. You can go to both through the side opening. It was a family business when he realized why Mason just disappeared. Mason got a haircut and cut his hair short, and over time, he had to grow a beard to help with him not being identified. White men growing beards is a trend making its way back into American life after about 80 years.

Robert bought a Gatorade and requested to see the manager or owner. A young man came out of a small office and asked, "What can I do for him." Robert showed his badge and told him his name. The Manager got nervous and said, "We are a good establishment." Robert responded back, "I need to see your video system, please, and do you save your video, or does it roll over?" The manager responded back, "I am sorry it rolls over every 24 hours." Robert looked down and replied, "Oh well, just following a hunch." Robert said, "Thanks," and headed to the exit when the manager informed him, "Sir, the bank across the street has cameras all over the place, so you might check with them." Robert smiled and said, "Thanks, and if you need anything, here is my card." The manager looked at the card and smiled, and put it in his shirt pocket.

Robert left and crossed the street to the bank. Robert entered the bank, went up to the teller, and asked for the manager. He showed his badge with his I.D. The teller stated, "Just a moment, sir." She used her phone and called the bank manager, who came over, introducing himself to Robert and asked, "What can I do to help." Robert explained he was investigating a crime, and I believe the suspect walked down this street but disappeared after entering the building across the street. The manager told Robert, "We hold all tapes for one year, and then they go to the corporate office." The manager also asked about the date and time he was looking for. Robert pulled out his notepad and told the Manager, "The suspect entered the building when and where and on what date." The manager told Robert he would have to get approval from higher up, so give me a few minutes. Robert went and sat down, and five minutes later, the bank manager came back and told Robert, "He was told no and that a warrant must be initiated before he could do anything."

Robert smiled and replied, "No problem," and pulled out a copy of the paper he took off Jackson's desk and called one of the numbers on the paper. The original was safely hidden for his protection. The Governor answered, and Robert identified himself. He told him what was going on and stated the name of the bank and how he was getting no cooperation. The Governor said, "Give him five minutes, and it will be taken care of," and the governor hung up. Less than five minutes later, the assistant manager came running up to the manager and advised him, "The corporate office is on the telephone." The bank manager left and then, a minute later, came back and informed him, "Whatever you need, sir, because I have been ordered to cooperate in all areas." So, they went to the video room and looked at the video for the date and approximate time Robert had asked for.

Robert observed Mason walk into the store, but he never came out. Then he saw a man with short bleached blonde hair come out. Robert smiled and said, "Bingo." He turned to the manager and stated, "I need a copy of this." The bank manager made a copy of it and gave the disk to Robert. They shook hands and exited the video room when the manager asked, "Detective, who did you call anyway"? Robert smiled and responded," You do not want to know." The bank manager quietly informed him," I understand, and if you need any more help, Detective, in the future, please let me know."

Robert then went back to his office and began his coded notes in case someone decided to see what he was doing. He taught himself to write in code while in the military. He hid the new disk in his box where nobody could take it. He then realized it was 4:30 PM, and he had a date in a few hours. So, he left the building, knowing he was now heading in the right direction. Slow start, but a start.

Chapter 5

Date Night

Robert went home and cleaned up and put on his nicest suit, and waited for his date to pick him up. He knew it would be an interesting night. She was a rich spoiled woman, and he was just an average person who loved pushing people's buttons when he could. Robert was known at work for being a smartass to people and especially to the higher-ups. He knew his job performance was what saved him from getting put back on patrol. At 6:00 PM, there was a knock at the door, and he went and looked through the peephole and saw Veronica Jackson in a nice black dress. He opened the door and smiled, and said, "Good evening. Would you like to come into my mansion?" She looked at him and responded back, "I have my own." Veronica asked, "I didn't think someone like you would have a suit." Robert locked the door and said, "Sarcasm, I guess it is going to be an interesting night." The chauffeur opened the door, and Veronica got in first, then Robert jumped in. Robert said, "I am impressed. Is this rental or all your dads?" She declared back, "It's dads."

There was very little talking in the car. Veronica, after a few minutes, asked, "Is there any news"? Robert responded back with a "yes." She turned her head toward him, and he explained how he found a new lead that was missed, and tomorrow he would pick up where he left off and why nobody could find him. She looked at him and said, "Why"? He looked at her and explained, "It would be in my report to my bosses, who will let your dad know. Robert stopped and remarked, "By the way, tell your dad those detectives following me could slow me down, and my self-preservation alarm might go off, and I might forget what I know on this case." He turned and looked at her with a serious look on his face and said, "Do you understand?"

"Yes, I understand," she responded.

Robert then got quiet and asked, "By the way, nice dress. Did you buy it off the rack, or did you buy it at the fancy dress store"? Veronica looked at Robert and responded back, "I never buy off the rack compared to you." Robert laughed, and Veronica asked, "What so funny?" Robert asserted, "Your snot nose attitude." She responded and asked, "What about yours?" He smiled and said, "Touche." He then changed the subject and asked, "By the way, where are we eating at?" Veronica spoke in French and said, *Veronique.* Robert said, "Wow, I am glad you are paying for dinner." Veronica shook her head.

Once they arrived at *Veronique,* the chauffeur opened the door, and Robert observed the driver with a grin on his face. However, he turned his head when Veronica got out so she could not see his grin.

Veronica walked in front as Robert followed a few feet behind her, not knowing where to go. While walking, he looked her up and down in her tight black dress with a deep cut in the back, and he smiled. He began looking around as the doormen opened the door, and they walked in. The Restaurant manager was in the front waiting for them. He reached out for Veronica's hand and said, "Thank you for coming. I have your table for two." He turned around and snapped his finger. A gentleman stepped up and told Veronica to follow him. He then looked at Robert and said, "I guess you too," sarcastically. Veronica smiled and followed the waiter into the restraint.

Once the waiter helped Veronica by pulling out her chair so she could sit down, he looked at Robert and said, "Take a seat." Robert smiled and wanted to say something, but he bit his tongue. Veronica, who was watching, said, "Is there something you wanted to tell him?"

"Yes, but why ruin a good night by me bouncing his head through the wall," Robert replied.

Veronica stated, "Thank you, the food is excellent here, and who wants it to be ruined by someone who's knuckle dragged on the ground." Robert laughed and said, "Yep, my knuckles drag, but I know when to lift them also." Veronica grinned and stated, "We will see."

The waiter returned and asked Veronica, "Would you like the usual, Madam? Veronica looked at Robert and asked, "Would you like to order?" Robert looked at the menu and suggested, "Well, since I will be having meat with blood," as he looked at Veronica, "I would go with red wine. How about Chateau Lafite-Rothschild 2018 wine." Veronica looked surprised, as did the waiter. Veronica remarked, "I will have the same." The waiter stated, "Very good, Madam," and he left. Robert stated, "This is a nice place. Do you come here a lot?" Veronica said, "Yes, I do. It's my favorite place." Robert grinned and said, "I totally understand. No riff raft in here like people like me." Veronica smiled and answered back, "Your words." Robert stated, "They did a good job kissing your butt when you walked in." Veronica smiled and stated, "They better; I own the place." Robert started to laugh and said, "Wow, I didn't see that coming." She looked at him and responded, "no doubt".

The waiter came back and brought the red wine in two large wine glasses. The waiter then asked Veronica, "What would you like for your meal?"

"Filet Mignon Medium well, with the vegetable of the day and a salad with no dressing."

"Very good, Madam."

He then looked at Robert and asked, "What would you like" with a snotty attitude.

"I will have the T-Bone steak, Medium rare, plain baked potato, vegetable of the day and a salad with balsamic Vinaigrette dressing." Then he stood up and waved the waiter over, and he whispered in his ear something as he put his left hand on the waiter's neck. The waiter went pale, and Robert sat back down, saying, "Do we understand each other?" The waiter responded back nervously, "Yes, sir," and scampered away.

Veronica looked at Robert and leaned in from her seat, and asked, "What did you say to him"? Robert told her, "We just had a man-to-man understanding of how life can turn out for some." Veronica leaned back and took her wine glass, and took a sip. Robert did the same and stated, "Nice wine." Veronica said, "Well, at least we agree on that." She leaned forward again and asked, "By the way, were your knuckles on the ground or up when you put the fear of god in him?" Robert thought for a moment and leaned a little in her direction, and said, "They were up because his head hitting the table would have told you they were down." She smiled and stated, "At least you know the difference in how to behave." Robert looked at Veronica and downed his wine, and told her, "I am also housebroken to," as he signaled the waiter, who stepped right over to him and said, "Yes, sir." Robert asked for him to bring the bottle. The waiter responded back by saying, "Very good sir," and left to retrieve the bottle. When the waiter returned, he returned he poured wine into both, Veronica's and Robert's glass, and he left the bottle on the table.

When the food arrived, Robert did not ask for any steak sauce because he believed in a classy joint like this. He did not want to give Veronica any ammo. The waiter then looked at Robert and respectfully asked, "Sir, is there anything else we can do for you"? Robert looked up and saw the waiter's name tag and told the waiter, "Wade, we are good, thank you." Wade looked down and said, "Very good sir," and walked away. Veronica started to sip her wine and almost choked on it, seeing the polite exchange between those two men. Veronica stated, "That was impressive." Robert closed his eyes, looked down, put both hands on the table, and silently prayed, ignoring what Veronica said. She looked at Robert, puzzled. Here was a man who had an impressive military and Police back grown, praying in silence like a child. She had never seen that, and he seemed not to care what the people who were looking at him thought.

Then after about 20 seconds, he opened his eyes and responded to her, "Yeah, it was," as he cut into his steak. Veronica looked at Robert with a puzzled look and asked, "What's with the praying"? He smiled and took a sip of his wine, and waited for what he knew was coming. She asked, "I thought praying before dinner went out of style"? Robert took a bite of his steak, chewed it, and then looked at her and said, "Lady, I give thanks for what little I have and what I have done during my life, but my soul is just as important or more so than my life." Veronica got quiet. She was puzzled about this cop whom she was eating with. So many conflicting things, but he did not care about people looking at him praying like a schoolboy.

Veronica started to eat, and very little was said as they consumed their meal. The waiter came by a few times and looked at Robert each time, and asked, "How was everything"? Robert would respond back, "Wade, it's good, thank you." Wade would answer back, "Thank you, sir." Wade did ask Robert if they would like some more wine since the bottle was empty. Robert looked at Veronica and answered back, "I believe we will. Leave the bottle." Wade snapped his fingers, and the wine steward came over and poured the wine and left the bottle. Veronica looked up at Wade and said, "Thank you," and Wade left. Veronica smiled and asked, "How's the wine, Robert"? Robert smiled as he was chewing his food and said, "That's the first time you called me Robert." Veronica smiled and then stated, "It must be the wine." Robert grinned and answered back, "Maybe."

When they were done eating their meal, Wade came back and asked, "Would they like any dessert"? Robert looked at Veronica, and she replied, "No, thank you." Robert stated, "We are good. Just the bill, please." Veronica drank more wine and started to ask questions about her brother's case. Robert smiled and told her, "I have been waiting on that and am surprised it took so long." Veronica tried to ask questions, but Robert would only say, "he will be giving her dad a report in 72 hours on what he discovered."

Veronica drank some more and was getting a real buzz on and started to ask questions about why he wasn't married and having kids. Robert laughed and responded, "I have not met the right woman." He took a big sip of wine and told her, "You women are complicated, and sometimes I work too much." Veronica told him, "That's a good reason." Robert then leaned over and asked her, "Well, you are rich and beautiful, and why are you not married with 2.5 kids and seeing the world with a rich husband"? Veronica laughed and stated, "I am picky, and you men are complicated." Robert smiled and told her, "Good response."

Robert leaned back in his chair and looked at her, and he realized she was just a scared woman not wanting to show her feelings due to concern she would be hurt. Veronica took another sip and said, "Robert, I noticed you are not drinking your wine anymore." Robert responded, "I have had enough." Veronica then looked down as Robert just looked at her. She looked at Robert and asked, "What are you looking at"? He then leaned forward and whispered, "Do you really want to know what I am thinking"? Veronica finished her glass and stated, "Yes." He whispered, "I see a woman who is scared of life and is afraid of being hurt." He stopped for a second, seeing what her facial expression was. Her face looked like someone who was lost. He then continued saying, "You want a man who would die for you and mean it. He leaned back for a second, then leaned forward again and said, "The men you dated talked the game but were nothing but soy boys who never take any risk and run away from a challenge because they might get a bloody nose." She looked at Robert and looked down, and she got quiet. He looked at her and then stated, "On that note, it's time to go." Veronica put down her empty drink and got quiet as the waiter came over and helped her up, and Robert threw down a 20 for the tip. Wade saw it and said, "thank you, sir, by the way, there is no bill."

Robert then escorted Veronica out the door to the limousine. They got in, and nothing was said until the limo stopped, and the chauffeur opened the door at Robert's place. Robert looked at Veronica and told her, "I had a good time, Thank you." Veronica looked at him through her buzz and said, "ok." Robert then got out and walked to his place without looking back. The limo door closed, and Veronica watched him go to his door without looking back. Then the limo headed back to her home while she thought about what he said about her. She didn't know what to say back to him because he was right. Since her mom's death and now her brother's death, she has felt alone, even with her dad, whom she loved.

Robert entered his house and threw his keys and wallet, and he unstrapped his gun and tossed it on the kitchen table. He then went to the fridge and grabbed a beer and popped the top off and went and sat on the couch and turned the tv on, and went to The Turner classic channel, which was playing The Searchers. He leaned back and watched the movie, and drank his beer.

He grinned a couple of times, thinking about Veronica during the movie and how the evening went. He felt he won her over to at least she would be less bitchy with him. Once he finished his beer he laid down and fell asleep on the couch. Before he fell asleep, he turned the tv off with the remote control. He knew the days were going to start being long.

Veronica, while watching Robert walk away, was surprised. He didn't even try and kiss her or anything. When she got home, she entered the house and saw her dad sitting on the couch watching television. Thomas asked, "Well, how did it go" with a smile on his face. Veronica said, "It went fine." Thomas saw she was intoxicated and said, "You are drunk." Veronica responded back, "Yes, on good wine." Thomas looked at the two maids that walked in, and Thomas told them to help her to her room. They responded back, "Yes, sir." Thomas asked, "Well, what is this guy like." She looked at her dad and, while being helped up the stairs and told him, "He is very complicated." Thomas shook his head and said, "Good night," and Veronica also said, "Good night," as the maids helped her up the stairs to her room, where they helped her out of her clothes and tucked her into bed. Veronica fell asleep immediately.

Thomas saw the chauffeur come in, and he looked at him and asked, "How did it go?" He gave a detailed report to his boss. Thomas told Jack, "Go ahead and call it a day." There was a section of the mansion where the maids, butlers and chauffeurs, and cooks lived. All the staff were married and worked for him. He even sent their kids to private schools. He believed loyalty was very important, and it goes both ways.

The quarters were like apartments for the staff. He had them especially made and attached to the mansion. Thomas sat on his couch and was surprised by his daughter's response about this Robert Bench character. He went back to his office after he turned off the tv and looked at the detective's jacket and looked for things to better understand who he was and why he does what he does. He was impressed by his background, blue-collar family, one brother and one sister, both younger than him but married with kids and good jobs. Roberts's military record was extremely impressive, and so was his police file. One thing is for sure his daughter does not intimidate him and neither does he. He found out why the Police chief said why Robert shows no fear, and Robert's words were always all men bleed red. Thomas understood the remark and knew this man was not someone to toy with. He then put the files down and went to bed.

Chapter 6

Time to Hunt

Robert woke up at 5:00 AM and went to the beach and ran his usual five miles on the beach and then went to the gym and worked out for a while. Once he was done working out, he went and showered, dressed, and headed to work. He wasn't hungry and didn't eat breakfast. Robert went to work on a rainy Sunday morning. Miami weather could rain one minute, then clear and nice 20 minutes later. He repeated going over everything over the two days in his head and wanted to be at his desk where he could start to watch more videos and start putting things together. He was puzzled about what Mason did and were he headed away from the scene of Dustin Jacksons' overdose. He wondered if there was more to this.

Did Mason use the drugs, too, and why did he leave everything where it was in the Hotel room and not try to remove any evidence? He looked at the videos and saw Dustin's wallet on the floor. There was no money in it. Was this a robbery or an actual overdose? They were college friends, so why would he not at least call for an ambulance and then high-tail it out of there? Something was just not right with this case. A junky falling off the wagon is not new. It happens all the time. He decided to look at the toxicology report on Dustin. He found out the alcohol level was .03, which is low, but the video showed Mason helping Duston to the room. He then looked down at the report and saw some chemicals. He did not know what they were. They were a small number., 0002 and .00005, and he was again puzzled.

Robert went on google and looked up the compounds. They had to do with animal tranquilizers. He then called the lab and talked to the doctor who was working on another case. Robert was told yes, those were for animals and very powerful. Robert asked the Doc, "How much would be needed to put a human out." The Doctor thought about it and stated, "A very small drop, about a tenth of a teaspoon." Robert thanked the Doc and hung up the phone.

Robert went back and looked at the video of the room. He observed Dustin was fully dressed, and the rubber band or anything a junky use to wrap around an arm was on his left arm. He sat back and saw the syringe in the left arm. Dustin was left-handed. Robert checked his papers, and he found them. It confirmed Dustin was left-handed. Why would he use his weak hand to put dope into his system? Users don't do that in most cases. He looked at the autopsy pictures and noticed there were no needle marks or scabs of any kind on his left arm. They were on his right arm and other places on his body. Between his Toes and his legs were marked up. He then realized this was a robbery and homicide.

Mason murdered Dustin for the clump of cash Dustin always carried. Mason did not grab the credit cards because he knew they would be traced. Dustin usually had a few grand in his pocket. In his statement, the bartender saw a large clump of money when Dustin bought the drinks. Robert new this was not a man who fell off the wagon and OD. This was definitely a murder and robbery case.

He put everything together and grabbed his key, and headed to the Jacksons' mansion. He called the Chief of Police and his boss and said, "I need you guys to meet me at Jackson's place in one hour." The COP at first asked, "Why?" Robert told them, "He knows what happened with old man Jackson's kid." The COP said, "He will be there, and it better be good. I am on the 10th green and doing good." Robert responded back, "The game has changed."

At 3:00 PM, Robert drove up and jumped out of his vehicle and went to the front door. He observed both the COP and his boss walk up, and they both said, "This better be good." Robert replied, "It is." The door opened, and the butler recognized them and said, "Please come in." They walked in with Robert falling in behind them. Robert asked, "Where is Mr. Jackson?" The butler responded, "In his office." Robert said, "Please tell him we need to see him immediately."

Then Veronica came walking down the stairs and ignoring the COP, and the Chief of detectives smiled and said, "Hi Robert, how are you doing?" Robert smiled and asked, "Good, how are you?" She replied, "Fine, you men here to see my dad?" The COP said, "Yes." She informed them, "Follow me, please." They followed her to the office, and the butler opened the door, and they walked in.

Thomas got up and shook everyone's hand, and approached Robert, and he shook his hand and asked, "How did the dinner go?" Robert smiled and stated, "Good food," and he looked at Veronica and said, "A good host." Thomas smiled and said, "No doubt." Thomas went back to his deck and asked, "Now, what is this all about?" Robert looked at everyone and stated, "I need to have everyone sit down, and I am going to talk while I walk and pace." Veronica stated, "I will stand." Robert went up to her and whispered and told her, "Either sit or get out." Veronica was shocked and sat down. Thomas loved what he just heard and saw. A man is putting his daughter in check. Thomas stated, "It's your show, Detective."

Robert looked around and said, "Please, nobody interrupts, and I am going to tell you what happened to your son Mr. Jackson." He started to pace and went over the date of the victim's death and how he left work to head for the White Sands restaurant with a bar. He explained how the victim was sitting eating his lunch when a video across the street showed Mason walking down the street and looking around inside the stores and restaurants. Mason was looking for a target to drug and rob. He walks by the restaurant and sees Dustin eating. Mason starts walking, stops, realizes who it is, and returns and enters the restaurant.

The bartender was interviewed and stated he remembered your son and Mason sitting and eating, but nobody was drinking. They ate at first, and then maybe they had one drink each. The video outside says an hour later, Dustin is seen by the video being helped down the street by Mason. Dustin appeared to be drunk and was taken to a Hotel about 100 yards down the road where Mason was staying.

The hotel video shows them going into room 202. One hour later, you see Mason come out of the room, putting what looks like a wad of money in his wallet, and he runs down the stairs, off the grounds, and down the street. After pausing, Robert continued explaining what he discovered. He discovered a video from a bank he went to, and it showed Mason entering the store and never coming out. However, what he did in the store was go to the barbershop, which is attached to the store. He had his long hair cut and bleached blonde. The video shows only one white guy coming out with a drink in one hand and a baseball hat he puts on his head. He walks to the bus stop, and when the bus arrives, he jumps on and heads down the road.

Thomas put his hands on his head and asked, "So you are saying my son was murdered?" Robert stated, "Yes sir, nothing made him fall off the wagon, and it was cold-blooded murder for money." Veronica started to cry, got up, and ran out of the room. Robert said, "I am sorry, sir." The Chief of Detectives asked, "Can we prove it in court?" Robert answered back, "I believe so." The Chief of Police told Robert, "You know your stuff, we will go with it, and I will get with the FBI to put out a nation man hunt for this thug."

Thomas told everyone, "I believe you have work to do." The Chief of Police said, "We will get the ball rolling," and they headed for the door. Thomas asked Robert, "Could you please stay for a minute?" Robert looked at the Chief, and they acknowledged him, and they left the office.

Robert closed the door, and Thomas looked up and said, "Thanks. You have taken a big load off my shoulders thinking it was something I might have done to have Dustin relapse." Robert said, "Sir, I just look at the facts and the evidence." Thomas stood up and said, "Please catch him." Robert answered back, "I will do everything I can," and then he headed back to the door. Thomas said, "Robert," and Robert turned around and said, "Sir?" Then Thomas told him, "I never saw my daughter ever listen to a man like you." Robert got quiet for a second and then told Thomas, "Maybe because she never met a real man beside you." Thomas said, "Thanks." They looked at each other with mutual respect.

Robert stepped out and heard the old man through the door start crying. He stood outside the door to think for a minute about his next move to capture Mason. At least the old man can feel better about not feeling guilty and believing he was to blame. It could have been anyone. Dustin Jackson was at the wrong place.

Robert felt bad for the old man, and then he headed to the front door to leave when Veronica came walking up to Robert and said through her tears, "Thank you." Thomas opened his door and stopped to watch and listen to his daughter and the detective interact. Roberts stepped forward, wiped the tears off her face, and told her, "It will all work out, I promise," and he walked out the door. Veronica turned and saw her dad looking at her. She saw he had also been crying. Thomas stepped over to his daughter, and they hugged each other, and he said, "That young man will get him, I have no doubt." Veronica sniffled and said, "I hope so." Thomas then smiled and mentioned how Robert was different, and Veronica answered, "Maybe." Then she let go of her father and went to head up stairs.

After Robert stepped outside the mansion, he saw his bosses drive away. He started to get in his car and said, "Damn it." He turned around and headed back to the front door and knocked on it. Veronica, who was heading back upstairs, turned around and yelled at the butler. She got it. Thomas was walking back to his office when he turned around to see who it was. Veronica opened the door and saw Robert, and she asked," what do you want, detective?" Robert said, "I will pick you up in three hours dress casually," and he turned away and headed to his truck. Veronica smiled and closed the door. He didn't even wait for a response from her. Thomas smiled as Veronica headed upstairs. Thomas stepped back into his office and went and reread the report he had on Robert Bench.

Chapter 7

Ice Melting

Three hours later, Robert knocked on the door, and instead of the butler, it was Veronica dressed in tight jeans, a shirt and high heels. She yelled out, "Heading out," and closed the door. Thomas, watching the local news, stood up and watched his daughter walk with Robert to his truck. He opened the front door for her, and she jumped in. She seemed to be happy. Robert went around and jumped into his side, and they headed out to a restaurant. He took her to the Texas roadhouse, where they had dinner.

While waiting for their dinner, they ate peanuts and started throwing them at each other. Robert grinned, and Veronica asked, "What?" He smiled and told her, "You seem to be having a good time." He knew she was melting and showing her true self, but he did not say it to her. She had a big wall for protection, and he could see it was big. He knew women with walls like that had had things happen to them, and trust was a big issue.

Once dinner was over, he took her to a Putt-Putt place. Veronica began laughing. She looked at Robert and asked, "PUTT PUTT, are you serious?" He jumped out and went to her side and opened the door, and said, "Yep, this will tell me if I can take you golfing." Veronica continued laughing. They spent an hour there, and he would putt left-handed to make it fair.

Halfway through, she would start to flirt with him while he was putting by shaking her butt or blowing in his ear to make him mess up. Sometimes it worked, and sometimes it didn't. When they were done, they turned in their putters and headed to the truck. He saw a few bricks come down from the wall.

Robert opened the door, and she got in, and he went and got in and started the truck up, and they headed to the exit. Veronica laughed and said, "Wait till my friends hear about this. A guy takes me to a Putt-Putt place on a date." He laughed and said, "It builds character." She laughed and shook her head, still not believing it, she didn't tell him, but she was having a good time.

When he saw him, he waited for people to finish crossing at the exit. James Duffy was a person he had been hunting for a long time before he turned over all his cases to focus on the Jackson issue. Robert stated, "Son of a bitch." Robert slammed the truck into the park. Duffy, who was in front of the truck, stopped and looked at the driver, and his eyes almost bugged out when he saw Robert Bench.

James Duffy stopped and looked around, and then he took off running. Robert jumped out and tossed Veronica his phone and said, "Dial 911. Tell them I need backup in pursuit of a murder suspect." Robert took off after Duffy down the street. After about three streets down, Duffy ran into traffic, dodging and weaving through cars slamming on their breaks. Robert did the same while pursuing Duffy. When they got to 9th Ave and Miami Ave, Duffy pulled out his gun and turned and fired two shots at Robert.

Veronica had called 911 and moved over to the driver's side, and drove the truck in the direction Robert went. She had 911 on the phone telling the lady what was happening and the direction Robert was running. Then Veronica saw Robert in the middle of the street as a person shot at him. Robert hit the ground and pulled his gun, and fired three shots into Duffy, who fell backward onto the pavement. Vehicles were stopping, and people were running in all directions.

She told the 911 lady what had happened and that they needed to send an ambulance and some police. Veronica put the truck into park, found the emergency blinkers, and turned them on. She got out and ran to Robert, who had a serious look on his face but with no fear. Robert was surprised when she ran up to him and hugged him, asking, "Are you alright?" Robert answered back, "Yes." He then asked Veronica, "Where the hell did you come from," as Robert walked over to the body and grabbed the gun lying next to the body. Robert looked at Veronica and asked, "Can I have my phone?" Veronica gave it to him while seeing how confident he was and relaxed like it was a walk in the park.

Robert looked at her and asked her again, "How did you get here?" He still didn't know she had driven his truck. She told him what she did, and he said, "Good job, and are you ok?" Veronica smiled and said, "Yes." Minutes later, police cars came from many directions and surrounded the area.

Once the police approached Robert with their guns drawn, he showed his badge, told the uniform, Sargent, what happened and handed over his required gun. Veronica asked Robert, "Why do you do that?" He remarked, "It's Policy. I have more guns anyway." She smiled and said, "I am sure," as she hung on to Robert. Robert told the Uniform Sargent, "He will be in the first thing to help with the paperwork." The sergeant told Robert he would do the rest.

Robert walked over to the passenger side and opened the passenger door, and Veronica got in as the media started to show up. Robert got into his truck, and they took off. Robert leaned over and popped the glove box open and pulled out a 9mm model 40 with a twenty-round clip, and put it in his holster while waiting on the red light. Veronica was looking at Robert and finally asked, "Why are you not freaking out about almost being killed." Robert smiled and told her, "I try not to think about it. Life is too short to worry about things like that." Robert glanced at her and told her, "I need to take you home." Veronica asked, "Can we go someplace else? It's still early." Robert grinned and asked, "How about we go dancing?" Veronica smiled and said, "Perfect, it's been long since I did that." Robert said, "I know the perfect place we can go." She smiled and said, "Let's go."

When they drove up to the dance club, he parked, and Veronica jumped out. Robert locked the truck, and they walked to the entrance in front of the huge line. Veronica asked, "Where are we going?" Then she pointed at the long line. Robert smiled, held her hand and told her, "Come with me." She was surprised Robert held her hand, and she smiled and said, "Ok," but a little confused.

They walked up to the head bouncer, and Robert and the head bouncer shook hands while the bounce pulled back the rope and told the other bouncer at the door to find them the best table and walk them in. Veronica looked puzzled but held onto Robert, who followed the bouncer to a table in the second level in the middle. Drinks were ordered, and they danced and danced throughout the evening. As the night went by, Veronica showed no attitude, while she was amazed at how he was during the evening after killing a guy and trying to show her a good time. As the evening went by, they danced and kissed each other extremely romantically in the middle of the dance floor. She was intoxicated but was having a good time.

They stayed till the club closed at 2:00 am. Veronica had many drinks during the evening, but Robert made his one drink last all evening and drank orange juice till they left. When they walked out, Robert shook hands with the head bouncer and a couple of others. They headed to the truck, and Veronica, who was extremely intoxicated, showed it. Robert opened her door, and she grabbed him and kissed him hard and long. Then she kissed him again and said, "I had a good time Robert."

While they were kissing, some people walking by yelled out get a room when Veronica stopped kissing Robert and yelled, "Fuck off." One guy said, "Excuse me," and started walking towards Robert and Veronica when Robert flashed his badge and his gun and told him, "Just go away. She is drunk." The man put his hands in the air, saying, "I am gone," and walked away.

Robert helped her into the truck, got her into the passenger seat, and hooked up the safety belt. Robert jumped in, and they drove off. Veronica started laughing and asked, "Where are we going?" Robert said, "To your home." Veronica started to cry.

Being drunk brought out her emotions. She said, "I miss my brother." Robert got quiet and told her, "I know. It's going to be alright." Veronica stopped crying and leaned over with her eyes closed and said, "You kiss good what else do you do good." Robert laughed and said, "Everything." Veronica said with slurred speech, "Sure, find my brother's killer, and then you can say that."

The truck got quiet, and after 20 minutes, he drove up to the Mansion and helped get Veronica out of the vehicle. She stopped walking, turned around staggering, grabbed Robert, kissed him passionately, and told him, "Make love to me." Robert kissed her and said, "One day, when the time is right." She stepped back, staggering and asked, "Why not know?" Robert stepped up to her and told her, "When you are sober." She then lost her balance, and he caught her.

Thomas was looking out the window watching the whole time. Roberts then carried her up the stairs, and the door opened with Thomas standing there. Robert asked, "Where is her room?" Thomas looked at Robert, then his daughter and told him, "Follow me". Thomas showed Robert, who was carrying Veronica up the stairs to her room. Robert took her to the bed and put her on the bed, and took off her shoes while her dad watched. Robert then covered her up and kissed her forehead, and whispered sweet dreams, and then Robert and Thomas walked out of the room and headed downstairs.

Robert headed to the door, and Thomas said, "Hang on a minute Robert." Thomas and Robert faced each other, and Thomas told him, "She is hurting and in deep pain because she lost her mom and now her brother." Thomas paused, then continued, "She needs a strong man like you to bring her alive." Robert shrugged his shoulders and informed him, "Only time will tell, and I am too busy for relationships."

Thomas got quiet for a second and stated, "Son, it happens when it happens, and there is nothing anyone can do about it." Robert shook Thomas' hands and said, "I must get a few hours of sleep. I am sure you already know about tonight." Thomas answered back, "Yes." Robert smiled and mentioned, "He knew about the bodyguards in the black Escapade who were following us all night and gave you the full report." Thomas smiled and told Robert, "The report shows you are a good cop, and by the way, how do you feel?" Robert said, "Tired it was a long night," as he turned and walked out the door to his truck. He started it up and thought about Veronica and what he and her dad discussed about her needing a good man, and then headed home. Once he got home, he sat on the couch for a few minutes and went over the chase and shooting in his head. He then went to his bed and crashed and went to sleep.

Chapter 8

Work and Veronica

The alarm went off at 6:00 am, and Robert went and stood in the shower to wake up. Thank God for hot water. He then went for a two-mile run on the beach and lifted in the gym. Robert was hurting and tired from last night. He went to IHOP and had an omelet and orange juice, and read the paper were he saw the shooting of Duffy on the front page and a picture of him standing over the body like Wyatt Earp. The paper mentioned how Detective Bench gets another fugitive. The article was more negative than positive, ignoring the rap sheet of the rapes and murders the man committed.

Once he got to work, he did his share of the paperwork from the night before. The Chief of Detectives came by and asked him if he was ok? Robert chuckled, saying, "He was ok, just tired from the long night." The COD snickered and said, "You were with a woman who met the description of Thomas Jackson's daughter last night, weren't you?" Robert stated, "Yea, she drove my truck while I ran after Duffy." His boss smiled and told Robert to make it a short day and go get some sleep. You look like you need it. Robert agreed and mentioned that he would hit the door when he was done with last night's paperwork. He tied off all the loose ends and looked forward to a good nap.

At about noon, he finished up and decided to leave and take a nap at home. He was heading home when he decided to drive down the road where Mason was on the bus. Robert drove down the road, and after about 10 miles, he saw a Greyhound bus station. He realized Mason had split town.

He pulled into the bus station parking, went inside the building, showed his badge, and asked to see the manager. Once the manager came over, Robert identified himself again and explained that he needed to see the manifest on the bus he was trying to gather information on. The manager apologized and stated, "We can't give that out." Robert, who was tired and short-tempered, told the Manager, "Listen, you can either get me the fucking copy of the manifest, or I make a phone call, and your higher-ups will not be happy with you quibbling over this and interfering with a murder investigation."

Robert pulled out his phone and a piece of paper and started to dial when the manager could see the officer was not bluffing. The manager said, "Please come with me." Robert put the phone away and the paper and followed the manager. They went to the desk, and the clerk was told to get the full manifest for every bus that went out from there, and he looked at Robert, who said 4 pm till 10 pm, which was the last bus. Once Robert received the papers, he said, "Thanks" to the staff and manager, and he left and went home. When Robert got home, he crashed on the couch as he was exhausted.

Veronica woke up at about 2 pm, showered, dressed, and went downstairs, where she saw her dad watching the local news. The news was talking about the shooting last night. Thomas looked at Veronica and asked, "Well, young lady?" Veronica answered him and said, "Robert was amazing," as she told her dad what happened, leaving nothing out. Once she was done, Thomas asked, "Besides that did you have a good time?" Veronica said, "Yes, I had a good time."

Thomas smiled, and he could read his daughter easily, and said, "Well, it must have been ok. You grabbed him and kissed him pretty well." Veronica said, "Dad, it was nothing. I was a little drunk, no more and no less." Thomas told her, "Honey, don't bullshit your old man. You had a good time, and you like being with him." Veronica tried to keep her wall up and said, "It's nothing and walked away." Thomas laughed as she walked away and then said loudly, "Bullshit." Veronica turned her head and told him, "Stop it," and went outside.

Thomas laughed again and went back to watching the local news. Veronica went and ate lunch, and she thought about what her dad said. She was curious about this detective. She smiled as she finished her food and went back to her room to talk to a friend on her phone about her date.

Around 5 PM, Thomas saw Veronica drive off with her two body guards tailing her from a distance. She did not know her car had a tracker on it, so her dad would always know where she was for her safety. There was also a camera in the car where he could always see if something was wrong. Technology can be good sometimes for the right reason. Kidnapping the rich still happened in America, something he always worried about. He always worried about his kids due to how messed up our world is? Thomas lost one child. He would not lose another.

Veronica drove her Lamborghini down the road and headed to Robert's place. She didn't know if he was there but wanted to surprise him. She lied to her dad about how she felt for Robert. Once she arrived in the parking lot, she went and knocked on his door, and nobody answered, but she kept on knocking.

After knocking for a few minutes, she heard Robert yell, "There better be a fire." He opened the door and stood there in his briefs, scratching his eyes, surprised, and asked, "What are you doing here?" Veronica smiled and said, "Nice briefs," as she walked in. Roberts closed the door and asked, "Hi, what are you up to?" Veronica asked him, "What are you doing?" Robert told her, "Napping because I was up at six this morning, worked out, went to work and discovered how Mason got out of town." Veronica asked him, "Do you bring your work home." Robert stretched and said, "Sometimes, but I am working on an important case." Veronica told him, "Good, get cleaned up. We are going out."

Robert looked at her and informed her, "Sorry, I have to go in and do some Police work." Veronica stepped up to him and kissed him, and said, "No argument." He smiled and replied, "Ok, you win." Veronica smiled and remarked, "Of course." Robert went and took a shower and got cleaned up. While Robert was showering, Veronica thought about sneaking in and getting in the shower with him, but her better judgment said, "No, not yet." She started to look through all the paperwork, and Robert highlighted and circled names and locations. It looked like Robert had narrowed it down to four people and places. Veronica was impressed by how smart and detailed Robert was. One bus went out west, one went north, and one went south to Key West.

Once Robert was cleaned up and dressed, they headed out, and Robert headed to his truck. When he stopped and looked around, he saw her walking to her car. Robert said, "No, I drive." Veronica said, "No, I am driving." Robert went and got in his truck and started it up. He then rolled down his window and told her, "Either I drive, or I go to work. You decide." Veronica called him some names in Spanish, and he laughed and told her in Spanish, "Piss off, and by the way, I speak Spanish fluently."

She was shocked and smiled. She got out of her car, went to her passenger side, and stood there. Robert smiled and said, "Fair enough." He got out of his truck and hit the lock switch, and went and opened her car door for her. Veronica smiled as she got in. Robert went and got in on the driver's side, started the vehicle up, and smiled.

They didn't say anything for a few seconds, then he looked at veronica and told her, "I had one of these," and she replied, "No, you didn't." He said, "I swear I really did. It hit the track fast and was quick, except it would crash all the time." She remarked, "bullshit." He smiled and said, "I swear, it was an amazing matchbox hot wheel." Veronica laughed and called him a smartass. Robert snickered, saying, "Yep, I have been told that a few times, even by my bosses."

He revved the engine up and asked, "Where do you want to go?" Veronica told him, "Just drive, and we will see." Robert headed south and went to the beach. She asked, "Why here?" Roberts said, "It's nice right now, and I think a good walk would be good for both of us after last night." Once they arrived at Lummus Park Beach, Robert took his shoes and socks off and tossed them on his seat while Veronica took off her heels and did the same.

They walked and talked for an hour or so and came to a beach restaurant selling seafood. Robert asked Veronica if she was hungry, and she answered, "Yes, you buying?" Robert smiled and told her, "All the fish and chips on me." They went and entered the restaurant, where they watched the waves. Robert asked her if she wanted a beer, and she said, "After last night, no alcohol for a while." Robert ordered a beer, and they had a nice dinner and talked about their families. Veronica was impressed by the Roberts blue color family and its encouragement of hard work. Veronica talked about her family and how losing her mom and her brother felt. Once they were done eating, they went back and walked on the beach some more.

Veronica stopped after a while and looked around. Her black hair blew in the wind, and she said, "I love the beach." Then she decided to run into the waves with Robert watching. He laughed, and she told him, "Come in," and he replied, "I can't. I got the keys and my gun." She called him a party pooper. He responded by saying, "Yea, that's me." She came out soaked, and when she walked up to him, they looked into each other's eyes, and they fell into each other's arms and kissed passionately. They fell to the ground partially in the waves and kissed for a few minutes in the sand as the waves came crashing in.

After five minutes of hugging and kissing, they got up, held onto each other, and walked to the Lamborghini. When they got to Robert's place, they got out, and she ran over to him and kissed him, and they went upstairs to his place and went inside. He locked the door, and they helped each other out of each other's clothes, and he lifted her in his arms and carried her into his bedroom. They made love like two lovers who had not seen each other in a long time. Veronica's two bodyguards were parked, saw the lights go off, and called Mr. Jackson and told him what happened during the evening. Thomas told them, "Stay there, and you guys rotate on sleep in case she comes home during the night." They responded by saying, "No problem, boss, as they hung up." Thomas smiled, and he went to bed, hoping this was the man who could win her heart and not break it. He just wanted her to be happy.

Chapter 9

The Search

The next morning Robert's alarm went off at 6:00 am, and he got up and jumped in the shower while Veronica was still sleeping. After showering, he heard the door open, and Veronica stepped in and opened the shower door with a smile on her face. She asked, "Where are you going?" He mentioned he had to get his work out and then go to work. Veronica smiled and requested, "How about coming back to bed and workout with me." He smiled and remarked, "Ok," they began kissing each other, and Robert turned off the water, and Veronica walked backward out of the shower with Robert kissing her. They went and made love some more.

Robert again stepped out of bed at about 8 am, took a shower, and dressed. Veronica looked at him and said, "Wait for me." She went and jumped in the shower, and 40 minutes later, they left. Robert walked Veronica to her car, and they kissed, and he opened the door, and she got in. Veronica asked whether you could come to my house for dinner tonight. Robert answered back, "I can't. I am heading to key west to follow a lead, and I won't get back until after midnight." Veronica asked, "Why Key West?" Robert told her, "Because it's one of the four areas I believe Mason went." Veronica asked, "How about tomorrow evening." Robert said, "I will be there, and what time." Veronica asked, "Is 5 pm ok?" Robert leaned into the car and whispered, "Perfect," and they kissed again, and she took off and headed home. Veronica smiled as she drove home. She felt happy being with this guy.

Robert went and jumped into his truck and looked and saw Veronica's two bodyguards following her from a distance. He snickered and told himself I bet they had a uncomfortable night, as he headed south on highway One to Key West. Veronica got home, parked her car, and jogged to the front door, where the butler opened the door and said, "Good morning Ms. Jackson." She smiled and said with a smile, "Good morning." When she walked in, she saw her dad coming out of his office, and he had a smile on his face and asked, "Well honey, how are you doing?" She smiled and informed him, "Doing fine, Daddy," as she headed up the stairs. Veronica stopped on the stairs and told him, "Robert is following up on a lead in Key West looking for Mason."

She told her dad, "I have invited Robert to dinner tomorrow." Thomas said, "Great, and what do you think he would want to eat?" Veronica said, "T-bone with salad, vegetables, and a plain potato." Thomas grinned and told her, "I will let the cook know, and where are you going?" She told him, "She is going to swim some laps in the pool, layout, and relax." Thomas said, "Ok." She went upstairs, and Thomas went back into his office and called his detective agency, and during the discussion, he told the person on the other line to send a couple of men down to Key West and told him why. Then he hung up, leaned back on his chair and thought deeply about how the investigation was going, and hoped Detective Robert Bench could find this guy.

While Robert was driving south, two more dead women washed up on the shores of a Miami beach, leading the total to six. The Police Chief met with his subordinates and initiated a task force about serial killers or killers killing young college women who disappeared at least two weeks before they were discovered. The FBI was brought in and gave a psychological profile of who the killer could be. In most cases, it's a white guy, age bracket, appearance, mother issues, intelligence, and other information. All the women were strangled to death; the autopsy shows were someone's hands.

This made the news and went national. Young women were told not to go places by themselves. The local university Police increased their patrols, and there was an increase of police patrols in all areas to protect the citizens and hopefully find and capture this person. The autopsy report, when released, documented all the women had been raped, but there was no DNA to help identify the person. There were no fingerprints or DNA found anywhere on the women's bodies. The local politicians started to panic, knowing this could hurt the tourist season, which was coming up ion a few more months.

Robert arrived at the Key West Police station to give them the courtesy he was in town and pass some photos around. He walked in and asked for the supervisor, and the Desk sergeant said that would be me, sir. Robert identified himself again, and the Desk Sargent smiled and asked, "What can we do for you." Robert handed him some photos and informed the desk Sargent, "I am trying to find this guy, he was wanted for murder, and I believe he might have come this way." When the desk Sargent saw the copies, his facial expression went from a smile to a frown in a blink of an eye.

Robert is new to that look from the Sargent who informed him, "That individual was here, and he robbed a restaurant, assaulted the bartender/Manager, and split." The Sargent looked at the photo again, then looked back at Robert and told him, "We have been looking all over for this turd." Robert got a little excited and asked, "When and where did this happen?" The Sargent stated, "Two days ago." Robert asked if it was ok if he saw the police report, and the Sargent answered back and said, "I am not supposed to do this, but since we are looking for the same guy, step this way, please." The side door opened, and Robert walked in and followed the Sargent.

The Sargent approached a detective, identified Robert, and told him, "Please give this man whatever he needs." The Sargent and Robert shook hands, and Robert said, "Thanks." The Sargent told Robert, "Good luck," and went back to his desk. The detective shook hands with Robert and said, "My name is Detective Thorn, but you can call me Tom." Robert said, "Thanks," and Tom handed

Robert the paperwork on the assault and robbery. Robert reviewed everything and looked at the up-to-date photo of Mason. He was right. His hair was cut short and blonde. He had grown a beard, and Robert was not surprised by that. He knew Mason would cut it now and not shave. He asked for a copy, and Detective Thorn said, "Go ahead and keep that one."

Robert asked, "Where was this place?" Tom said, "Follow me, and I will take you out there." So, they left the station, and 20 minutes later, they pulled up to the restaurant. They both went in and identified themselves as a waitress and

the manager. Robert asked a few questions like, "Did this guy use any credit cards, or was it all cash?" The manager stated, "It was all cash."

The Manager explained how the guy stood at the bar all night and only had a couple of drinks and watched people dance. He didn't talk with anyone, and the guy seemed to be a loner, and he seemed to be a little unclean. Tom asked, "What do you mean unclean?" Robert interrupted and told Tom, "He probably had not showered in a couple of days and was looking for easy money."

Robert shook Manager's hand and looked at Tom, and told him, "I will be here for a few hours and will drive around." Tom told Robert, "If you need anything, call me." Tom handed Robert his card, and Robert handed Tom his. They shook hands and went their separate ways. Robert went to his truck and called Mr. Jackson.

When Jackson answered the phone after three rings, Robert said, "This is Robert." Thomas told him, "Hello, Robert. How is it going down there?" Veronica walked in and listened. Thomas told her, "It's Robert." Thomas said, "Go ahead, Robert." Robert said, "Mason was here in Key West two days ago. He robbed a restaurant which tells me he was short on money." Robert continued and told Thomas, "I am going to drive around for a while and see what turns up here." Thomas got quiet and said, "Keep me informed." Robert then asked, "Is Veronica there?" Thomas told him, "Yes, hang on," Veronica took the phone and said Robert, how are you doing? Robert told her, "I am getting close, your dad will explain the rest, and I have to go. Talk to you later," and he hung up.

Veronica was disappointed that Robert did not talk longer but knew it must be important. She hung up the house phone and asked, "Dad, what's going on." Thomas looked at her and told her Mason was in Key West two days ago." He took a deep breath and said, "Robert is getting closer. This young man is amazing, isn't he?" Veronica looked down and smiled and then looked at her dad and told him, "I hope so." She then left her dad's office. Thomas picked up the house phone and called his detective agency, and notified them to get every available man down to Key West. He explained that Mason was spotted two days ago. Thomas told the person on the other side of the phone, "Find him. Do you understand me? My patience is almost run out." The man on the other line said, "Yes, sir."

Thomas was impressed with Robert but wanted Vincent Mason dead or alive, preferably dead. He turned on the local news and heard about the serial killer who killed Six young girls. Thomas called Veronica's bodyguards and told them, "They need to be really close to her for his daughters' protection, and she no longer goes anyplace by herself." He took a deep breath and told them that when she takes the limo, you guys are in the limo with her." They answered back, "Yes sir," and walked out. He yelled out and said, "Find her keys and give them to me."

Robert sat in his truck, looking at the photo of Mason, and tried to imagine what he would look like at this moment. He then figured he would not go anyplace were he could be recognized easily. Robert felt Mason would be at the beaches to hide or at some low-cost cabins or cheap apartment rentals. Robert went and spent the day walking around the beaches through the many crowds at the beaches.

He started with the farthest and worked his way back. He had no luck when around 435 pm, he saw a man in his mid-20s with short hair who looked like he was washing his shirt in the water. Robert laughed and said to himself, "Well, let's sit back and see what this guy does and if He could get a better look at him." So Robert put his shades back on and put on a hat he had in his back pocket, and laid out like he was sleeping on the top of a bench.

The guy got out of the water and dried off, and looked around nervously. He got dressed and he looked around and headed towards the docks where fishing boats docked. There were also cruise ships hooked up, either dropping off passengers or picking them up. Robert observed him walking away, so he followed him. Robert grabbed a beer can out of the trash can and acted like he was just a person enjoying the beach with a beer heading back to the docks. Robert followed this guy for about 200 yards when the guy turned around to look around. Robert kept walking, and the individual looked at the water and then behind him and saw Robert. At first, he suspected nothing because the guy looked like just a guy enjoying the beach with a beer.

Then he recognized Robert by how he walked and his appearance. Mason new who it was and took off running. Robert threw the beer can and took off running off after Mason. Robert's hat flew off, and the pursuit began. It was an endurance run. People saw one man chasing another man, and both men were on a full sprint. Mason saw the piers and headed towards them, and when he got to it, he plowed through the crowd, hit the security guard who approached him, and began running down the Main Dock.

Robert blew through the crowd in pursuit of Mason, and The other security guard called for assistance and checked on his partner. Robert was gaining, and then Mason ran through several stores on the Dock with Robert on his tail. Mason ended up back on the Dock and saw a cruise ship heading out but was riding close to the dock. He ran through the entry point without being checked, the alarm went off, and the CBP were in pursuit of both men who ran through the security checkpoints and the building.

Robert was about 20 yards behind Mason, who was tired, made it to the outside dock, ran, jumped onto the cruise ship outside, and held on while catching his breath. Robert jumped and saw Mason's right leg, surprising Mason, who almost lost his grip. Robert tried to pull Mason off the latter, and then Mason kicked Robert in the face causing him to fall into the water.

Mason looked down and smiled and shot Robert the finger, and he climbed up the latter and jumped over the rail, and disappeared. Robert swam to the dock, climbed out, and then realized there were 20 law enforcement officials pointing guns at him. Robert raised his hands as they yelled at him to get on the ground. He followed instructions, and he was handcuffed.

His gun was discovered, and someone said Gun, and it was removed. Robert yelled, "I have a knife in my left boot and one inside my belt." Both knives were removed from him while he lay on the ground, cuffed. Robert tried to identify himself, but he was met with sarcasm. Robert realized he had taken his badge and ID off and left them under his truck seat for some stupid reason. Robert was helped up and taken to the local Police station for processing.

He kept saying, "I need my phone call," while in the holding tank. An unidentified Officer told him he would get one on their time. Robert laughed while sitting in the holding tank. He knew they were right. Many movies and TV shows make it seem that you are allowed a phone call immediately. It does not work that way. Four hours later, he was allowed to make a phone call. He called Mr. Jackson, who told Robert it would be taken care of. He was disappointed Robert had just missed getting Mason, but he knew Robert wouldn't quit. Robert was like a dog with a bone. He was focused.

Thomas called the Governor and told him what happened, and the governor said he would make some phone calls. Then

Thomas called Veronica and told her Robert wouldn't be here for dinner. He is in a holding cell and explains everything Robert tells him. Veronica was happy Robert was doing what he promised he would do, and he was getting close to catching Mason. She asked her dad, "Is he ok" and Thomas said, "Yes, he is fine, just pissed off he came up short." Veronica smiled and told her dad, "Robert will get him one way or the other." Thomas said, "I hope so."

Chapter 10

Bahamas Run Down

An hour later, Robert was released, and all charges were dropped. Robert sat at the desk of Detective Tom Thorn, who came in to help clean up the mess after being called in by his COP. Robert told Tom, "He needed to know where that boat was going since it was too late to call it back." Tom told him, "He already checked. It's going to Nassau in the Bahamas." Robert asked, "Could he use their phone and call his boss so he could brief him on what had happened and what he was going to do?" Once Robert made contact with his boss, Robert was told, "Hurry up with this case because we have our 6th body of college girls, and he needs all hands on deck with this one." Roberts said, "He saw it in the news today and understood." Then Robert hung up.

Robert immediately called Mr. Jackson and told him, "I need a private jet to pick me up here and take me to Nassau, Bahamas and let the police down there know I am coming and who we will be going after." Thomas said, "He will have his private jet there in about an hour," and hung up. Thomas called both US Senators of Florida to help smooth things over in the Bahamas for Robert and his men when they flood the island. He then called his Pilot on call and told him what he needed to do as quickly as possible.

Veronica, standing there listening, said, "Daddy, I am going." Thomas told her, "No, let Robert do his job." Veronica said, "I am going no ifs or butts about it." Thomas looked at his daughter and said, "You care about him," she got quiet and then shook her head up and down and said, "Yes, Dad, I really do."

She went and grabbed some clothes and had her driver take her to Robert's place to get some of his clothes. She had the manager of Robert's place let her and then headed to the Executive Airport, where she boarded her dad's jet. The staff took her luggage and secured it. The pilot asked, "Ma'am, straight to Key West first," and Veronica answered, "Yes, as fast as you can." The pilot looked at the copilot and told him, "Let's get going." Five minutes later, they were in the air when Veronica realized ten men were in the back of the plane going over what was needed while in the Bahamas.

Robert had the local police take him to his truck, and he drove to the airport. He grabbed his badge and cleaned his gun while he waited for the plane. Robert also oiled and cleaned his two knives. About an hour later, he saw a plain land, and the pilot disembarked and yelled, "Robert Bench." Robert waved his hand so the pilot could see as he walked over to the plane. Once he started boarding, a woman stepped to the door and said, "Hi, Robert." Robert smiled and asked Veronica, "What are you doing here?" Veronica laughed and told him, "I brought the cavalry to help out." She said, "I have to take care of my man," and she kissed him, and Robert replied, "I have to take care of you." Veronica smiled and answered back, "Maybe." They boarded, and he looked in the back of the plane and saw ten big men. He figured those were old men Jackson's men sent to help.

He went and introduced himself, and before takeoff, they seat-belted themselves in, and the plane took off for the Bahamas. Robert briefed the men on everything they needed to know. Veronica interrupted Robert when he paused and told everyone, "My dad had the Bahamas PM notified we are coming, and we will get all the cooperation we need." Once the plane leveled out, Veronica and Robert relaxed in their seats, and she started to talk when Robert fell asleep. She snickered and realized how exhausted he must be.

Veronica got up and asked the stewardess for a blanket, and after a blanket was brought to her, she covered Robert, who was out like a light. Veronica watched Robert sleep and realized what she told her dad was true, and she truly cared for these men. She then called her dad and told him where they were and how things were going. Then she closed her eyes and fell asleep.

An hour outside Nassau, the co-pilot came and woke up Veronica and informed her, "Ma'am, we are an hour out." Veronica told the copilot, Thank you". She woke up Robert, and they got cleaned up in the plane restroom. The men also got ready. Once the plane landed and stopped, the door opened, and the head of the Bahamas law enforcement and others were waiting. Veronica stepped down the ladder, and the Chief held her hand as she stepped down. He introduced himself to Veronica and told her, "Welcome to the Bahamas, and we are at your service, Ms. Jackson." Once everyone else stepped off the plane, she introduced each person. Then she looked back at the Chief, who said, "The boat will be here in three hours, and the boat will dock at approximately 8:00 A.M." He looked around and he explained, "A coded message was sent to the cruise ship about a wanted person on the boat and gave new instructions on docking."

They drove to the dock and waited. The Bahamian Security Forces were waiting with small watercraft and vehicles. About 15 minutes out, the Chief received a phone call from the cruise ship about a white male mid-20s jumping off the boat and being seen swimming what they believed was Cable Beach. The chief told him, "Continue with the docking instructions." He stepped over to Veronica and Robert and explained what he was told. Robert immediately ran for a vehicle and jumped in, and Veronica yelled, "Robert, wait." He ignored her as she ran to the Vehicle and jumped in just as Robert took off for the mentioned beach area. He was driving backward due to the dock not allowing him to turn around. The Bahamas Police jumped in their vehicles and headed to cable beach.

Veronica buckled up, looked at Robert, and asked, "What the hell are you doing?" Robert flipped the vehicle around on the disembark dock and slammed the gear forward, and the car headed to Cable beach. He had been here many years ago in the Navy, so he knew the island. He worked his way down West Bay Street and turned right on Skyline Drive. He felt lucky because it was early, and there was very little traffic and no big crowds yet. While speeding down, Skyline Driver started approaching cable beach and slowed down, and started to look around for Mason. Robert looked around and then suddenly saw a white male with soak clothing walking down a street.

Robert turned the vehicle in his direction and sped towards him. Mason heard the car and turned around, and started running. Then Mason stopped and jumped a fence into an open yard that led to another street. Robert jumped out and yelled to Veronica, "Get on the car radio and let them know what direction Mason was heading." Robert jumped the fence and looked around and saw Mason running towards the beach. Robert ran in his direction, trying to catch him. Veronica jumped into the driver's seat and backed the car up, and yelled on the radio what was going on. She backed the vehicle up backward when she slowly stopped at the intersection, and when she stopped, Mason opened the door and pushed her over, and jumped in.

She saw him brandishing a knife in his hand and commented, "Hello, it's been a long time Veronica." Mason backed into the main street and threw the gears first when Robert suddenly jumped on the roof. Veronica was in shock at what was happening. Mason sped down the street with Robert hanging on to the roof. When they ran into morning traffic, Mason slammed on the brakes and saw Robert fly over the front window onto the ground.

He grabbed Veronica by the hair and dragged her out and looked at her face to face, and told her, "Let's go for a walk." He dragged her into the morning crowd which had been building. Robert stood up and saw Mason, with Veronica as his hostage, walking into the crowd. Robert heard sirens in the background, and he got up and ran in the direction Mason and Veronica went.

Mason worked his way around the crowd and heard the sirens getting closer as he headed to the beach. While walking fast with Veronica holding her long black hair in his fist, they made it to the beach, and he saw a boat with an operator about 30 yards from the beach. Robert pushed through the early beach crowd, ran onto the beach, and pulled his gun.

Mason realized he would not make it to the boat, so he turned around and put the knife against Veronica's throat and yelled, "Well, supercop, drop it, or I give her a new hole." People stopped and watched and filmed what was going on. The security forces arrived, and they made their way through the crowd and circled Mason. Mason yelled out, "Drop your weapons, or I will kill this bitch." Then Mason kissed her right cheek and declared to her, "I always wanted to do that in college, but you were too snooty bitch." Robert walked close with his gun pointed down. Mason yelled again about weapons being dropped, and he slightly cut a nick on her neck. The security forces looked at their boss, who said, "Weapons down, but do not drop them."

Mason looking at Robert, told him, "I am not joking, supercop. I will kill her in 5 seconds. Robert walked slowly towards Mason, and he raised his gun. Mason told Robert, "Are you ready to see her die," he yanked her backward and put the knife against her throat. Robert could see the fear in her eyes and heard Mason count, "One, two, three fo." Mason never said the full word four because Robert pulled the trigger and shot Mason in the head, and as Veronica fell to the ground, Robert kept pulling the trigger and put five more rounds into Mason's chest as he fell to the ground dead. Robert stepped over and helped Veronica up, and they walked away. Robert didn't even look at Mason. His only concern was Veronica and getting her out of there.

Robert stopped and turned to the Police chief and told him, "The body is yours," Robert led Veronica through the crowd as people filmed. Robert flagged down a taxi, and one stopped, and he told the driver, "Take us to the airport." The taxi driver was puzzled but followed instructions. When they got to the plane, Robert helped Veronica, who was still in shock, up into the Jet. Robert looked at the Pilot and told him, "Take us home." The Pilot looked at Ms. Jackson and said, "Yes, sir." The Pilot signaled to the crew, let's go. They revved up the engines and took off for Miami.

Chapter 11

After Math

While on the plane, he laid Veronica on the couch and grabbed the blanket he used, covered her up, and fell asleep. Robert called Mr. Jackson on his cell phone, and when Jackson got on the phone, he sounded pissed off. Thomas asked Robert, "How could you put her in harm's way like that?" Robert responded back and told Thomas, "Shut the fuck up, old man, and I will tell you what happened." Mr. Jackson yelled back, "Who the fuck do you think you are talking to me like that?" Robert told him, "Either shut up and listen or I hang up." Jackson asked, "Was she right now?" Robert said, "She is asleep, and we will be there in 45 minutes, so have a car there, and by the way, your men are back in the Bahamas." Jackson calmed down and said, "Ok, Detective, tell me everything that happened."

Robert left nothing out and explained everything in detail as a good detective would. Jackson said, "Thank you, Robert, for doing what you did, but I don't want to see you again in my house." He paused and continued speaking, "I can't forgive you for putting my daughter in harm's way." Robert said, "Whatever, Mr. Jackson, I am bringing her home," and he hung up. He was pissed off about what was said between Mr. Jackson and him. He just leaned back and closed his eyes to relax.

When the plane landed and stopped, the door opened, and Robert helped Veronica down the stairs and to the limousine that was there. Mr. Jackson got out, and Robert looked at him, and then he whispered something to Veronica, who leaned forward and kissed Robert, and she whispered the words, "I love you," and then her dad helped her get into the limo. Mr. Jackson closed the door and went to the other side, and the limo and escort drove away.

Robert watched the vehicles leave and headed to his Vehicle with Foster waiting for him. Foster went down and picked it up. Foster and Robert talked for a while, and Foster jumped into a patrol car that drove up, and Robert went home. While driving home, his cell phone went off, and it was the Chief of Detectives. He asked, "How was he doing?" He mentioned how he has been watching all the videos on the news, YouTube, Facebook, and Twitter. He told Robert, "What happened in the Bahamas has gone worldwide on you taking out Mason and saving Jackson's daughter." Robert declared, "Boss, I am tired and do not feel like talking." The COD said, "I will see you in the morning for your report." Robert answered, "I will be there at 8," and then Robert hung up.

When Robert got home, he went and laid down on his bed and took off his boots, and set his alarm for 6 am. He lay down and saw the look of fear in Veronica's eyes. He felt bad about what had happened, and he realized he truly cared about her, and finally, he fell asleep after going over again on what had happened.

Once the limousine made it to their home, Mr. Jackson helped Veronica out of the vehicle, and they headed to the house. Her dad helped Veronica up the stairs, and the door opened. The staff came out and helped bring her in and up the stairs to her room. She stopped and turned. She stopped talking for a second, took a deep breath, and then said, "I acted stupidly and put myself in that position." She whispered, "Dad, I love him and will only marry him," and then she turned around, and the maids helped her upstairs and put her to bed.

Thomas turned around and went to his office and called around to thank the people that helped with his son's case. He called the Police Chief, saying, "I want to have a press conference tomorrow at 0900 am with you, the Mayor, and the Chief of Detectives." The COP said, "He will make that happen." Then Jackson hung up the house phone and leaned back and thought about what Robert said and the words Veronica used. He was grateful she was ok, but he was pissed off with Robert for having her in that dangerous position she was put in.

He made more phone calls to have his detectives, and stewardess returned back to Miami. Thomas then called the Bahamas PM, thanked him for his help, and let the security forces know how appreciative he was. He asked the PM, "Is there anything I could do to help the people of the Bahamas, Mr. Prime Minister?" The PM said, "Actually, well, sir, we could use some help with our water system on a couple of the outer islands, and we could use some financial assistance with that." Jackson asked, "Will 200 million be enough" and the PM responded by saying, "That's more than enough." Thomas Jackson said, "Use the remaining amount for the poor in your country." The PM again thanked Mr. Jackson and told him, "If there is ever something you need, just call." Then both men hung up, and Thomas did some work on his computer, and about 9 pm, he went to bed after checking on Veronica.

Robert was awakened by his alarm at 6:00 AM, and he turned it off and jumped into his workout clothes. He drove to the beach and ran for five miles. After his run, he went and worked out hard with weights. He knew he was in for a very along day. Once he got cleaned up, he stopped by IHOP and had a vegetation omelet with orange juice. He read the paper and saw a photo of his shooting Mason with Veronica being held by Mason. He read the story in the Miami paper, which was pretty well written. I guess to many video tapes out there to keep things from being twisted without any distortion or lies. He was glad that the case was closed and finished. It was a long and a big pain in the ass case with too many politicians involved, and at least he did not have to use the piece of paper the politicians signed.

Once he was done eating, he left his usual three-dollar tip and headed to work. When he arrived, he saw the media all over the place, and he turned into the police parking lot. He headed to his desk, and people he passed patted him on the back and told him a good job getting that scum bucket. Robert shook hands with some of them. When he got to his desk, he saw cut-out photos of his blasting the dirtbag. Robert grinned and worked on his case to finally closed it out.

Robert watched the Conference, which was very black and white. When the press asked about him, they said he was on the side doing his job closing out the case. Then the media pounced and asked what about the murders of the college girls up and down the Florida coast. The COP stepped up and announced, "We are working with the FBI, and it looks like more young girls were killed in the northern part of the state over the last year with a grisly number of around 20-25 girls." The press asked, "Why is it taking so long, and is Detective Bench going to assist on the case?" The COP said, "We have a lot of men on the case with the FBI, and we will use all available tools we have in our arsenal."

He paused and looked around and continued and stated, "All the departments involved in the state-run task force are working together to find the perp or perps." One reporter asked if you think more than one person is doing this. And the Chief of Detectives stepped up and said, "You never know. We are looking at all possibilities, including copycats." Then another Reporter asked, "Is Detective Bench going to be involved after shooting Vincent Mason?" The COD stated, "He is working on the paperwork on the case of Vincent Mason, who was responsible for murdering Mr. Jackson's son."

A reporter yelled out, "Mr. Jackson, are you glad Detective Bench killed Vincent Mason?" Mr. Jackson stepped up to the microphone and paused before speaking, saying, "I am glad justice was done." Then the same reporter asked, "How is your daughter doing?" Mr. Jackson responded, "She is at home resting. She was in a difficult and dangerous situation that happened to her." Another reporter asked, "Why was she there with Detective Bench?" Mr. Jackson said, "Next question."

The reporters got quiet for a second, and a reporter asked, "Is his daughter dating Detective Bench?" Mr. Jackson paused and answered with, "Next question." One more reporter asked, "Mr. Jackson will you give Detective Bench the millions you promised anyone who would get Vincent Mason Dead or alive?" Then he asked, "Also did Detective Bench execute Vincent Mason with extreme prejudice?" Mr. Jackson said, "Mr. Bench refused the money and saved my daughter's life." Then another reporter asked, "Why was your daughter there?" Mr. Jackson looked at the COP, who stepped up and stated, "The press conference is over. Thank you for coming."

Robert chuckled and went back to finish the paperwork he was trying to get done. A phone call came into the investigative department about two more missing girls being found on the beach. Everyone ran out of the room and headed with lights and sirens to the crime location. The press saw all the vehicles heading out with lights and sirens, and they ran to their vehicles and tried to catch up. The COP asked an officer who came running up, "What was going on?" The officer stated, "Two more missing girls washed up on the beach." The COP looked at the Mayor and said, "This is getting out of hand." The Mayor looked back and said, "We are in trouble if this is not fixed."

Robert heard what had happened and kept on working on finishing his paperwork. He hoped the bosses would not ask him to help because he just wanted a break to do some old-time police work. At about 5 pm, he finished his reports, dropped them off at his boss's desk, and headed home. While heading home, he thought about what Veronica whispered to him and about everything else that happened with Veronica. She was a brave person, and she did not even know it. He figured he would have to figure out how to see her in the future.

Chapter 12

Roommate

When he drove up and got out of his truck, he headed to his door and put the key in, and the door opened, and there stood veronica. She was in one of his shirts and wearing shorts, and was barefoot. She stepped up to Robert, kissed him passionately, and told him, "I love you, Robert. You don't have to say that to me right now, but I can wait". She grabbed his hand and brought him inside, and he closed the door and saw dinner on the table. He asked, "Did you make it?" Veronica responded, "Yes, I did," with a smile on her face. Robert told her, "It smells great. What is it?" She told him, "It's a Cuban dish my mom used to make."

Robert looked around and saw two huge suite cases and a couple of small ones and asked, "What are those for?" She told him, "They are my clothes. I am moving in with you." Robert was surprised and asked, "Why?" Veronica said, "Since my dad does not want to see you, and I love you, I decided to come and live with you."

Robert did not answer, and She looked at him and asked Robert, "Is that a problem?" Robert looked at her as she looked at him, and he stepped up and grabbed her and kissed her passionately, and asked, "I hope you don't snore." She smacked his shoulder and said, "I don't." Robert asked, "How do you know you don't?" Robert smiled. Veronica asked, "Do you?" Robert using a line from the three stooges, said, "I stayed up all night once, and I didn't snore once." Veronica laughed and said, "That was stupid." Robert smiled and stated, "Get used to it."

She kissed him and asked him to "Lift the suitcases and put them in the bedroom." He started laughing and stated, "Already giving orders, and we are not even," he caught himself and looked at Veronica, who was smiling, putting out the silver ware. Robert put the suit cases in his bedroom and then sat at the table next to veronica and reached for her hand and held it and prayed to himself, and she looked at him. Then he let go and started eating the food. He was amazed at how good it was and told her so.

Once they were done eating, they both cleaned the dishes and put them into the dishwasher. Veronica asked do you wash then as soon as they go in or wait till its full? He said when it's full. She said, "OK," and then she wiped the table off while Robert went and sat on the couch.

Once done, she sat beside him and asked, "What do you want to do?" He smiled and hesitated and asked her, "How did your dad take it when you told him you were moving in with me?" Veronica went into it, and heading out to the taxi, he told her she was always welcome to come back anytime, day or night. She hugged her dad and kissed his forehead, and said, "I love you, but I love Robert." Her dad told her, "He loved her too." She told her dad, "You have been waiting for me to find a good man who would love me, and I know he does by how he does things around and acts around me, so you need to get used to it." Her dad asked, "Don't you want your car?" She said, "No."

Then she asked the driver, "To get her suitcases and put them in the vehicle." The driver did that and asked, "Are you ready," and she gave him the address. The driver put it in his GPs and drove. Thomas Jackson was not happy with Robert, but he was glad his daughter was happy. He just hoped their relationship did not fall apart. If that happened, he would do what any father did to a man that hurt his only child, especially a daughter.

Thomas went back inside to do some work. He knew Veronica was on her own. He froze all her credit cards and bank accounts. Veronica new he would do that when he didn't get his way. He did it to her brother until he went on the right path. She told Robert, "She only has the money in her purse and no accounts," due to her dad doing what she knew he would do. Robert smiled and told her, "I guess you will be taking care of the home." She chuckled, saying, "I guess that will be my job, and by the way, what time is wake up?" He told her, "6 AM." She smiled, looked at him, and whispered, "Maybe we need to go to bed to get a good night's sleep." Robert looked at her and whispered back, "I agree." He grabbed her hand, hit the light switch and turned into the bedroom and pushed the suitcase off the bed, and turned off the light as he helped her out of her clothes, and she helped him get out of his. They made love and fell asleep in each other's arms.

What she did not know was the necklace Veronica had on. There was a tracker on it that let her dad know where she was at all times. Before Thomas went to bed, he turned on his computer and checked to see where she was at. The computer showed she was at Robert's place. He then turned the computer off and went to bed. He used technology to know where she was always. He lost his wife and son. He would not lose her, even if he were mad at the man she loved.

At 6:00 A.M, Robert woke up when the alarm went off. He got up and got ready to go for a run. Veronica got up and told him, "I am going with you," and he started to snicker and said, "Ok, but please try and keep up." She laughed and told him, "She will," and he answered back, "We will see." Once they got in the truck, they headed to the beach. After they arrived, he parked, they got out, and they began stretching. After about 10 minutes, Veronica asked, "How far?" Robert grinned and told her, "Two and a half out and back." She smiled and said, "That's easy." Robert laughed and responded by saying, "We will see."

Veronica started running to the beach, and Robert headed in her direction and ran just behind her. He noticed after a mile out, Veronica was staying steady and kept on going while he continued to run behind her. When they got two miles out, she kept the same pace, and he was impressed with her running skill. When they got to the two-and-a-half-mile spot, they turned around, and she kept the same pace, and he decided to pick up the pace, shifted gears, and passed her, but she pushed herself and was right behind him. When they got to the last mile, he picked it up to a full sprint, and Veronica picked it up, staying right behind Robert. When they got to the quarter mile left, she passed him up, and he picked it up, and they raced to the finish line. He beat her by about five feet and began walking, cooling off.

After a few minutes of walking and catching her breath, Veronica walked up to him and told him, "Not bad." Robert stopped, looked at her, and said, "Not bad, you did great where did you run at?" She smiled and told him, "She ran track in college." Robert smiled and stated, "Surprises keep coming." They both walked a little bit down the beach and then turned around. Veronica asked, "What's next?" Robert said, "It's weight time." She said, "Ok." They got in his truck and headed to the gym, where he lifted, and she did her own workout.

After a couple of hours, they headed back to Robert's place and got cleaned up. When Robert got out of the shower, Veronica already made bacon and eggs. They ate, and she asked, "If she could go to work with him?" He immediately said, "No." Then he explained, "He was trying to finish up a couple of cases and hoped to make a couple of arrests today." She smiled and answered back, "I understand." She did ask, "If she could use his truck?" Robert told her, "Yes, and why?" She told him, "I want to go see my dad and collect a few things." Robert told her, "Sure, just drop me off at work."

When they reached the station, he put the truck in park, leaned over, and kissed her. They kissed for a moment, and she told him, "Please be careful." Robert told her, "I always am." She laughed, saying, "Yea, right." He jumped out and she moved over to the driver's seat. He waved, and she waved back and drove off. A couple of his friends walked by and asked him, "How the hell did you end up with that?" He responded by saying, "I still do not know how and what I did." They walked into the building, and Robert started working at his desk. He felt things were getting interesting with her. He wondered what other surprises he would discover being with her. Like all men, he asked if he would screw it up.

Chapter 13

Bodies and the Search

Over the next five months, Robert would be out the door at a regular time to be home for dinner. Everyone noticed it and was amazed at how mellow Robert had become. He did his job and enjoyed his life with Veronica, who made him happy. Unfortunately, four more girls washed ashore dead over the next five months, and the investigation was not going anywhere. Robert was not assigned to the case or helping the Taskforce investigating the crimes. He had his own cases he was working on.

Then one day, while at his desk, he heard a commotion, and he looked up and saw all these men come walking into the investigation department. He saw the Mayor, the COP, the COD and the state governor who walked in, and he definitely did not look happy. They walked past him and headed to the conference room. The COD looked at Robert and told him, "Come with us, Detective. Your vacation is over." Robert said, "Shit," and got up and followed them into the conference room, and everyone, including Robert, sat down with the Governor at the head of the table. The Governor asked, "Can someone close the door" and one of the Governor's bodyguards closed the door and stepped out. The room got quiet, and most of the people looked at the governor.

The Governor stood up and looked at Robert and told him, "Mr. Bench, your reputation for catching murders and garbage is well known and documented." He paused and looked around the room, and continued, "This state is in dire straits over these murders, and nobody is close to catching whoever is doing this today then we were months ago." He slammed his fist down on the table and stated, "People are going to other states instead of here, and it's hitting businesses hard, and I am hearing it from businesses and the dam press, locally and nationally." He sat down and said, "The Task force is striking out, and I have had it up to here," as he pointed at his head.

He again looked around the room and back at Robert and said, "I want you to help out and do whatever Voo Doo you do to end this nightmare." He paused and continued by saying, "I know you are playing house with Thomas Jackson's daughter, and you have been living the good life." Robert told him, "I do my job, and I close out and catch the people on my cases, sir."

Robert was getting annoyed by the Governor and finally stated, "Enough of the BS crap. What do you want from me?" The Governor smiled and said, "Outstanding a man that does not blow smoke up my ass," as he looked around the room. People looked down from his angry glare. While putting both hands on the table, Robert stood and asked, "What do you want from me, Governor?" He paused as he looked right at the Governor, "Just spell it out." Robert voted for the guy and was a fan of the governor, but he was still a politician. The Governor told him, "I want you to hunt down this person and get him or her at all costs."

Robert walked around the room up to the Governor, who stood up, and they looked each other in the eye. Robert, in a strong tone of voice, told him, "I want a piece of paper with your signature and that man," pointing at the state Attorney General giving me full immunity from all things legal or civil that I do. The Attorney General stood up and yelled in a pissed-off tone of voice, "Hell no, I would never hear the end of it if this goes wrong."

The Governor and the AG were in the same party, and the Governor, who was pissed off due to the political mess this was causing, said, "Sit down and shut up." The Governor, looking at the AG, told him, "You will sign it and if you want to succeed me down the road." He paused, then told him, "If you do not, your career will be over today." The Mayor and others at the conference table looked around at each other, enjoying the show, but nobody said anything.

Robert said, "I am waiting," he added, "I want my LT when I am done with this." The Governor looked at Robert and told him, "You must be looking at marrying that girl." For the first time, Robert admitted to himself that's what he wanted to do but told the Governor, "You never know." The Governor then looked at the AG, who took a deep breath then said, "Ok, but he looked at Robert and added, "Detective, do not fuck this up, and I will get it written up, Detective."

Robert told the AG, "No, I will type it up." The AG told Robert, "We will get it to you later today." Robert again said, "No, You people are politicians. I will do it and write it in plain English without the political BS you guys have a habit of saying in your writings."

He stepped out and came back 15 minutes later with a memorandum written by him using the words he wanted and passed it around the room for all their signatures as witnesses. Then the Governor signed it, and the AG hesitated, and the Governor told him, "Fucking sign it," and the AG signed it with concern on his face.

Robert watched the paper get signed, then took it and told the men in the room, "I will start first thing in the morning, and I work alone." He looked at his boss and the COP and told them, "I want this office with three computers hooked up together with all records of the cases." The COP told him, "You will have it all sitting here ready to go first thing in the morning." Roberts then added, "Gentleman, we are done for now. You will get a report from me every 72 hours starting from tomorrow on what and why I am doing it."

Robert looked at his boss and told him, "I will take the cases I have and put them on your desk, boss." The COD smiled and told Robert, "That sounds good." Right before Robert left the room, the COD said, "Robert," and Robert answered back, "Yes sir," and the COD told him, "Thanks." Robert smiled and said, "Welcome," and he walked out of the room.

Robert cleared his desk, took his cases, and put them on his boss's desk. Everyone watched, and one of Robert's friends stated, "I guess you are going to help with this, Robert," Robert gave a thumbs up and then said, "See you guys tomorrow," and left to head home to spend the rest of the day with Veronica.

He had some things to do first before he started his work on this case. He called Veronica on his cell phone and asked her to pick him up. She said, "She would and asked if everything was ok?" Robert told her, "It's all good." Veronica said, "I will be there, but it will take about a half hour. I am with my dad." He said, "Sure, I will meet you out front." Veronica said, "I love you," and Robert was quiet for a moment, and then he surprised her and told her," I love you too, sweetie."

Veronica hung up her cell phone and, with a big smile, told her dad, "I have to go pick Robert up." With a puzzled look, Thomas asked, "Why the smile?" Veronica told him, "That's the first time he ever said he loved me." Thomas grinned and asked, "Things must be going well with you two?" She responded and stated, "Yes." Thomas told her, "I know I told Robert I do not want to see him, and I do not want him inside my home, but I was angry as a father worried about his daughter and the only child I have left."

Veronica stood there looking at her dad, and then she stepped over to her dad and told him, "I understand. That's why I am not mad at you." She said, "Daddy, I love this man, and you will have to grow up and accept it." She further added, "I am going to say yes whenever the day comes, and he proposes to me." Veronica looked into her dads' eyes and told her dad, "Robert brought me back to life. I felt like I was dying inside, and he has done something to me I thought nobody could do." He hugged her and told her, "I am happy for you. Please tell Robert it is done with. I only want my daughter's happiness, and please come to dinner tomorrow night." Veronica stepped back, smiled, and then hugged her dad tightly. He smiled and kissed the top of her head, and said, "I just want you to be safe and happy." She then let go and told him, "I have to go." He smiled, saying, "Please drive safe."

Chapter 14

Surprises

Veronica jumped into the truck as her dad watched her drive off. He was surprised their relationship had gone this far. Most rich kids would be shocked by getting cut off financially, but she wasn't. She visited all the time but not once asked for help in any way. He is happy and thrilled that she is happy. Thomas figured his anger had gone far enough, and he needed to move on from what happened to his daughter. She was happy, and that is what is important to him.

He stood there thinking about what she said, and he smiled and went back to his office, opened up her accounts with the bank, and reactivated her credit cards. He put all her things back to normal. She was happy, and he was amazed that he had not once complained about not having access to his money.

Once Veronica arrived at the Police Station, Robert walked out and jumped into the passenger seat. Veronica asked, "What do you not want to drive?" Robert answered back, "No, I have to do some thinking while we head home." Veronica said, "Good," and they headed to his place. Robert did not say anything and looked out the window as she drove.

She wondered what he was thinking about the whole time they headed home. When they got to Robert's place, he got out, walked up the stairs and to the door, and walked in. Veronica watched him and was amazed at how deep in thought he was. Robert went and sat down on the couch and just looked at the tv, which was off. Veronica said nothing and sat beside him, whispered into his ear, and told him, "Everything will be ok."

Suddenly, Robert turned his head towards her and got down on one knee and asked, "Will you marry me?" Veronica was surprised and was in shock. He pulled out a ring he had brought a week earlier, and Veronica started crying, put her finger out, and immediately said, "Yes." Robert stated, "I can't afford some big super ring, but, on cops, pay, it's the best I could do." She kissed him over and over and told him, "I don't care. You love me and want me to be your wife." She wiped her tears and said, "Yes, yes." They hugged and kissed and made promises to each other. Robert sat back, and Veronica laid down on his lap and looked up at her new engagement ring, and she smiled at him.

Veronica got quiet for a moment and mentioned her dad wanted them to come for dinner tomorrow night. Robert was surprised and asked, "Why?" She repeated what her dad told her, and she figured it was real between us, and he needed to move on from his daddy's anger. Robert laughed and told her, "That's great, but unfortunately, I have some bad news," and she sat up and said, "What's wrong?"

Robert looked at her and told her, "I am sorry to spoil the moment, but tomorrow I start on those missing girls' cases who are ending up dead on the beach." Veronica shook her head and said, "It's been awful, and I have been following it, those poor girls." She then said, "How does that affect you and me?" Robert told her, "I need you to stay with your dad because I will be working long shifts and won't be able to spend much time with you." He kissed her and told her, "I would feel better if you were with your dad instead of being here by yourself." She smiled and looked at her ring, and said, "Ok."

Veronica looked at her ring and asked, "Can we go out to dinner and celebrate?" He smiled and said, "What, no wife slaving over a hot stove?" She smacked his shoulder and said, "No, never going to happen." He told her, "Let's go, and what are you craving?" She told him, "Chinese food." Robert said, "Let's go," and grabbed his truck keys. They headed out and went and ate. They came back after eating and went to bed early since Robert needed to get as much sleep as possible due to the long days he knew were going to happen.

However, she rolled over onto him and took her shirt off and said make love to me. Robert whispered back and told her, "I have a headache." Veronica said, "What?" Robert laughed, saying, "Just letting you know how it sounds when women play that." She laughed and said, "Fair enough." They made love, and when they were done, they fell asleep with Veronica holding onto Robert looking at her ring finger before she closed her eyes.

The next morning, they woke up, went running together, worked out at the gym and went home and cleaned up. Veronica made breakfast, and they loaded up some of her stuff in the truck and they headed to her dad's house. When they arrived, the butler opened the door, and Robert brought in one of Veronica's suitcases and put it down.

Thomas, who was in his office, heard some noise and walked out of his office and asked, "What was going on?" Veronica ran to her dad and told him, "Look at my ring." Thomas smiled and said, "I guess this is congratulations." Veronica said, "I am moving in for a while. Robert is working on the murder case with all those girls." Thomas stuck his hand out, and Robert shook his hand, and Thomas said, "Congratulations." Robert smiled and said, "Thank you, sir." Thomas told Robert, "Call me Dad," Robert said, "I can't. I already have a dad. How about Robert?" Thomas smiled and said, "Fair enough, Robert, I understand." Robert sensed some uneasiness from Mr. Jackson but knew there would be some.

Robert stepped up to Veronica and said, I have to go. I will see you in a couple of days." Veronica asked, "Why not sleep here?" Robert insisted, "It would be better if I don't." Veronica frowned and said, "Ok, please call me when you can." She thought for a moment and asked, "Can I bring you lunch or dinner?" Robert told her, "Call first, and we can try and get together," and he headed to the door. She walked him to his car, and they kissed each other, and she asked, "Please call me." Robert told her, "He will call when he can." They kissed again, and he got in his truck and drove to work.

Veronica walked into the house, looking at her ring, which was perfect. When she stepped in, her dad was getting ready to head to the office and asked her, "Would she like to come and do some business work since she will inherit everything?" She smiled and asked, "Can I go change?" He told her, "Make it quick." She went upstairs, and 30 minutes later, she came down the stairs in a business suit.

Thomas smiled and said, "Let's go to the office." Veronica told him, "You can brief me on what I have been missing in the car." Thomas signaled to the chauffeur and the bodyguards, and they left the house. Once they were set, they headed to the big tower he owned in downtown Miami while he briefed Veronica.

Robert arrived at work and went into the conference room and saw all the files and everything he needed. Foster Thomas, a good friend of Roberts, came in and asked Robert, "If you need any help, let me know." Robert said, "I appreciate it, and I will need some help here and there and going out and checking the crime scenes." Foster was on the task force, but he knew Robert was a force all his own, and he also saved his life years ago and would never forget that. Foster also new Robert had no problems breaking the rules to get the bad guy. He wasn't like that. He believed in the rules but understood sometimes things had to be done because criminals do not follow any rules, which is something some politicians do not understand.

Chapter 15

Worse Then Believed

When Foster left the room, Robert started to go through the files of all the girls. He was looking for things not brought up or discovered in the investigations. He went to one of the big boards on the wall and put all the similar stuff of all the homicides on one. Robert also located a map and put it up, and pulled out different color pins, one color for each crime scene. He also taped paper around the maps so he could write notes when needed next to the maps. He looked at all the information he had, and so he sat down, and he sat down and started to go through one folder after another.

At around noon, there was a commotion outside the conference room, and there was a knock on the door, and Robert yelled out, "Go away." There was another knock, and he said, "Go away. Are you deaf?" There was a third knocking on the door, and Robert got up and said again loudly, "Are you deaf?" And he opened the door, and Veronica was holding a subway sandwich. Robert asked her, "How did you get through the entrance point?" I showed them my ring and said, "This is my pass." He laughed as she came into the room. She looked around at everything and said, "What a mess you need a secretary." He laughed and told her, "Yes, unfortunately, I could use one, but I have been getting all the information gathered from all the murders."

Robert admitted he had lots of work, and he as to go through this stuff to start organizing it. She asked, "Do you have 20 minutes to split a sandwich because I have to get back to work also". Robert looked puzzled as he sat down with her. She explained, "She is at the Tower working with her dad on some things, Important stuff, but not like what you are doing."

They ate and then talked for a few minutes, and she looked at her watch and stated, "I have to go." He told her, "I can walk you out," and she smiled and said, "Absolutely." Then she asked, "When do you want to get married?" Robert told her, "When I am done with this case." She kissed him and told him, "I will start getting things ready." He stated, "Good, but not until I am done with this case, then we can go to a good warm climate someplace and relax." She whispered in his ear, "Not too much relaxing, I hope." He smiled and kissed her and said, "Just a little." He walked her to the limo, kissed her, and she got in the limo, and it drove off. People looked at him, and he said, "What?" They shook their heads and asked, "How?" He shrugged his shoulders and stated, "Who knows," and then went back to work.

Later, he saw Foster and asked him, "Hey, let's go and see a couple of the crime scenes." Foster said, "Good, I will get a car." When Foster showed up with the car, Robert jumped in the passenger side and said, "Let's go." Foster smiled and said, "No problem." Robert called his parents while Foster drove and told them he was getting married down the road, and he already proposed and had known her for a while. His parents were happy, and his mom asked, "It's about time." She then asked, "Will we have grandkids?" Robert said, "Mom, let's do one thing at a time." His dad asked Robert, "Who is she, and what does she do?" Robert told him, "She works for her father in the sports business and investment firms." Robert left out how wealthy her family was and who her father was. Then Robert cut them off and told them, "I will call the rest of the family later." He said, "He loves them, and he will talk to them later," and hung up.

Foster laughed and told Robert, "It sounded like you didn't tell them who she really is." Robert answered by saying, "Yea, I know. I figure over time that they will figure it out." Robert called his brother and sister and left messages about him getting married down the road. His brother and sister have their own families already. He was the last one, and he was always getting pestered, but he stuck to his guns on meeting the right women. He was shocked at who it turned out to be.

Foster drove out to the first scene with Robert and looked around it, houses, buildings, and everyone around. They walked to the next scene, which was close by and after a ten-minute walk, they each looked around at the houses and buildings. Then they went to the next one, which was only five minutes away, and they walked to it and repeated what they had done at the other sites. Robert asked Foster, "Where are the other locations" as he pointed to the opposite side of where they parked. They were all within a two-three-mile radius of where we parked our vehicle.

Robert looked at his small map, which had other sites up the coast and when they occurred. They each happened in different periods of the last couple of years, actually four years, and when law enforcement tripped over that they had a serial killer in Florida killing young women. He looked at the folder, and all of them were young college women. All were smart girls with high GPAs and no criminal records. All from good families. All were raped and strangled in pairs. None of the girls knew each other. All different races and all had boy friends who were cleared with solid alibies.

Robert said, "Let's go," then he told Foster, "You need to get with the FBI and see if there are similar cases all the way up the Atlantic coast of girls found dead, naked and on the beach." Robert explained to Foster how he believed this was not just our problem, and he bet if a national check were done, this would be worse than we know. Foster asked Robert, "Are you serious?" Robert looked at Foster and told him, "Brother, I have never been more serious."

They headed to the car, and he called the COD and told him, "Boss, I believe this is worse than I thought." He continued by saying, "Foster is going to notify the FBI and also put out a bulletin to all law enforcement all the way up to Maine about similar cases. Robert paused and told his boss they might as well do the same thing on the west coast because this just didn't start here." He knew people like this always start small and work their way to bigger things. The CODs said, "Shit, I hope you are wrong." Robert responded, "I will bet you a dinner at the Texas Roadhouse." When Robert's Boss said, "Hell no, your hunches usually pan out." The COD asked whether Foster was there. Foster said, "Go ahead, boss." The COD told Foster, "When you get back, start making those phone calls, and he will start making his." Foster started the vehicle, and they headed back to the station.

Thomas Jackson and Veronica walked into the main corporation meeting room, and Thomas sat at the head with his daughter next to him. Thomas looked at the President of his company and said, "John, go ahead and let's get this briefing on the way." John stood up and started talking about the profit margin with the salary caps for each team's estimated profits for the year and the other companies which came under Jackson enterprises. When John was done, he went and sat back down and turned it over to each team's General Managers, who went over players they had signed, what type of contracts, and players they will let go when their sports seasons were completed.

Then Veronica's cell phone went off. She looked startled but grabbed it and apologized, and answered it. It was Robert. The conference room got quiet. Veronica told him, "She was in a meeting." Robert apologized and said, "I will be here all night. This is worse than I thought." He paused for a moment, and he told her, "There are more dead women, I believe, in other states." Veronica said, "Ok, and be careful." He told her, "I love you." She smiled and told him, "I love you, and I will call you later." Then she hung up.

The room was quiet for a moment, and then a Vice President stood up and said, "Ms. Jackson, we have a rule enforced by your dad no cell phones in the meetings." She looked at him, and before she could say anything, Thomas put his hand on hers and said, "Young man, who owns this business?" The VP sat down and responded by saying, "You do, sir, but your rules." Thomas cut the VP off and looked at everyone before speaking. He then explained to everyone, "This is my daughter, and she will be sitting in my seat when I choose to hand her the rain." He took a slight breath and asked, "Does everyone here understand that?" Everyone was quiet. He looked at the VP and repeated his question, "Does everyone here understand what I just said?" The room was full of 'yes sirs'. The VP gulped and weaseled down in his chair.

Thomas stood up and told everyone, "If she wants to bring in a phone so she can talk to her future husband, it's her right." Then he said, "Honey go ahead and sit on my chair and take charge. I will be in my office." Thomas then walked out. Veronica looked at her dad's chief secretary and asked, "Are you ready?" An hour later, the meeting was over, and Veronica stood up, left, went to her dad's office, and briefed him.

Once she was done briefing her dad, Thomas acknowledged the information, stood up, and told Veronica, "I have a great Idea. How about we fix this big office, and we split this office so you can start learning the job." She agreed and believed it would be a great idea.

What she did not tell her dad was she had an alternative plan: to put Robert in here with her, working together so he would not have to put his life at risk anymore. She also wanted kids, and her goal was to get Robert into her business and spend time with the family instead of risking his life doing what he does. She hoped her plan would work out, but she knew Robert was stubborn and loved his job. Sometimes men have to do it themselves and not be pushed by a woman into something they might or might not want to do.

Chapter 16

Worse Than We Thought

It was 10 pm when Robert reviewed some papers when the phone rang. It was Foster. Foster told Robert, "You are right. SC and Georgia have reported they had similar cases and are sending the information to the FBI." Foster asked, "How did you know?" Robert told Foster that scum like this just doesn't keep doing this for no reason, and they always start small. They move around in most cases. Robert told Foster, "I was Just playing the odds, and Let's call our bosses. We need to do a press conference on this so it does not come out and blow up in our faces." Foster said, "Ok." Less than thirty minutes later, Foster called back and told Robert, "They are having one at 09:30 am, "It look good for the press. You will be answering some of the questions." Robert stated, "I do not do interviews." Foster laughed and told him, "The Police Chief said you would say that, and he will tie you to the stand if he had to." Robert said, "Shit, alright," and hung up the conference phone.

For two hours, he looked at the timelines of all the bodies washed ashore in Florida. The new number was 32. He noticed as the season was slowing down, the murders slowed down. At midnight he took his shoes off and crashed on the conference room couch and reached up and turned off the light switch.

After a few minutes, his cell phone went off. He recognized the number, answered it and said, "Hello." Veronica asked him, "What was he doing?" Robert told her, "He just laid down on the couch in the conference room." She asked, "Why don't you come home?" He said, "He can't. He had a press conference at 9:30 am and had to get up early to work on things." Robert asked her, "Where is she?" She told him, "In bed naked, waiting for you."

Robert got quiet for a moment and said, "I wish I were there, but I can't tonight, but I will be there for dinner tomorrow. How about that?" She stated, "Great." She knew he was tired and told him, "Love you, and I miss you." Robert said, "I love you too." Veronica then asked, "How many kids do you want?" Robert laughed and told her, "Two or three." Robert said, "Good night," and Veronica said the same thing, and they both hung up. Robert fell asleep, and Veronica smiled and thought about what Robert said about kids. She then went to sleep.

The next day, Robert got up at 6 am, showered, and got ready for the press conference. While he was sitting at the table, Veronica popped in and brought him breakfast. She was dressed up, and Robert asked, "Where are you going?" She smiled and told him, "Dad and the limo are outside, and we are going to the Tower for another meeting." She kissed him and said, "You look tired." He replied, "Thanks," and he started eating, and he got up and hugged her and swallowed his food and kissed her. She kissed him, turned around to leave, and said, "See you tonight." Robert smiled and told her, "C-YA," as Veronica hurriedly walked out.

At 9:15 am, Robert put down a folder he was going through and headed out to the Press conference. Once he got there, he stood behind all the brass and the Mayor. After the press conference started, the Mayor started by explaining how hard the city is working to assist law enforcement in ending this crime of violence toward women. He continued talking about how this has hindered local businesses due to people going to other areas or states.

During the meeting, Veronica was listening to everyone talking around the table, and her dad was listening to what everyone was saying as they went around the table. Veronica had the big television on so she could watch what Robert said when he came on. The TV was on mute, and she would glance at the screen every few minutes.

When it was her turn, she went over issues with the profit margin and why some funds in advertising have not been used but have been sitting there doing nothing. She looked at the advertising manager and asked, "Why is it sitting there doing nothing?" The manager answered, "Well, ma'am, we were using that as an emergency fund in case it was needed." Veronica told him, "Every department is given a set amount, and if you are not using it, I will use it for something else as of now." The manager looked at Thomas, and he said, "Don't look at me. She has a good point, and I guess next year's budget, you use your money better."

Thomas looked at Veronica and asked, "What is your plan for the money?" She told him, "I believe we use it as a contribution to the cancer children's hospital, and it gives us a tax deduction, and it goes to a noble cause and looks good in the community." Thomas grinned and told her, "Run with it, honey." The manager sat back in his chair and said nothing, knowing he messed up and should have spent it.

When the Chief of Police finished, he said, "I will have Detective Bench come up and speak." Robert stepped up, and Veronica immediately hit the mute button and interrupted the meeting. Thomas said, "Do what she says," everyone went quiet. Robert started by saying, "Good morning, and I want to say since I have been on this case assisting the Task force, I have discovered a couple of new things that everyone needs to know." He took a big breath and looked around, and said, "What I am going to say is not guesswork or will be politically correct, this is a big mess, and it's going to be ugly."

He stopped again, cleared his throat, and said, "These gentlemen behind me have not been briefed completely by me on everything, and I want to make this perfectly clear this city is not out of danger." The press and the Police brass, and the Mayor looked at each other. Roberts stated, "These women are not the first victims of this person or persons. After going through paperwork and going to some of the crime scenes, I believe most states all the way from Florida to Main have been hit with this type of crime." He paused and looked at all the reporters, who were flabbergasted.

He continued and let the Press know, "The FBI is checking with all similar cases up and down the Eastern coast."

The press was quit as they listened to the Detective. The brass and the Mayor had a shock look on their faces as Robert talked. Robert added, "The FBI is following my advice and checking the western Pacific states for victims being murdered the same way." He stopped talking for a moment, so what he said would sink into everyone's head. He then apologized by saying, "I am sorry this has shocked everyone, but with all law enforcement working together, hopefully, we can end this." He stepped back from the microphone and stepped back and added, "I have one more thing to say. It appears that the crimes have slowed down for now. Maybe it's the weather or the economic downturn due to the crimes, but we will look at all avenues."

Robert looked around and announced, "Now, I will take questions." The press all raised their hands and started asking questions. Robert pointed to the close, and the reporter asked the detective, "Will there be more victims?" Roberts responded, "Unfortunately, yes." The people behind him were still flabbergasted by what Robert was saying. The COP stepped up, and Robert looked at him, basically saying don't. Robert was asked by another reporter's question, "How many victims does he believe there are overall?" Robert paused before speaking, knowing he would be lighting a political fuse and saying, "At least 50-100 at least." He heard some reporters saying, "Oh my God." Robert told the press, "He received the news before he came out. There were a total of 16 in Georgia and 12 in SC, which have similarities." Robert stated, "One more question."

One Reporter asked, "What advise does he give to women in the city and surrounding area?" Robert paused and looked around at the press, looked down, thinking and then he looked back up and told them, "All women should be in groups when they go outside, and I want to finish and say they do not target groups three or more, and none of the women knew each other." He explained to everyone just in case the criminal or criminals change their MO. Robert finished up by saying, "He encourages women to go in groups of three or more. This will help hinder and make it harder for the perp or perps." Robert turned away and went back to the office. He knew his bosses would be pissed off, but he did not care. He needed to get the information out so it would be harder for more women to be killed.

Veronica and everyone in the meeting room were shocked about what they heard from the News Conference. Thomas looked at Veronica and told her, "He could tell Robert's bosses are pissed at him for doing what he did." Veronica told her dad, "She could tell also, but Robert knows what he is doing. He just wants to save lives." Thomas looked around and told everyone, "The meeting is over, and I want you to send everyone home to be with their families, and they can do their work at home." Thomas and Veronica got up and went back to Thomas's office.

Robert went to the conference room and returned to work when everyone barged in and looked at Robert with angry and pissed-off expressions. The Mayor started by yelling at Robert, "What the hell did you just do, and why?" Robert explained himself, and then the COP started chewing him about authority on what he was doing.

Robert was 6ft-2 and stood up and got in the COP's face and said, "That piece of paper you all signed, including the governor, do you want this resolved or don't you?" The cop stepped back and said, "Robert, you could have briefed us." Robert responded, saying, "There was no time." The COD stepped between them and told both men, "Let's all just calm down and figure out what needs to be done." Robert looked at the COP and told him, "Sir, I would go out there and tell those reporters still gathered out there and tell them you are putting all police on 12-hour shifts and no days off and all vacations suspended until this is over to show everyone how serious you take this."

The Mayor grabbed the chief and said, "That's good let's go." They ran out there and released a follow-up, saying, "We both come to the same conclusion that all officers will be on 12-hour shifts with no days off and vacations suspended until further notice."

Chapter 17

He works, they plan.

They headed back to the conference room, closed the door, and the Mayor said, "It's done." The COP stated, "He will get with all precincts and increase patrols on all the beaches." Robert looked around and stated, "Gentlemen, I apologize for the headache, but it needed to be done to save lives." The COP told Robert, "You can be a prick sometimes, but the only thing that saves you is you are good at what you do, and can you give me a time line on when we can end this." Robert said, "Boss, not soon enough." The COP asked, "Robert is there anything you need?" Robert answered by saying, "I need all video up and down the beach in the area around the crime scenes, Before and after, and I do not care how old or new." He turned to the COD, who walked in and told him, "I need a flight to SCN. Myrtle Beach for a few days to check the crime scene there." The COP said, "Done. When do you need to go?" The COP was told, "First thing in the morning." The Mayor told the COP, "He will call our Governor, so he can call the SC governor to get all the help you need." The Mayor then left with the COP.

Robert told his boss, "I need to take Foster with me." The COD stated, "Done," and, "When do you want to leave?" Roberts told him, "6 am sounds good." The COD said, "I will let Foster know, and is there anything else?" "Yes, one more thing, see if the FBI has more information on the rest of the east coast and out west, and I need an FBI agent assigned to assist me." The COD laughed and stated, "I will try." Robert told his boss, "Tell whoever that if they don't, my next press conference will be throwing them under the bus." The COD smiled and said, "No mercy, right?" Robert smiled and stated, "Mission first." The COD then walked out.

Veronica called Robert, but he didn't answer because he was talking with his bosses. She tried again, and Robert answered and said, "Hello." Veronica asked, "Baby are you alright?" He told her, "Absolutely, my bosses pissed their pants, but what's an ass chewing." She asked, "Are we still having dinner tonight?" Robert said, "I will be there about 5 pm, and he said he had to go," and hung up. Thomas looked over at Veronica and asked, "I thought dinner was later?" Veronica smiled, and Thomas grinned and said, "Never mind, I get it."

Robert went back to work, and Foster came in and told Robert, "I have the folders from SC and Georgia. They just arrived from the FBI." Foster added, "It looks like more cases up the coast have been reported to the FBI." Robert shook his head and stated, "I hate being right, and this tells me we are running out of time before the person or persons move to another state or even a country." Foster sat down, handed Robert the folders, and asked, "You believe they will move on at any time?" Robert said, "Absolutely, just look at the trail of death which has been left by this scum." Foster asked, "One or two people." Robert replied, "I believe it's two." He mentioned they could be friends, brothers, cousins, men, women, anything, So we need to shift gears." Robert told Foster, "I need you today. Get with the task force and let them know we are looking for at least two people." Foster got up and said, "Done," and left.

Robert called his boss and told him, "We are looking for at least two people." The COD asked, "Why two?" Robert explained, "The girls show up dead in pairs every time." The COD told Robert, "It makes sense because it would take two men to drag those bodies around and dump them so close together at the same time." Robert added, "This appears to happen in many places." His boss hung up and made some phone calls to the FBI. When he called the FBI, they had no problem assigning an agent to them from the task force. Then he made other phone calls to his higher-ups.

Robert went through as much as he could before he left to have dinner with Veronica, and he wanted to be there on time. When he arrived and got out of his truck, Veronica ran out of the house, jumped into his arms, kissed up passionately, and told him, "I missed you." Robert kissed her back, and he let her down, and they went and walked into the house. They walked to her dad's office, opened the door, and walked in. Thomas stood up, reached over the desk, and told Robert, "Nice to see you. I hear you have been busy." Robert grinned and said, "Yes, earning my paycheck." Thomas told them to take a seat, and everyone sat down. Thomas got straight to the point and asked, "So, when do you plan on marrying my daughter?" Robert looked at him and said, "I told her whenever this case is solved." Thomas stated, "Good, that gives us time to start preparing."

Thomas asked, "Will it be a church wedding, and what type?" Roberts told him, "He has not discussed really anything else with Veronica," and Thomas replied, "He understood." Thomas got up and told Robert and his daughter, "I will let you two deal with that." Thomas left the room to go and check to see if dinner was ready.

Veronica and Robert looked at each other, and she told him, "Let's go for a walk while they are setting the table." Robert smiled and followed her out of the office. They went and walked around the compound holding hands. Veronica asked, "How did things go after the briefing?" Robert laughed and told her, "My ass was chewed, but it had to be done to save lives." She leaned in, kissed him, and asked, "Once this is done and we get married, would you consider retiring and coming to work for my dad?" He stopped and looked at her with a serious look on his face. She looked down and then back at Robert and said, "It was just a thought." Robert looked into her eyes and then stuck his hand out and touched her face. He knew she wanted to hear something positive, so he leaned in, kissed her, and told her, "We will see when this is over." She smiled and knew it was not a yes or no, but at least it was in his head.

They walked and talked about what type of wedding they wanted. Robert said, "He could not afford an expensive one." She laughed and told him, "Don't even worry about that. My dad already told me he will pay for it all." Robert smiled and said Well, in that case, "Ok." He told her, "He insisted on a church wedding." Veronica replied, "Super, I agree." Robert said, "I have no doubt you and your dad want to put it together." He then said in a firm tone of voice, catching her off guard, saying, "I will sell my place, and we can get a bigger place due to future kids." Veronica started to talk, and he caught her off and told her, "I don't want to live here. I insist on our own place." She stopped, looked at him, and asked, "Can we talk about that later?" Robert told her, "No, our place." She looked down, and a smile came across her face, and she told him, "Well, there is still time to change your mind." Robert laughed and replied, "Sure," as they went to the house to eat.

While everyone was eating, Thomas asked, "How is the investigation going?" Robert looked up and told him, "Its ugly, the worse one I have ever been involved with, too many victims." Robert added, "He was going to N. Myrtle beach to check some of the crime scenes there." Veronica put her fork down and asked, "How long will you be there?" Robert told her, "Foster and he and an FBI agent are flying there in the morning in an FBI jet and coming back in the evening sometime." Veronica asked, "When will I see you?" Robert said, "In a day or two."

Robert added, "When he gets back, I will stay at my place for a few hours and then head in to work early." Veronica looked at Robert and asked, "Can we spend the evening together?" And Robert smiled and told her, "Absolutely." Thomas interrupted and asked Robert, "How was the food?" Robert turned his head, looked at Thomas, and said, "It's excellent. I appreciate you inviting me to dinner." Thomas smiled and replied, "You are welcome, and I am glad you are here." He then looked at his daughter and Robert and said, "I am done, and I am going to leave you two alone and do some work in my office." He stood up and went to his office, and closed the door, to his office.

Robert looked at Veronica and asked, "What do you want to do?" He mentioned TV, going to the movies, walking and talking. Veronica got up, grabbed his hand, and told him, "Follow me." They went to the stairs and walked up them while she held Robert's hand with a smile. She took off her shirt and her bra as they headed upstairs. She then disrobed her dress as it fell on the stairs, and Robert said, "I guess you have other plans." She smiled and asked, "Do you have plans for the night?" She stopped and looked at him, and he picked her nude body up and carried her to her bedroom and whispered to her, "He will be spending the night with the woman he loves." Veronica smiled and kissed him. They entered the room, and he closed the door, and they went to bed.

Chapter 18

Searching for clues

The next morning Robert got up at five and took a shower in Veronica's bathroom, and he was amazed at how big it was. He showered, got back into his clothes, and kissed Veronica, who was still in bed. She kissed him and said, "Be careful." He told her, "I promise," and Robert headed down stairs and went to his apartment to change clothes and grab a to-go bag. Once he did that, he headed to the private airport and met Foster and the FBI agent Johnson Fox. They boarded the FBI Jet and headed to South Carolina. During the flight, they discussed some evidence and all possibilities.

Once they landed at Myrtle Beach airport, the local law enforcement introduced themselves, and after introductions, Robert asked them, "Please take them to a couple of them to-go crime scenes." When they got there, they got out and walked the beach to the exact locations where the bodies were found. Robert and Foster looked at the folders they had, and while Foster went through them, Robert looked around and all the houses, rentals, and hotels.

Robert realized the houses were similar to the ones in Florida and were close up to the beach. They went to both crime scenes, and he realized it was the same way as they were in Florida. The houses were in the middle, and hotels were to the left and right of them. He noticed an open spot where it looked like a house collapsed into the ground. The N. Myrtle Beach Police Officer, Mr. Atkins, said, "The house collapsed into the ground for some strange reason, and it's been a big puzzle to everyone." Robert asked, "Are all the other houses ok?" Atkins answered back, "Yes, they were checked by the city inspectors."

Robert went up to the hole in the ground full of rotted wood and other material. He looked at a spot that looked like there was a dip in the ground and asked what was right there as he went into the dip. Atkins stated, "They do not know." Foster was listening, and Robert and Foster looked at each other with a puzzled looks. They walked towards the beach and then to the location of the first two bodies and told Foster, "Stand right here." He then took some photos in all directions.

He walked to the second spot and took more photos. The house was in the middle. He grinned and said, "Bingo." He walked up and told the officer and notified him, "You need a construction crew to get here and go through this and remove by hand as much as possible and as soon as possible. I believe we just found where those two girls were murdered". He also told him to have a forensic team on standby.

Everyone was surprised and looked at each other, and the officer called the chief and told him what was going on. When he hung up, he told Robert, "The Chief is getting people out here asap to help clear it and have a forensic team ready to respond." The FBI agent asked, "How do you know this?" Robert told him, "I bet you a dinner you will find a dug-out basement that leads to the beach because none of these other houses have basements due to flooding."

Robert looked at Foster and asked him, "I need you to stay here and observe and take photos of what is found." Foster laughed and replied, "I am glad I packed." Robert added, "I need to head to Savannah, Georgia and go to the place down there and check their crime scene and see what is similar there that matches this place and Florida."

A police car took them back to the airport, and while they were en route, Robert called his boss and informed him of what was going on and what had been discovered. The COD said, "Ok," and he asked, "Where are you heading to at this moment?" Robert told his boss, "The FBI agent was on the phone with the task force informing them of other related crime scenes, and the forensic team will be standing by once the caved-in house is cleared out.”

Robert and Agent Fox, when they arrived at the airport, thanked the officer and boarded up for Georgia.

An hour later, they landed at Savannah airport, and the local Police, with Two FBI agents, were waiting for them. They introduced each other, loaded up, and went to the crime scene area. Robert was shown the two separate locations, and he went and looked at the homes on the beach. They were the older type. Robert asked, “If they had basements?” He was told no by the police, who stated, “They would flood if they did.” He went and checked at both locations and looked at the homes. There was an empty spot in the middle of the other homes.

Robert went up and looked at where the house used to be. He observed a huge dip in the ground and asked everyone who followed him, “What happened here?” He was told a strange fire started under the floor and burned the house down, and it collapsed. Robert asked, “Was there anything left.” He was told ‘no’. Robert was puzzled, and he finally asked, “Isn’t it strange that a fire would leave a big hole in the ground.” Everyone agreed it was suspicious.

Robert looked at Agent Fox and notified him, “We need to head down to Daytona Beach.” Robert looked around and notified them, “Gentlemen, this is where your homicides happened. I would call your Forensic teams to dig around here.” Then he looked at Agent Fox, stating, “We need to go quickly.” They were brought back to the airport, and Agent Fox called his boss and notified him, “They need a team and gave the location of the suspected murder location,” and then hung up. They got to the plane and loaded up. The FBI jet took off, and they headed to Daytona Beach. Once they landed, it was starting to get dark, so they checked in at the local Holiday Inn. They ate at the local Oriental Restaurant, called their bosses and made notes for the next day. There was small talk about the case, but they were just too tired to talk about things.

Robert got a phone call from Foster right before he was going to call Veronica and said, "They received new information that Virginia Beach was another spot." Robert replied, "Copy," and said, "I guess I will meet you in the morning tomorrow." Robert asked, "How was the work going on the site?" Foster told him, "Slow, but they should be done in a couple of days. I will let you know what we find." Foster asked, "What should we be looking for?" Roberts responded by saying, "A basement and a tunnel out to the beach." Foster was surprised but got it, and they hung up.

Robert then called Veronica, and they talked for a while. She asked, "When is he coming home?" Robert told her, "Maybe tomorrow night." He then explained he must go to Virginia Beach to another crime scene. He paused and told her, "I am piecing it together on where they were and what they do." Veronica told him, "Good, and I love you. Hurry home." Robert said, "Good night," and she told him, "Good night." The same thing and they hung up. Robert closed his eyes and went to sleep.

Robert woke up at 6 am and got ready to check out. He went downstairs, ate, and waited for Fox to come down. After about 20 minutes, Fox came down, and they took a cab to the airport. The plane was fueled up and ready to go. They loaded up and headed to Virginia Beach, where the local FBI would be there to pick us up.

After a few hours, they landed at the Virginia Beach airport and unloaded. The FBI agents met them, and they loaded up on the tarmac and headed to the crime scenes. Once they arrived, Robert knew what needed to be done while he was there. Once they arrived at the locations, he took photos and some video and went to a home that burnt down mysteriously. However, in this case, the burnt-down house was still there. He walked around, and after going to where the girls were found, he took more photos and looked where the house was each time.

He had all the information he needed for now and approached the FBI agents and told them, "You guys need to get your teams here. This was where the crime scene was, not just the beach." He told them, "You will find a dug-out basement, which is why the house has a huge dip in the ground." The FBI agents started to make phone calls about what they were told. Robert called his boss and told him, "You need to measure where the houses are from where the buddies were discovered and get warrants to search all the homes within 250 yards of where the girls were discovered."

There should be three or four homes to search. The COD asked, "Are you sure?" Robert told him, "Yes, you need to move asap and have the SWAT teams raid the homes all at once." Robert paused and stated, "Look for a hidden basement in one of them, which was dug out and leads to the beach." Robert new time was short. He looked at the agents and told them, "You need to get the names of the last group of people that lived here right before the fire." Robert took a breath and told the agents, "They are the killers."

Chapter 19

Preparations

Robert sat down on the beach, and he watched people on the beach looking at him, and he looked back at them. They had a 'Who are those guys look'. After 5 minutes, he got up and said, "It's time to go," and he then said, "Guys do your stuff. I am going home." Robert and the agents headed to the cars then Fox and Robert loaded up on the jet. Fox asked, "Where do we go next?" Robert told him, "Home." Fox asked about the other places. Robert replied, "In due time, the goal is catching them right now." Robert looked around and told Fox, "The other places are just more ammo for the Federal death penalty." Atkins agreed.

Once they landed at the airport in Miami, Robert saw a limo outside, and he unloaded his stuff. He saw Veronica jump out and run to him. She kissed him, and he kissed her back. He didn't ask how she knew he was heading back. He didn't care. He looked at Fox and asked, "Can we give you a ride?" Fox told him, "No thanks, my ride just drove up." Robert looked, and it was another FBI car. Robert told Fox I would see you later. They waved, and both parties went their separate ways. When Robert got in the limo, Veronica was all over him, and he told her, "Hold on, honey, I have to call my boss." She smiled. Robert called and asked his boss, "How did the raids go?" The COD told Robert, "They found the house and the basement and a tunnel to the beach." Robert asked about the crime scene and told him, "I will be there first thing at the location, and you might want to tell the Chief and Mayor to be at the office at 08:00 am so that I can brief them first thing."

The COD told Robert, "It looked like whoever was there was in a hurry and packed and left." Robert said, "Damn," and then he told his boss, "We need all the video from around there so we can see what they look like." The COD told Robert, "They are already doing that as they spoke with warrants yesterday for all videos." The COD told Robert, "Good job." Robert told his boss, "No, we missed them." Robert stated, "They are on the move, and now we have to figure out who they are and where they are going." His boss agreed and told Roberts, "You did what nobody else could figure out, and I will call the Chief so they can be better prepared than last time." Robert answered back, "Ok," and hung up.

After he hung up, Veronica began kissing him, and he kissed her just as much. Veronica asked, "How much time do we have?" Robert told her, "I have tonight, but I have to be at work bright and early." She said, "Good, we can eat out and then go home." Robert asked, "My place?" Veronica told him, "How about my place?" Robert then pulled a quarter out and flipped it. She picked heads. He smiled and showed her the coin. She smiled and told the chauffeur, "Take us home, please." Robert laughed and whispered, "You win."

She smiled and asked Robert, "After dinner can we go to a movie?" He told her, "Sounds good." Robert asked her how about an early picture? She told him, "That's fine." Veronica understood he was extremely tired from his work. Then she whispered in his ear, "You will need some energy tonight." He kissed her and said, "Sounds good." When they made it home, they went straight to the couch, and Veronica informed him, "I have been planning everything, so you don't have to." He kissed her forehead, and she continued explaining how they would get married at the local church. She then told Robert, "Her dad will send out invitations to everyone and give him a list of who wants to be there and especially your family."

Robert leaned back and told her, "Keep going." She said, "We will have the reception here, and then, we will fly to wherever you want to go." Robert asked her, "Where would you like to go?" She was smiling and told him, "Since you asked, how about we take a European cruise for two weeks." Robert told her, "That's a great idea. You set it up, and it's a go." Veronica got quiet for a moment and finally said, "Now for the serious stuff. My dad wants to talk to you about something." Robert asked, "What?" She looked down because she felt embarrassed and said quietly, "It's about a Prenup." Robert laughed and told her, "Is that all?" He looked at her and told her, "Come on, let's go and talk to your dad." She asked, you mean right now, Robert?" They stood up, and she told him, "But he wants to talk to you alone." Robert told her, "Bullshit, this is about both of us," as he took her hand, and they went to her dad's office.

Chapter 20

No Greed

They knocked on the door, and Thomas yelled, "Come on in." They entered, and they sat down. Thomas asked, "What's up, guys?" Robert told him, "The prenup." He looked at both Veronica and Thomas and told them, "I want both of you to hear what I want." Thomas leaned back, tossed his pen on the table, and asked, "How much?" Robert looked at Veronica, and then he looked at Thomas and stated, "Nothing." He paused and told Thomas, "No matter what happens with our marriage, including divorce, "I want no allowance, no money, no nothing." Veronica's face had a puzzled look on her face as Robert continued talking. He told both, "If we get divorced, and we have kids, we have joint custody, and she pays for the private school that we both agree on." He paused again, looked at both of them, and said, "We must agree on all things dealing with the kids, and If we can't agree, then it does not happen."

Robert stopped for a second to let what he said sink in and then stated, "One last thing, the kids cannot move to another state or country without my approval." Thomas looked at him, and Veronica's mouth opened. Robert again said, "I do not want one dime, write it up, and I will sign it without argument also. Since she has the money, if my insurance does not cover it, she pays the difference." Robert smiled and then told both of them, "I will step out and let you talk about it." He then walked out and closed the door. He knew they were surprised about what he said, and he meant every word. He just wanted happiness that he knew she could bring to him. Her money is irrelevant.

Veronica was shocked. Thomas grinned and said, "Wow, I did not see that coming." Veronica looked at her dad and told him,

"I know now he truly loves me for who I am, not what I have." Thomas replied, "I agree. Wow, not one dime and how many men would say that?" Veronica told her dad, "Not many, that is for sure. Most would want something and try and milk it." Thomas asked her, "Is there anything you disagreed with?" Veronica said, "No, I knew he was not a selfish man." Thomas told her, "I will have the lawyers write it up and get it taken care of."

The door opened, and Veronica had a smile on her face and told Robert, "Please come in." Robert knew they were in shock. He would not want anything, but he didn't want anything. He felt it was the right thing to do. He and his dad talked about it a few days ago, and his dad laughed and told his son, "You are doing the right thing."

Robert entered the huge office and asked, "Well, what will it be?" Thomas came up to him and shook his hand, and told him, "We both agree, you just proved to me and to her you truly love her." Thomas looked at his daughter and then said, "99% of the men would want millions. You amaze me, Robert." He then asked, "Robert, please sit down." After they sat down, Thomas told Robert, "You are truly amazing. You also turned down 100 million for something you did anyway." Thomas told Robert, "I know you like your job Son, but when you choose, I want you to come and work for me." Robert looked at Veronica, and she smiled because she did not see that one coming. Robert grinned and said sir, "I want to thank you, but I have to say no at this time, but maybe down the road." Thomas replied, "I understand."

There was a knock on the door, and Thomas said, "Come in." The butler came in and stated, "Dinner is served, sir." Thomas told him, "We will be right there," and the butler left and closed the door. Robert told Thomas, "Veronica and I will not be living here. We will sell my townhouse and look for a three-bedroom, two-bathroom house after we get married." The room got quiet. Thomas looked at Veronica with a surprised look, and she whispered into her dad's ear and told him, "Relax, Dad, I still have time to change

Robert's mind." Thomas said, "Ok," and he looked at Robert and told him, "Son, I would prefer you two be here, but I am sure you two will talk about it," he then said, "Let's go eat. I am starved."

Once dinner was over, Robert and Veronica left in his truck and went to a movie she wanted to see. They shared popcorn and a seven-up, and they both enjoyed the movie and talked about it on the way to her home. Once they arrived at Veronica's home. Veronica asked, "Are you staying with me tonight, right?" Robert asked, "Are you sure?" Veronica smiled and said, "It's time for bed. I know you have to get up early." They entered the mansion, and she held his hand up the stairs, and they went into her room.

Thomas heard them come in and went back to working on the paperwork he needed to get done. He was happy his daughter had a man she was in love with, and he knew Robert loved her. He liked Robert and was not afraid to put his daughter in line when needed, and she knew Robert would stand up to her when he felt she was wrong or being bossy.

Chapter 21

Fear of Copycats

Robert woke up at 6 am, cleaned up, kissed Veronica, and went to work. He arrived at 7:30 am and went to the conference room, where he started to go over the maps and where all the crimes were committed. At 08:00 am, the Mayor walked in with the Police Chief, the Chief of Detectives, a couple of FBI agents and, one of them being Agent Fox. Everyone sat down, and Robert began the debriefing of everything which he discovered and the results of it.

After about 30 minutes of going over everything he had, he turned to FBI agent Fox who added they had all the false names of the people who lived in all the suspected homes. He went over the information the FBI had put together with the Task Force that an older lady and a son rented those houses out, and after six months on average, they leave and work their way to the next spot. There were other places up the Atlantic coast in other states all the way up to Maine, and those houses are being searched with warrants as we speak. Robert interrupted and said, "I doubt you guys will find a house." Fox asked, "Why?" Robert told him, "It looks like they destroyed the house with all evidence and left, but only time will tell if that's fact or not."

Robert told the men in the room, "Know, gentleman, I am ready for questions." The Mayor started and asked, "What does this mean?" Robert looked around the room and back at the Mayor and told him, "For now, the murders should be over for a little while." The Mayor responded back by asking, "How do you know this?" Robert went to the map and showed all the places they were at and how after a period of time, the houses mysteriously were destroyed, and the suspects moved at least 50 to 100 miles to the next target.

Robert then looked at Agent Fox and asked, "Can the FBI's Behavioral Analysis Unit do a profile of mother and son profile on these killers?" Agent Fox replied, "Absolutely." Agent Fox stepped out and called Washington and sent them copies of what he had. He was told it would be a few hours and they will send a profile back in 24 hours.

While Agent Fox was out, the Mayor looked at Robert and asked, "What are the odds they have moved on?" Roberts thought for a moment and stated, "80%." The Mayor asked, "Why not 100%?" Robert told him, "Nothing is 100%, and anything can happen." The big question going around the room was what direction they were going and are they still in the country or did they leave. The Mayor looked at Detective Bench and asked, "What do you think, Detective?" Robert told him, "He believes they have moved on, but he has no idea what direction they went." The Mayor stood up and looked at the Police Chief and told him, "Let's do a news conference at 3 PM and let the people know it's safe and the murderers have moved on."

The Police Chief stood up and replied, "Sir, I don't believe that's a good idea yet, sir." Robert watched the Mayor and POC argue about it while the COD sat back with his arms crossed with a ticked-off look on his face. After a couple of minutes, Robert had enough of playing nice. He yelled out, "Enough." Both the Mayor and COP stopped arguing and looked at Robert. The Mayor stated, "Excuse me!" Robert told the Mayor, "A press conference is fine, but we must not let the people know things are safe. They are not." The Chief of Police looked at Robert and told him, "Explain himself." Robert told them, "There are so many variables that could happen, for example, copycat crimes, and it would come back on you, Mayor, and I agree with the Chief." The Mayor scoffed and asked, "What the hell do you recommend, Detective?" Robert sat down and looked at everyone with an irritated look on his face having to deal with a typical Mayor not using any common sense God gave him.

Robert said, "First, we release to the press all information about the mother and son suspects." He looked at the Mayor and continued saying, "We tell the press that these two are suspected of multiple crimes up and down the eastern states." However, we do not mention how they destroy the houses and move on and go to another area". Robert stopped for a moment, then told the Mayor, "We explain how we just missed them, but we collected enough evidence to prosecute them once they are captured." Robert took a deep breath and said, "We add it's believed they are still in the area, but possibly they left the area also." He thought for a moment and told the Police Chief, "Put out the usual extremely dangerous and do not approach and call the Police immediately if it's believed the population observes the suspects."

Robert then walked up to the Mayor and told him, "If you say they are gone, and something happens, don't think this will not come back and bit you, It will, and your political career will be over." Robert looked the Mayor in his eyes with a don't fuck with me look.

The Mayor stepped back and sat down and looked at the COP, and said, "Unfortunately, this insolent SOB is right." He then looked at Robert and told him, "I will do a brief talk, then Detective, you will give the basics." The COP and the COD laughed out loud, breaking the tension in the room, and the COD said, "Robert, it looks like it's your show, don't fuck it up." Robert looked around the room and stated, "Fair enough."

Around noon Agent Fox received an email from Washington giving a new profile on the suspects. Agent Fox read it and printed it out. He went and looked around the offices for Robert when he observed him coming out of the COD office. Agent Fox gave it to Robert, who looked it over, and they headed to the conference room. After Robert read it, he asked Fox, "If there was any news from the west coast." Fox smiled and said, "Yes, We had similar cases in Santa Barbara, Contra Costa County, and up north by Portland and Seattle."

Robert got quiet for a minute, and he put the profile down and said, "You might want to check with Canada Law enforcement also." There is possibly a chance all this started in Canada. Robert stated, "There is no way they just popped up in Seattle and went South, and they headed to the east coast." He took a deep breath and mentioned, "I also need you to check their facial features and see what European country their backgrounds might be." Agent Fox replied, "They might not be from here." Robert told him, "We need to cover all the bases. At this time, anything is possible." Agent Fox got up and went to make phone calls on the questions Robert asked for."

When Fox left, Robert took a break and called Veronica. Veronica didn't answer, so he figured she was busy with her dad in a meeting or something. So, he went up to the food machine when he heard some guys whistling, and he looked up, and Veronica was walking towards him. She was flipping off the guys who whistled and looked at Robert and gave him a big kiss in front of everyone. She had a bag of food for them to eat. They went to the conference room, and they ate lunch together. They talked, and she told him, "I will be in a meeting all afternoon." Robert told her, "He had a news conference at 3 pm." Veronica said, "You will do good," and she asked, "How was the case going?" Robert replied, "We just missed catching them, but unfortunately, they got away." Veronica told him, "You will get them."

They ate, and then she jumped up and headed out the conference door and then suddenly Veronica told everyone, "Listen up." The whole room got quiet, and she told them, "Robert and I are getting married soon, so hurry up and catch those dirtbags so I can marry him sooner." Robert smiled, and everyone clapped and hooted. A couple of guys yelled out, "How the hell did Robert land her?" Robert smiled, and he shrugged his shoulders. Veronica turned and kissed him and then left. There were some comments made once she left, and Robert stated, "Fuck you guys," and went back into the conference room.

Later on, Robert was met at the outside Press Conference outside by the FBI, the Mayor, COP and the COD. They all shook hands as the press took photographs and the tv networks did their filming. The COD pulled Robert aside and told him, "The Mayor is pissed at you for putting him on the spot, but he hesitantly agreed on what you said because it made the most sense for his political career." Robert grinned and replied, "I am just speaking the truth, boss." The COD told Robert, "I know, and you know, but our bosses are politicians, nothing more, and most politicians could not find their asses without a flashlight, which means the chief also." Robert looked at the COD and whispered, "Wow, are you going out on a limb here?" The COD smiled and whispered, "I said that because I know that's between you and mean."

Everyone stood in the back as the Police spokeswoman stepped up to the mike and introduced herself and what the press conference was about. She then introduced the Mayor, who stepped up and started by saying, "Good afternoon, and we have some good news today and a lot of information to be forwarded to you." He looked around at all the reporters and added, "I want to thank all of the law enforcement agencies' hard workers who have worked on this serious and tragic situation that has struck many communities." The Mayor looked at his notes and stated, "Due to the diligence of these agencies, we have discovered who they are and where they have been." He took a tiny breath and finished up by introducing the Chief of Police, who stepped up and discussed his department's actions.

The Police Chief stepped up and said, "Thank you, Mayor," and went into what his department and others did, mostly talking about the raid and thanking the FBI and other departments for their assistance. Then he called up the Chief of Detectives, who came forward and thanked the Chief of the Police and Mayor for their support during the investigation. Then he cut himself off and told everyone, "Ladies and Gentlemen, I will have the lead detective step up and go over what helped make a difference in this case. He looked over and asked, "Detective Bench, please come forward and discuss the case, please."

Robert stepped up and shook his bosses' hands and stepped up to the mike. Veronica was in her meeting, stopped, hit the volume, and watched Robert give his briefing. Robert started with the bad news, and the media was shocked by how many bodies there were and how large the manhunt was due to all the crime scenes.

Robert went over how the Task Force figured out the location of the crime scenes, how the information was gathered, and how the raids of the house on the beach were used to hide the missing girls and kill them. Foster, who got back from his assignment, came up on the stand, covered up the mike, whispered, and told Robert, "They found evidence with DNA on it and fingerprints, and it's being forward to the FBI to process the new evidence."

Robert smiled and told Foster, "Good job," and Foster started to turn around and walk off the stand when Robert grabbed him and pulled him back. Foster was surprised, and Robert turned to the media and told them, "We do have some new evidence from the crime scene in another state." Robert introduced Detective Foster, who has been working on the task for. Robert then said, "All this new evidence will be forwarded to the FBI, and they will come up in a moment to discuss how the evidence will tell if it is victims or possible suspects."

Robert standing next to Foster, told the press, "We are ready for some questions." One reporter asked, "Are the suspects still in Miami?" Robert replied, "As I told my superiors, it is still possible, we do not know, but anything is possible." Another Reporter asked the Police Chief if he agreed with the Detective. The Police Chief got quiet and said, "A smart cop would still believe they are still here." The Police Chief stated, "Better safe until more evidence shows they are truly gone."

Robert stated, "Next question." Another reporter asked, "Are the murders over?" Robert said, "No, if they are not here, they will kill someplace else." A TV reporter asked Detective Bench, "Will you keep hunting for these people if they are out of the city limit?" Robert responded by saying, "As long as my bosses allow me to." The COP looked at the Mayor, who was not happy with Robert's response.

Robert hesitated and then continued speaking, "I have no doubt my fellow detectives and myself will never stop hunting for these people." He knew he pissed off the COP, but he did not care. He then said, "I want you, the media, to understand this, it is possible this is not over, and I encourage the media to do the right thing and keep the people informed of facts and not opinions." He paused for a moment and looked around.

He continued, "We are not out of the woods yet, so please, everyone keep taking safety percussions, and I urge all parents to watch out for their daughters." Robert finished by telling everyone, "My biggest fear is a copycat, which sometimes happens, so everyone keep your guard up and Thank you." Robert walked off the stage while the press yelled out more questions that he refused to answer. Then the FBI agents stepped up and discussed what the FBI was doing to help locate these individuals and how the evidence will be treated. Once the FBI was done, they turned it over to the Police spokeswoman.

The Police spokeswoman stepped up to the mike and thanked everyone for coming, and everyone else walked off the stage. Veronica looked at her dad, who said, "Robert looked good, but I think he threw a zinger at the Police Chief and Mayor." Veronica smiled and told her dad, "My Robert did well." Thomas smiled and replied, "Alright, everyone, let's continue with the meeting."

Chapter 22

Putting the Puzzle Together

When Robert made it back to the conference room, he sat down and put his feet on the table, and waited for his bosses to come in. Ten minutes later, his bosses came in, including the Mayor, who was smiling and talking with the Police Chief.

Everyone sat down, and Robert lowered his feet and started answering questions about what was next in the investigation. Robert answered the questions with ease, and then he stood up. He told the men in the room, "I have a date, so that I will start up first thing." Before Robert left, the Mayor asked, "Detective, how long do we have before the next death?" Robert looked down and told him, "I will try and figure that out tomorrow and just make sure all the local videos around that house are grabbed so we can review them." He smiled and stated, "I am going home. Good night, gentlemen," and he walked out.

Robert went to his home and relaxed, and fell asleep. He was exhausted and needed rest, so he closed his eyes and napped. A couple of hours later, there was a knock on the door, and Robert got up and slowly went to the door and opened it. Veronica was smiling, and she walked in and asked, "Are you ok?" Robert told her, "Yea, just tired." Veronica came up and kissed him and asked, "How about we stay in tonight, and I cook you dinner?" Robert smiled and said, "Sounds good." She opened the door and waved for the chauffer to leave. Veronica took her coat off and told Robert, "Go ahead and take your nap. I will make dinner." Robert went and laid down in his bed, and he was out cold.

Veronica made dinner and went and woke up Robert by kissing him. Robert woke up and kissed her, and played with her hair. He got up and asked, "What's for dinner?" Veronica told him, "Come to the table and see." When they got to the table, he saw some lasagna. He looked at her and said, "Wow, you put a lot of work into it." Veronica smiled and said, "Sit down and tell me how it tastes." Robert sat down and grabbed her hand, and said a prayer in silent. He then let go, and he dug in. He was amazed at how good it was. He told her, "Honey, this is super." Veronica smiled and replied, thanks. I am glad you like it." They discussed how she made it, and then she changed the subject and asked about his News Conference, and they talked about it. Veronica looked concerned and asked, "Robert is this eating you up?" He told her, it's stressful, but I want to get these animals, and I know it's going to take a lot more work to get them."

Once dinner was over, they took the red wine they were drinking and went and sat on the couch. They talked about their wedding and where they were at with it. Robert was told how Veronica and her dad were almost done putting it together. They were just waiting on the date. Robert told her, "I know I said when I am done with this case, but I do not know how long it will be." Veronica got very quiet and then said, "I know. Whenever you are ready is good with me." He looked into her eyes, and he could see the love in them.

He got quiet for a moment and realized he always seemed to melt when he looked into them. She looked at him, and she had tears coming out, and he asked, "Why are you crying?" Veronica told him, "I do not want to lose you." Robert smiled and replied, "You are not." He took a slight breath and told her, "I just want you to know that I won't be able to see you a lot for a while. I have to find these two before more girls lose their lives." Veronica stated, "I understand."

Robert looked into her eyes again, wiped the tears from her eyes, and said, "Let's do it no matter what," and he pulled out his cell phone calendar and stated, "How about 65 days from today?" Veronica smiled and asked, "Are you sure?" Robert replied, "Yes, it's time. Let's get married." Veronica was all over Robert, and they mad love on the couch and worked their way into the bed room during the night.

Around 6 am, Robert's alarm went off, and he looked at Veronica, who was asleep, kissed her, went for a run on the beach, and lifted weights. Once He was done working out, he headed home, and when he walked in, Veronica was already dressed, and she made breakfast, and they sat down to eat. Veronica asked, "Why didn't you wake me up?" He told her, "You were in a deep sleep, and I knew you were tired." She told him, "For now on, get me up when you get up so we can work out together."

She asked, "If you are worried about me out running, you just say so," with a smirk on her face. Robert laughed and stated, "Sounds good to me." Veronica asked, "You promise, and he said, "I promise." Once they were done eating, he showered and got dressed for work. He dressed casually instead of in a suit and tie because he knew he would put some work on the case. He also packed a small bag in case he needed to clean up if he crashed into his office after a long day.

They loaded up in Robert's truck and headed to Veronica's work, and he dropped her off, and they kissed for a few minutes, and they each said they loved the other. The doorman opened the door. Veronica got out and waved back at Robert. He waved at her back as he watched her disappear inside the building.

When he arrived, Robert headed to work and parked in the police parking lot. He got out, went inside, went to his boss's office, closed the door, and sat down. His boss looked at him, and Robert told him in a couple of months, he will be getting married, and he will be sending out invitations down the road, and he said he hoped COD Gomez would come. Gomez responded, saying, "Absolutely, and she will make you a good wife." He then asked, "Will you have kids?" Robert smiled and told him, "Yes, we both agreed we want two or three." Gomez told Robert, "Sounds good, but what about this case?" Robert mentioned, "That's why I am dressed casually. I am going to do some digging." Robert then got up and told Gomez, "I will keep you informed."

Robert went to the Conference room, sat down, and called Foster, who was at the Task force work area, and asked him, "When could you step over and discuss some things." Foster stated, "He would step over in a little while." Robert trusted Foster, and they seemed to get along on most things. He always said anyone who agrees with another person all the time is a kiss-ass or a 100% idiot. He was raised if you stand your ground with facts to stand out. But if you argue with no facts and only emotions, most people will look at you as an idiot.

Robert saw a new package on the table, and he opened it and saw the new report on crimes in California, Washington, and Oregon. He was amazed these people still had not been caught. A mistake, a screwup, a cop tripping over a crime scene, something. He then went to the map on the wall and attached the new maps to the wall. Robert understood these new findings. They could be the one little thing that help lead to catching the suspects.

Robert sat back down, pulled out his notepad, and started writing notes about the similarities. He wrote down the population within a mile of the crime scenes and, what type of construction, how close to the beach the houses were. Robert noted the feet size of the house, how many rooms there were, police patrols in the area, foot or vehicle, and Universities close by or Junior colleges. He also looked up the racial makeup of the local populations and the racial makeup of all the victims. Robert also documented the times the suspects stayed in the homes, which he knew was always around six months.

Robert was amazed that not one neighbor saw one suspicious thing or heard anything unusual. He further noted all the people who lived next door to all these locations needed to be reinterviewed and do better background checks. He told himself that's a good job for the FBI.

Robert called Agent Fox, who answered and asked, "What's up?" Robert told him, "I have a big job for the FBI." Fox laughed and asked, "What is it?" Agent Fox was told, "He needed to get your people to get the list of all the names of the neighbors of all these homes next door and questioned them again." Agent Fox told Robert, "That's a big task." Robert replied, "It needs to be done. Maybe we can find out where they actually came from and where this thing started because someone talked to one of them or overheard something they thought was meaningless." Fox said, "I will call Washington and see if I can get them to get agents out shaking trees." Robert stated, "Tell them it's urgent before the next bodies start popping up." Fox told Robert that he understood, and he hung up.

Robert then put his cell phone down, leaned back in his chair, and looked at his notes for a few minutes. They knew what they looked like. It was time to turn up the heat on them even more. Then he saw it. All main roads had at least three ways out of town if they needed to flee. Those two's driver's licenses were in Florida, so he also needed to see if they had a Georgia license and then follow it from one state to another with all those items helping.

Chapter 23

Getting Tougher

Robert called his boss and FBI Agent Fox and Foster over. Twenty minutes later, everyone was there. Robert went over the escape routes, looked at his boss and explained, "We need to find out any video from these three points leading out of town." He paused for a moment and continued talking, "If there is video, it will possibly show what type of car they used to get away." Robert told everyone, "The car we impounded had fingerprints and DNA, but we have not received any information from Washington on any matches." Robert told Agent Fox, "You need to kick them in the ass so we can know who we are actually dealing with, and you need to check out the states where these people came from, including other countries."

He then asked Foster, "To get help checking these other areas out, including banks and stores, because these banks and stores are by these intersections because I doubt they went through the towns." He looked around for a moment and told everyone, "They probably used the bypasses since they are the quickest, but they still have a couple of four-way stops, as he pointed on a GPS map." COD Gomez told Robert, "I am impressed." Robert scoffed and replied, "Sorry, boss, it doesn't matter unless these ideas help catch them."

Once the COD, Foster and Fox left the room, Robert sat down again. Robert then popped up because he forgot to tell Foster something else. He opened the door and said loudly, "Hey, Foster, please check all stolen vehicles from the time that place was hit till 30 minutes after." Foster turned around, smiled, replied, "Copy," and returned to the Taskforce area.

Robert yelled out to his boss and told him, "Let's go for a ride." Gomez thought about it and asked Robert, "What kind of trouble are we looking for?" Robert stated, "Hopefully, the worse." Robert grabbed his truck keys and his radio, and they left the building. After driving away from the station, they headed west to HWY 41, crossing the Everglades.

When they made it to the intersection of 997 and HWY 41, Gomez observed a Corrections Facility, and he pointed, and Robert told Gomez, "Before you say anything, I agree. Let's check it out." They entered the parking lot and parked. A roving patrol Officer came by and asked, "How can they be helped?" They showed their badges, and the C/O told them, "That's the entrance, and take care," as he rode off.

Both Gomez and Robert entered the main entrance, and the Front Lobby officer asked them, "How can I help you?" They showed their IDs and requested to see the Captain. The officer asked, "What should I tell him? It's about a gentleman?" Chief of Detectives Gomez told him, "We need to see the video over the last couple days of the main road to see if the criminals we are chasing went this way." The officer replied, "No problem, sir." The front lobby officer called the Captain and notified him who was at the entrance and what they requested. The Captain told the officer he would be up front in a few minutes. The C/O hung up and repeated what the Captain said. The Officer asked, "If you gentleman would like to sit down, please do," and he asked them, "Would you like some coffee?" Gomez said, "No, thank you, we prefer to stand."

Captain Johnson walked through the sallyport in a suit and tie a few minutes later and looked very professional. He walked up, introduced himself, and shook hands with both gentlemen. The Captain asked, "What could he do for them?" Robert told him, "We would like to check your video over the last couple of days of two criminals we are looking for and want to see if they went by this place." The Captain asked, "Just the ones covering the outer areas?" Robert replied, "Yes because we believe they came this way." The

Captain told Robert, "I am sorry unless I get a court order or the AG or Governor authorized it, my hands are tied."

Robert immediately asked the Captain, "May I use your phone?" Captain Johnson looked puzzled and stuttered and said, "Yes." He turned around and told the front lobby officer, "Dial whatever number the Detective wants." Robert pulled out a piece of paper and told the officer, "Dial this number." The phone rang in the Florida state Attorney General's Office, and the AG answered the phone. Captain Johnson told the AG, "Captain Johnson identified himself and what prison he was at and notified the AG." I have two gentlemen here wanting to see outside video of the road, and before the Captain could continue, the AG asked, "Is one a Detective Bench Captain?" Captain Johnson responded, "Yes, sir." The AG told the Captain, "Give him whatever, and I mean whatever he needs," and the AG hung up.

Both Detectives at the same time looked at Captain Johnson and asked, "Well?" Captain Johnson told both Detectives, "Please secure your handguns and cellphones in those gun lockers, please." Robert and Gomez complied and followed Captain Johnson through the metal detectors after signing in as visitors. The staff they passed in the corridors wondered who they were and what was going on. However, two inmate orderlies knew who Detective Bench was and knew he was not one to mess with.

They worked their way to the camera room in the Prisons investigation unit and shook hands with the investigation staff. The Captain notified the Chief investigator for the institution, "Help these gentlemen in reviewing the video, and that is a priority." The intel officer asked, "Gentlemen, I need the location, date and estimated time frame." Robert notified the officer of the date locations and then told him, "We appreciate you people helping out." They spent the next four hours looking at the video with no luck, and when they were getting ready to finish up, Gomez saw something.

He observed a big man in the car with an older lady, but it looked like another person was in the back seat. Robert requested a printout of that. They noticed about a half dozen cars with people who could be them, but the cars were full of people, and the cameras were too far back to give an actual proper view of the people in the cars. After a minute, he had a colored photo but could not tell if it was them. He showed it to Gomez, who looked at it and told Robert, "Maybe, but it looks like there are people in the back seat." Robert agreed but decided to hang onto the photo anyway. He put it in his folder with the rest of the photos, and after finishing up, they thanked everyone and headed out. Once they got their weapons, they headed back to Miami.

Robert was disappointed and a little irked because none of the vehicle pictures could show the plates of the vehicles, and not one photo of a guy and an older woman they could actually identify. He sat driving and thinking all the way back to the Police station. Chief of Detectives Gomez also didn't say a word and just sat there thinking about the video they had watched. When they drove up, Robert saw Veronica walk out of the station towards her limo, and he honked his horn as he drove into the parking lot. Veronica didn't see or hear the honk and got into the limo, and it drove off. Robert parked his vehicle, and both men got out and went inside through the side door.

Robert went to the conference room, sat, and looked at the Florida map. He still believed in his three-way routes theory. He looked at Key West but believed it didn't make sense since they could easily get caught trying to leave. There was only one real way out if a person had to get out quickly. He kept looking at the map and felt the next stop could be Naples, a rich area with homes of all types on the beach.

The question was, are their homes like what they have been using, and how the hell are they paying for all of these homes? Robert picked up the conference room phone and called the Taskforce room, and FBI Agent Davis answered. Robert asked for

Agent Fox. Davis told Robert, "He is not here, and who is this?" Robert replied, "Detective Bench." Agent Davis informed Detective Bench, "Agent Fox had to go to Washington for a couple of days to brief the Director." Robert asked, "Can you guys get all the information on how these clowns paid for all these homes either by, Checks, cash, credit cards, or whatever?" Agent Davis stated, "No problem, but it will take a couple of days." Robert said, "Fine. Also, if it's money orders, find out what banks and Post Offices they used, including any video."

As the evening was going by, he was going through the packets from Virginia beach when Veronica knocked and walked in. Robert looked at the clock, and it was already 9:20 PM. Robert rubbed his eyes, smiled, and asked, "How are you?" Veronica had a big bag from her Restaurant of Italian food. Robert smiled and told her, "Great, I am hungry time has flown by." Veronica smiled and told Robert she was fine. You look so tired, honey." He grinned and stood up and kissed her. They sat down, and she pulled out everything and set the food out like they were at a nice restraint. She also pulled out a bottle of wine and glasses, lit a candle, and turned off the room light. Veronica said while sitting back down, "She came by today, but you were not here, and the other Detectives told me you and your boss went to check on some things." Veronica asked, "Did it work out?" Robert took a deep breath and informed her, "No, it did not, but I think we were heading in the right direction." Veronica leaned over and kissed him, and told Robert, sorry it did not work out, but since we can't go out to eat, I brought the food here".

They ate and talked about her day and how things were going at her work. She explained to Robert, "Her dad is letting her take more control of the business, and she feels some of the men and women on the board are jealous because they felt they should be making the decisions she is making." Veronica bit her lip and stated, "I feel knives in my back all the time." Robert looked at her and chewed his food. When he swallowed his food, he took a sip of the red wine and said, "Honey fuck them, your dad owns 100% of the company, and you are his daughter, run it and the hell with them and tell them off."

Robert told Veronica, "I piss people off every day, especially my bosses, and I do not care." He grinned and told her, "How he gets called every name in the book, and his bosses know I do not give a shit because that's how I keep my sanity." He paused and notified her, "You will be my wife soon, so toughen up, and if you have to get tough, do it." She smiled and reminded him, "When you called me a bitch when we met." Robert replied, "Absolutely, be one only when you have to."

He told Veronica, "Stand up in front of everyone, including your dad, so that he can see and back you up." Robert explained to her, "Tell everyone your dad owns this company, and you are his daughter who is being groomed to take over, and if anyone of you does not like it, fucking resign right now or shut up and do what you are told." Veronica laughed as Robert finished by saying, "Make eye contact while you are talking to them and look at each one of them, and if no one says anything says good and let's move on, then go back to whatever the meeting is about."

Chapter 24

Wrong Place and the Wrong Time

Both Robert and Veronica got quiet for a second, and they started laughing, and she started to choke on the wine going down, and she stood up smiling. She told Robert, "I love you, and you will make a good advisor when I take over." He asked, "What's my pay?" Veronica told him, "You figure it out." Robert smiled and replied, "Sounds good to me." Once they were done eating, the COD, who was also working late, walked in and informed Robert, "There has been a shooting on Highway 41 about 60 miles west of Miami. It could have been them."

The COD looked at Veronica and back at Robert and continued explaining, "A police officer had pulled a vehicle over and described a couple of Caucasians in the vehicle, and before he could finish, the transmission ended. It matched a stolen vehicle from the area of the crime scene on the beach."

Gomez went into more detail explaining why the local authorities there believed it could be the suspects when Robert interrupted and asked, "Why did it take so long to notify anyone?" Gomez answered and told Robert, "They found the patrol car and the dead cop inside the vehicle in the swamp, and they had been looking over the last few days for the officer."

Veronica stated, "Oh my God, his poor family." Robert asked, "How did they find him?" His boss told Robert, "A fishermen's boat ran into it when he was trying to get closer to the shore, and when He used his big flashlight, he saw the patrol car." Gomez paused, looked at his notepad and continued speaking and told Robert, "The guy marketed it on his GPS then went to notify the Police due to the poor signal he had on his cell phone." Robert asked, "Was he shot?" Gomez told him, "They pulled the vehicle and the officer out of the swamp and found two bullet holes in him through the front window." Robert stood up and asked, "Are they still at the scene?" Agent Davis walked in, and when Gomez started to tell him what happened, Agent Davis stated, "Sorry, I already heard." Robert looked at the agent and told him, "Let's take the chopper." Agent Davis chuckled and stated, "Sounds good, Batman. What's next, the bat boat?" The COD laughed and told Davis, "That's a good one. I need to remember that one," as Robert kissed Veronica and told her, "I have to go." Agent Davis told Robert, "I am not Robin. Just remember that."

Robert called the Miami Dade chopper on their radio channel and asked, "How are they on fuel?" The Copilot responded, "They are refilling at the moment." Robert replied, "Meet me and the FBI at the Main station house in 15 minutes." The chopper pilot acknowledged, "10-4."

Robert helped Veronica clean up and then walked her to the limo, which just drove up. They kissed, and Robert thanked her for dinner. They each told the other they loved the other, and they kissed. Robert observed the chopper getting ready to land when Robert kissed her again and said, "I will call you." Veronica smiled and said, "When you get back, call me, I do not care what time." He smiled as he was heading away and replied, "Ok."

Robert ran up the stairs and into the building to the roof. Once to the top, both Agent Davis, who was waiting for Robert, got in the helicopter. Robert gave the location, and they took off. Veronica had the chauffer stand by as she wanted to watch the chopper leave. Once it was out of site, she told the chauffeur, "Ok, take me home."

While heading home, she realized how hard Robert pushed himself and thought about her plan for Robert. She hoped it would work and that Robert would realize it was best to work for her dad. Veronica worried he could drive himself into the ground working, But she will try to persuade him when the right time comes.

Veronica new he would make a great husband and a great father. She didn't tell him tonight because he had to go, but she was pregnant. She intended to be a mother and was not upset about getting pregnant. She wanted it, the baby.

After Robert put on his headset, he called his boss and told him, "I believe it's them because it's on HWY 41." Gomez replied, "Then we were right." Robert agreed. Robert told his boss, "Agent Davis is in the air heading that way. Please brief the chief and have him warn the Naples PD they might be heading their way or might already be there." Gomez replied, "Copy out." The FBI Agent asked, "So, you think they are in Naples?" The FBI Agent was told, "It fits, but the big question is what type of housing can they afford to start over again, and where is the money coming from?" Robert wanted to find out because that was a key piece of evidence.

The pilot got hold of the HWY Patrol as they were getting ready to land on the still-blocked road. Robert told the pilot after landing to "Stand by and wait." The pilot gave the thumbs up that he understood, and he turned the engine off, and the pilot and copilot waited. Robert and Agent Davis disembarked and headed towards the gathering of the cops on the side of the road. The Captain of the HWY Patrol came forward, and everyone identified themselves. Robert asked, "Can I see were this happened?" Captain waved and said, "Follow me, and I will have my LT go over everything." The Lieutenant stepped over, and the Captain identified the FBI Agent and Detective Bench. The Lieutenant showed them where they believed the police vehicle pulled over the car in a traffic stop. He explained, "The vehicle camera was ripped out of the car, and the police officer's body camera was also taken."

Robert looked at Agent Davis, shook his head in disgust and commented, "It's them, I have no doubt." Agent Davis got on his cell phone and called the FBI field office in Naples and advised them that the suspects were heading their way. Then he called Washington. He talked to Agent Fox, and suddenly, he heard the Director of the FBI come over the phone speaker and tell Agent

Davis, "This is the director. How are you?" Agent Davis replied, "Fine, sir. Detective Bench believes they are headed or are in Naples at the moment, and we are at an officer-involved shooting, and Detective Bench believes it was them." Then he advised the Director, "The vehicle camera and the officers' cameras were taken before the vehicle was pushed into the swamp."

The Director said I would call the Region office to get every agent to western Florida. He also said he would get hold of the U.S Marshals involved also. The director said good job keep up the good work, and find these animals. Agent xxx said yes, sir. The director notified Agent Davis, "That Agent Fox is heading back tomorrow and bringing more agents with him." Agent Davis thanked the Director, and the phone went dead. Agent Davis informed Detective Bench, "The FBI will be flooding into the west coast of Florida, and more agents are coming with the U.S. Marshals." Robert looked at Agent Davis and said, "Good job."

Once the LT showed them everything. Robert stood around and looked at the crime scene. He asked, "did the Police officer have a vehicle like the ones those officers have"? The LT informed him, "Yes, he did." Robert advised them, "To put a vehicle right here." The LT remarked, "We did that." Robert told him, "Do it again." So the LT hesitated and notified the local officer to put his vehicle in the same spot as before. Once that was done, Robert asked the Police officer, "How much room do they normally leave between the Police vehicle and a car they pull over?" The Police officer informed Robert about the car length so they could see the whole vehicle.

Robert went and checked the dead officer's car out and looked at the seat. Then Robert got into the other car and looked straight ahead. He asked the Police officer, "how big was the officer? Robert was told about your height. He fixed the seat to a similar spot in the other car, and he just sat there, rowed up the window, and turned on the air conditioner.

He looked and concluded it was not the passenger who did the shooting. It did not match the angles. It came in low due to the angle of the shot that took the top of the officer's head off and the bullet he was told was in the vehicle's roof. He figured the shot came from the back seat, so whoever was in the back seat did the shooting. The question was why the glass on the ground was only from the police car.

He turned the vehicle off and got out. He walked slowly and looked at the arrows from the crime lab, showing the angle it came from. Robert said loudly, "Damn." He looked around and announced, "Somebody was hiding in the trunk vehicle and fired the three rounds." Robert stated, "Let me guess, no shells." The LT replied, "No shells." Robert scratched his head and asked himself if there could be more than two, but no evidence showed that anywhere.

Robert questioned the LT again and asked, "How many people did the officer say before he was killed in the car?" The LT remarked, "Only two white people. He didn't say male or female." Robert looked at the crime scene and was puzzled. Maybe the guy got out quickly, had the gun low, and was shooting as he brought the gun up. Maybe. It happens all the time.

He shook hands with the LT and Captain and asked them, "When you are done, send all your crime scene information to this email address on his card." The Captain advised Roberts, "I don't think I can do that?" Robert stopped, turned around, and retorted, "Captain, just do it alright. I promise it will be ok." The Captain hesitated and replied, "No problem, we all want these animals." Robert stepped back over and shook the Captain's hand again, and remarked, "You are absolutely right thanks again." He signaled the pilot of the chopper, and the chopper started up. Robert and Agent Davis jumped in, and the chopper returned to Miami.

Chapter 25

Burning the House Down

When they made it back at 2:30 AM, the chopper landed, and Robert told the Pilot, "We are done for the night," the pilot and copilot were relieved and told Robert, "Thanks," as they winded down the chopper. Robert went back to the conference room, and Agent Davis went home. Once Robert entered, he looked at the map and told himself I hope they do not start up again. Robert then called the HWY patrol and requested any information on any vehicles stolen or missing along HWY 41. The officer on the line advised Robert he would get back to him.

Robert felt they would try and dump the vehicle in case he gave a full description and maybe grab another one. Robert was going through evidence when the phone rang. It was 4:30 am when he looked at the clock on the wall. Robert answered the phone and said, "Hello." Veronica came over the phone and asked, "How was he doing?" He shared with her how he felt and how the investigation was going.

The other conference room phone rang, and Robert told veronica, "Hang on." Robert answered the phone, and it was the Police officer he called about vehicles being stolen. The Officer informed him, "There was a theft and a shooting 25 miles down the road, and Somebody broke into a house and killed the old couple there and stole their vehicle, and burned the vehicle they arrived in."

The bodies were found the next day by family members who were worried about them. Robert asked for the address and told the officer, "Make sure it is sealed off, so I can get the FBI there tomorrow with their evidence people." The officer agreed and hung up.

Robert called the late-night officer in the Task force and notified him, "They killed an old couple," and told him the address. He advised the officer, "When the FBI gets there in the morning, they need to get the evidence team out to that address, and it has already been secured." Robert then said, "Hell with it, give me Agent Davis's number." Once he got it, he hung up and called Agent Davis and woke up the sleeping agent. Robert identified himself, and Agent Davis asked, "Don't you ever sleep?" Robert commented, "No, I am a vampire." He heard Veronica laugh on the other phone. Robert explained what was happening and told Davis he needed to get the FBIs evidence of people there by sunlight, and the town closest was Ochopee. The house is about 6 miles outside, just east of the town back in the swamps. Agent Davis told Robert, "Copy," and hung up.

Robert got quiet and then remembered Veronica was on the other phone. He went back and asked, "What was the laughing about?" Veronica commented on the vampire part and asked, "When will you bite me, Count?" While rubbing his tired eyes, he told her, "I would love to right now, but I have to get cleaned up and drive to this town to be there when the FBI evidence team arrives."

Veronica told Robert, "Please do not run yourself into the ground. Come home, please." He replied, "Honey, I am fine. I tell you what, When I get back tomorrow, I will take the rest of the day and night off." Veronica told him, "Great, we have a lot to talk about." Robert replied back, "Go to sleep, and I will see you later." Veronica whispered, "I love you." Robert responded by saying, "I love you too." He told her, "I am going to go take a shower, change clothes and head to Ochopee. See you later." Veronica said, "Be careful," and Robert replied, "I will be," and hung up, after which Veronica hung up and lay there worrying about him.

She could not sleep. She wanted to tell Robert so bad she was pregnant, but she will wait till dinner and tell Robert and her dad. She then finally fell back asleep. Veronica was worried about Robert, but she knew he could care for himself.

Robert pulled out a card from a friend who did IV drips of vitamins that help pick you up and are legal. He woke his friend up and said, "I need you to come to the Main Police station and hook me up and Just tell the front lobby you are to see me." His friend commented, "Robert, do you know what time it is?" He laughed and replied, "Yes, I still need you down here, I have a long day ahead, and I am about to fall on my face chasing those murderers." Lawson was irritated but told Robert, "Give me an hour." Robert asked, "How much?" Lawson quoted 500, and because it's you, 375". Robert replied, "Fair enough. See you in an hour."

Robert grabbed his bag, went to the showers, cleaned himself up, and got in new clean clothes. Then he went back to the conference room, and Lawson was escorted by an officer. They stepped out of the conference room, and Lawson notified Robert, "Hey, that room is good." Robert smiled and stated, "Top secret stuff in there. I might have to kill you if you saw anything". Lawson chuckled and said, "You probably would," and he pointed at a desk. They went and sat down, and Lawson hooked up the IV and ministered several vitamins into Robert's system to help with energy and stamina—all legal and approved.

Once they were done, Robert stood up feeling much better. The police officer watching stated, "Wow, how much?" Robert counted out 375 and gave his friend another 25 for coming early. The officer laughed and remarked, "Never mind, that's too much on my Rookie pay, maybe in a few years." Lawson gave the officer his card and told him, "Call me. We can work something out." They shook hands, and he was escorted out of the detective area and back to the entrance.

Robert went and signed out a vehicle and headed to Ochopee. He finally arrived around 830am and saw the FBI evidence teams drive up with some big trucks and vehicles. Robert got out of his vehicle and showed his ID. The Agent in charged identified himself, and they shook hands. Robert explained what he believed and anything they found might help resolve the case.

The agent in charge went up to the poor officers who were watching the house all night and identified himself and told them, "They can go once their reliefs get there, then they are to inform their reliefs on what is required of them." The two officers returned to their car and went to the entrance to prevent anybody else, including reporters, from getting in if they showed up.

The FBI Evidence Response team went through what was left of the smoking ashes of the house. Theis included taking photographs of the burnt bodies and then had the bodies placed in a special plastic material to help preserve the bodies as best as possible and not lose any evidence which could be lost. The FBI observed the couple was still in bed when they were shot multiple times. There were no other bodies discovered in the house during the thorough search.

The remaining ashes of the house showed no evidence that could be used to show who the assailants were or if they took any other items from the house. Anything with fingerprints or DNA was collected to be examined at the FBI lab. While looking around for any evidence, an FBI evidence team member found a DVD recorder melted and upside down in what would have been the far right part of the house. It must have been covered and fallen to the ground after the shelf burnt.

Robert followed the melted wires to the far front right side of the house if you were looking from the front. A melted small 4-inch camera was found. He yelled out what he found and hoped it showed something. Robert stepped over and looked at the video system, and smiled. He stated in a firm tone, "Get that to the FBI lab as soon as possible." The DVD still might have something important on it, like who entered the house and killed those people. He was hoping the suspects didn't see the camera. Hopefully, the victims hid it well.

As the day passed, they found little evidence of anything else major. The Fire inspector explained, "The fuel source was gasoline, and it seemed they did not care about hiding it." He showed a can found in the middle of the floor in what was probably the Livingroom. Robert shook his head in acknowledgment. These two elderly people were growing old together, living their lives when these animals did this with no remorse.

Chapter 26

Big Announcement

Later in the day, he decided he was going to head back to the office. He told the FBI agent, "Send me the autopsy report when it's done, please." The agent smiled and asked, "Why don't you come to work for us?" Robert grinned and snickered, "Thanks but no thanks." He knew he would probably fail the lie detector. He was no boy scout and occasionally stepped outside those grey areas a few times. It was nothing like planting evidence or setting people up. He truly believed that was a no-no. However, putting his hands on a criminal who deserved his ass kicked. Yea, he has done it but is more careful now due to cell phones everywhere. He knew those days of throwing an extra punch were basically over. Too many thugs around.

Once he got in the car and headed back to the station. He called FBI Agent Davis and advised him to check for all cars stolen and their locations. Over the next 72 hours, Robert paused for a moment and then mentioned, "The suspects might commit several crimes to keep us confused or guessing in what direction they are headed." He still believed in the Naples area, but that could change if the houses did not fit their way of doing things.

Once he hung up, he went to his place, showered and changed into casual clothing. He didn't take a nap because he knew he would not get up, so he headed to Veronicas. Robert pulled over a couple of times to make notes on things that popped into his head about all those homicides.

He then realized what if they came back this way. So, he called Agent Davis and requested a list of all stolen vehicles along Highway 41. Agent Davis got quiet and asked, "Do you think they might come back this way?" Robert suggested, "Yes if there is no place for them to keep doing what they are doing."

Robert requested the FBI get with the state patrol and notify them to increase patrols along the Highways to Naples and Tampa. Agent Davis replied, "Sound good." Robert added, "Hell, let's go for all stolen vehicles all the way to Tampa and all vehicles stolen for the next 72 hours to 96 hours in southern Florida." Davis informed him, "It's going to be a big folder," and Robert remarked, "Yea, it's big, but we can thin it out over time."

Robert hung up and drove back on the road, and ten minutes later, he drove up and got out of his truck at Veronica's home. She was walking around the compound with her dad when she observed Robert drive up. Veronica ran, and she hugged and kissed him when he got out of his truck. She kissed him all over his face and told him, "I have missed you so much." Robert squeezed her and said, "You feel so good, and I missed you too," as he kissed her lips.

Thomas came walking up and asked, "How's my future son-in-law"? Robert put his hand out, and they shook hands. Thomas looked at Robert and could see he was exhausted, but he didn't say anything. Veronica looked at Robert and remarked, "Honey, you look so tired." Robert smiled, telling her, "He was fine and will get a good night's sleep tonight." They headed to the house, and the butler opened the door as they entered the house.

Veronica announced, "It's dinner time. I am starved." Robert replied, "So am I," as they went and sat down at the big table. Once everyone sat down, Thomas asked, "How was the investigation going?" Robert suggested, "It's not good." He shook his head in disgust and informed Thomas, "They killed two old people who lived off the highway and burned the house down." He took a sip of water, and he was more detailed and explained they stole the old couple's vehicle after burning up the vehicle they stole in the Miami area. Thomas asked, "Do you have any idea where they are going?" Robert informed Thomas, "Either Naples or Tampa," but then Robert got quiet. Thomas looked at him, and then

Robert looked at Thomas and told him, "My gut keeps telling me they might come back this way."

The food was brought out, and Robert saw a huge T-Bone steak on his plate, and he smiled and said, "Just what I needed." Veronica had a Filet Mignon, and Thomas had a NY strip. Robert stated the vegetables were good. Then a salad for everyone was brought out. Veronica was eating while her dad and Robert talked about the case. Once they were done eating, Veronica began by saying, "Since I am here with the two men I love. I want you two men to know something." She smiled and announced, "I am pregnant," she stood up and told them, "She was about six weeks along."

Thomas jumped up, kissed Veronica on the cheek, and hugged her. Robert was surprised, and he finally stood up and gave Veronica a kiss on the lips and smiled. Veronica got quiet and asked Robert, "Are you not happy?" Robert grabbed her, kissed her, smiled, and told her he was just surprised and asked, "Is it a boy or a girl?" Veronica informed him, "She did not know." She seemed worried that Robert was not happy. He looked at her and told her, "He is definitely happy and that he is just surprised and tired."

He looked at her and Thomas and stated, "You know what we need to do is get married as soon as possible." Thomas smiled and commented, "That's an outstanding idea." Veronica looked into Robert's tired eyes and asked, "Are you sure?" Robert kissed her lips and replied, "100% in about two weeks." Veronica smiled, teary-eyed, hugged Robert and beamed, "I am so happy." She hugged her dad, who said, "I will make the calls tomorrow."

Thomas stood there and asked, "Small church or big?" Robert looked at Veronica, who smiled and replied, "Let's go big." Thomas then asked, "Where do you two want to go for your honeymoon?" Robert looked at Veronica, who informed her dad while looking at Robert and declared, "I always wanted to take a Mediterranean cruise," as she reached up and kissed Robert. Thomas informed them, "I am paying for it." He then suggested,

"How about a private yacht? Robert and Veronica looked at each other when Thomas explained, "I have a friend who has one over there, and I have no doubt you two can borrow it." Veronica smiled and asked Robert, "What do you think?" Robert looked into her eyes and commented, "Your happiness is the most important thing to me." She smiled and got teary-eyed again and kissed Robert. She told her dad, "Yes." They then all walked over to the couch and talked about the guest and other things.

As the evening went by, Robert was getting tired. The Butler bought their remaining red wine for dinner, where they drank it and saluted Veronica and the new baby. Around 9:00 P.M., Robert was getting extremely tired, and Veronica noticed him almost falling asleep during the conversations. When she advised her dad, "Roberts is tired, and it's time for bed." Robert remarked, "I should stay the night at my place," when Veronica said loudly, "No, you are sleeping here." Robert smiled and stated, "Yes, dear." Thomas laughed and told them, "I will do some work and make phone calls to get this going." Veronica led Robert upstairs and to their room.

When they entered the bedroom, she shut the door, kissed him, and asked Robert, "Are you sure about this?" Robert stepped up to her and reached and held her face softly and reached down and kissed her lips and whispered, "I have no doubts." They helped each other out their clothes, and he lifted her, carried her to the bed, laid her down, made love, and fell asleep next to each other. Veronica woke up an hour later and watched Robert sleep, and he looked so tired. She got out of bed and turned off her alarm so he could sleep in. Veronica leaned over, kissed him, and whispered in his ear, "I love you, Robert." She then laid back down and went to sleep.

Chapter 27

Day Off

Robert woke up around 11:00 am and jumped out of bed, realizing he had slept in, and he saw Veronica was not in bed. Robert went and took a shower, and he noticed his clothes had been washed, dried and folded. He got dressed and went downstairs and noticed nobody was around. One of the maids came in from the kitchen and notified Robert, "Ms. Veronica is outside in the pool, and Mr. Jackson is at the Tower." She said sir, "Would you like some breakfast?" He replied, "No thanks, I will eat lunch whenever it is served." She replied, "Very well, sir." Robert informed her, "Please call me Robert." She smiled and stated, "Yes, Mr. Robert." He said, "Just Robert." She smiled and notified him, "There are rules in this house, and we are not allowed to use first names the way you want them." Then she walked away.

Robert shrugged his shoulders and said, "Whatever," and he went out to the pool and saw Veronica swimming laps. He stood there by the pool, watching her go back and forth for a few minutes, when she stopped and looked up and saw Robert. She swam over to the side where he was watching her and asked, "How long have you been watching me swim?" He grinned and told her, "For a few minutes." She asked, "If he was coming in?" He told her, "No swimming trunks." Standing in the pool, she looked up at him and replied, "Just come in the way you are." He laughed and responded, "That's ok. I am fine watching you." She smiled and asked, "Are you sure?" He again answered, "Yes."

She smiled in a flirting way, took her top off and threw it at him, and asked again, "Are you sure?" He laughed and stuttered and replied, "Yea." She then took off her bottoms and threw them at him, and she remarked, "Now, are you really, really, sure?" Robert kicked off his shoes, socks, shirt, badge, and weapon, tossed them on the ground, and jumped in. They were back upstairs ten minutes later, making love and ordering the lunch meal to be brought to her room. They stayed in bed all day and evening and ordered dinner to be brought to the room.

When Thomas made it home, he asked the Butler where he was everyone. He pointed up stairs. Thomas laughed, saying, "I guess they are not coming down." The maid walked by and told him, "She was swimming in the pool, then he came down and then 15 minutes I saw her walking up the stairs naked, and he was soaking wet from the pool walking behind her, and they went back to her room." The maid headed to the kitchen. Thomas smiled and said to himself, "Well, at least things are going well."

Thomas went to the office and told the butler he would eat in his office, and the butler responded, "Very good, sir." When Thomas sat down at his desk, he did some work and then made some phone calls about his daughter's wedding. He decided to look at his will, which needed to be changed due to the loss of his son. He was going to split most of everything with his two children and the rest to charity causes. Unfortunately for Thomas, that would never happen. He made some changes to his will and gave his daughter 80% of all he owned and his future grandchild 20% of all his holdings. He set it up where his daughter would be the conservator of his grand child's 20% until the child reached twenty-five.

If something happened to his daughter, his grandchild would inherent it all in a trust until the child was twenty-five. He had where a trust would supervise all holdings and funds. Robert would get a fixed amount to raise the child in case of the death of Veronica. But besides that, Robert would get nothing. He set it that way because he felt Robert would not want anything. A man that turns down 100 million would undoubtedly not want anything to do with the business. He could be wrong, but it's what he feels at this time. Once he was done, he sent it over a secured line to his lawyer, who would make the corrections so he could sign it.

Thomas stayed up late and crashed into his office on the couch. He was happy his daughter was going to be married to a good man. He was also happy he was going to be a grandpa. Like those love birds upstairs, he wondered if it was going to be a boy or a girl. Before he fell asleep, he said, "Lights off," and the lights dimmed.

The next morning Robert woke up at 6:00 AM and got dressed. Veronica asked, "Where was he going?" He replied, "I have to get back to work." Veronica asked, "Can't you stay a little longer?" Robert stood there and smiled and advised her, "I have to go." He hesitated for a moment and told her, "Some people are going to lose their lives soon, no matter what I do, but it's the ones down the road I am trying to save."

She sat up in bed and asked, "When will I see you again?" He told her, "I will be here tonight unless something unfortunate happens." She stated, "Ok," and they kissed. Veronica then asked him, "What do you want for dinner?" He turned and said with a smile, "You?" She smiled back and replied, "Food, dummy." He said, "Definitely surprise me." She said, "Ok." She jumped out of bed, and they kissed for a minute, and then he let her go and headed out the door and down the stairs.

Thomas was up and eating breakfast and told Robert, "Good morning." Robert said good morning back. Thomas asked if he wanted any breakfast, and Robert replied, "No thanks, I have a long day and have to get going." Robert remarked, "See you at dinner." Thomas replied, "C-Ya." Robert went out the front door, jumped in his truck, and started it up.

He sat there for a minute, warming up the truck while thinking about getting married in two weeks. Robert knew he had to call and tell his parents, brother, and sister. He started driving and figured he would call them in a couple of hours once he started his work. He laughed to himself at how surprised they would be about his getting married and when they found out who he was marrying.

He figured he would water down who Veronica and her dad were. They will get the shock of their lives when they come down here for the wedding. Robert knew he would have to tell them he was going to be a daddy. His mom's strict Roman -Catholic views cause a slight problem getting Veronica pregnant before they get married, but he had no doubt she would get over it quickly. They have been wondering for a long time when I would ever meet a girl to marry. His mom says, "You are so picky." He always told her, "In today's world, you have to be."

While at work, he was looking at all the stolen car lists all the way up to Tampa. He compared the cars stolen earlier by the suspects with the cars that were stolen lately. Using the computer, he removed all the sports cars and vehicles that would draw attention to themselves. He made a list of all four-door stolen vehicles, which was a lot, but it cut the number to 89%.

Most car thieves steal certain types of vehicles and usually, in most cases, leave simple mom-and-pop type cars alone. Not fancy, and defiantly those vehicles do not get a second look from the Police unless they are driving extremely recklessly. Robert then removed the stolen vehicles, but the witnesses or video cameras of the thieves knocked it down to 96%. So that left about 28 vehicles.

Robert checked if anyone was killed or had their vehicles stolen, and no owners were missing or dead. Robert called the Taskforce and put a list out to all law enforcement to focus on these 28 vehicles. The information went out statewide within 30 minutes. He felt it did not need to go nationwide since he believed the suspects were in some places in Florida. He knew the national media would put it on the news cycle anyway. They always put the bad things on nationally.

Robert looked at the Florida map on the Gulf side of the small towns and bigger cities. He was curious about what type of buildings were on that side and how close they were to the beaches. The internet helps, but eyes on does a better job, and he wants to see the possible roads they might have taken.

In an insistent tone, he called his boss and stated, I want to go to Naples and the Tampa area for a few days and check the houses on the coastline. Gomez advised Robert, "I will call the Chief so he can call their Chiefs to get all the corporation you need." Roberts said, "Thanks and don't forget Tampa also." Gomez notified Robert, "I will get with Agent Fox so he can have a chopper in both areas on standby for you." Robert stated, "Thanks, I will head that way tomorrow, and I plan to drive to see things on the ground also." Before Robert hung up, he requested to bring Foster with him?" Gomez replied, "No problem and I will tell him to be here at 8 am." Robert said, "Make it 6 am. I want to leave early to get through the crappy traffic." Gomez replied, "Done," and both hung up.

Robert grabbed the equipment he needed, like binoculars, maps, notepads, and a video camera. While walking to his truck, he was going over what he would be doing tomorrow. He wanted it to be productive and not a waste of time. He jumped into his truck and headed to Veronicas. While driving, he realized he did not call his parents and brother and sister, so he called his parents and told them he was going to get married in two weeks. Surprised, his dad asked, "Son, are you sure she is the one?" Robert laughed and advised him, "Yep, she is the one."

He didn't tell them she was pregnant because his mom would have a fit. He would tell them sometime after the wedding, like a week or two. His mom asked about kids, and he told her, "If it happens, then you will be a grandparent. Only time will tell." They talked for a few minutes, and they said their good byes. He told them they would stay at his place.

He called his brother and sister, and they were happy for him. There was the usual it's about time and more talk about how many kids' stuff. He had a good discussion with each one of them. When he arrived at Veronica's, he got out and went and knocked on the door. The butler opened the door and said, "Come in, sir. You are expected." Robert replied, "Thank you."

Chapter 28

Family and Surprises

Robert walked in and saw Thomas sitting on the couch, watching the news. Thomas got up, and they shook hands. Thomas asked, "Can we go for a walk," and he told Robert, "Veronica is upstairs getting ready for dinner." They went outside, walked by the pool, and started walking around quietly when Thomas asked, "Robert do you have a problem with me calling you son?" Robert looked at Thomas and replied, "You can call me whatever you want, sir." Thomas stopped and looked at Robert and requested in a serious tone. "Please call me Thomas." Robert looked at Thomas and agreed, "Ok, Thomas." Thomas smiled and stated, "Good, that's a start."

They went back to walking when Robert asked, "Thomas, what's up?" Thomas told him, "He is one of the wealthiest persons in America and the wealthiest in Florida, and I own an Empire with thousands of employees all over the world." He took a deep breath, paused momentarily, and continued, "I was hoping to have my son and daughter split it all when I step down or die. Unfortunately, I only have Veronica, and she will inherent the whole ball of wax."

Robert kept his mouth shut and listened. Thomas told Robert, "I want you to know I have changed my will to make sure it all goes to her. It's not personal, but when you have kids, if something ever happens to her, the kid or kids will inherent all of it." Robert grinned because he knew what was coming. Thomas stated, "I know you are not greedy, or you would have taken the millions I offered you a while back."

Thomas stopped and looked at his future son-in-law, saying, "No matter what, you will get enough money to raise your children and send them to private schools and the top colleges, and they will inherit everything when they are 25." He told Robert, "A Trust is being set up as we are talking by my lawyers, also the prenup between you and Veronica." Thomas stopped for a moment to try and read what Robert is thinking, but he could not tell. He then mentions, "I talked with Veronica and told her you get nothing if it does not work out, and you will have joint custody but not have to pay for anything for the kids." Thomas stopped and asked, "Son, I hope this does not change anything between you, Veronica and me." Robert smiled and told Thomas, "We are good. I have my career."

Thomas chuckled and remarked, "Since you mentioned that I know Veronica talked about coming to work for me, and you said no." Both men stopped walking, and Robert listened to everything Thomas said. Thomas said, "Veronica told him you do not want to live here. May I ask why?" Robert looked at Thomas and told him, "Call it independence. I don't want to intrude on you or pressure you if Veronica and I have disagreements and argue, which a couple always do".

Thomas laughed and replied, "He agreed that all couples argue and say things they don't mean, and they say the best part of fights is the making up." Thomas paused and stated, "Please, Robert, I would love for you to come and work for me so you can make more money to spend on her." Both men started laughing at what Thomas said.

Robert, still laughing, told his future Father-in-law, "I tell you what, let's meet halfway. We will move in here so you can see your grandkids anytime you want. Still, I will stay and do what I am doing." Thomas smiled and remarked, "Great, one out of two is a good start. Let's go eat." While heading back, Robert remarked, "The Prenup and wills are what I would do if I were you." Thomas stopped and looked at Robert and told him, "Thanks, that means a lot."

They entered the house and headed to the main table, where they saw Veronica coming down in a sexy knee-high dress. She smiled, came down the stairs, got between both men, kissed them on their cheeks, and then kissed Robert on his lips.

She steered them towards the table and declared, "I have two men that love me, and let's eat." They sat down, and the food was brought to them. Robert looked at Veronica and told her, "You look good, but you always look good." Veronica smiled and replied, "After dinner, we are going dancing tonight." Robert was tired, but he said, "Sounds good."

He knew she wanted to spend more time with him than they had been. During the dinner, Thomas mostly listened to the couple talking. Veronica looked at her dad and then back at Robert, asking, "If he told his family?" Robert replied, "Yes, they are happy, and the top words were. It's about time, and how many kids do you plan on having?"

Veronica asked, "Did you tell them about the baby?" Robert told her, "No," and he explained, "My mom is a strict Catholic, and I believe in due time." Veronica looked puzzled, and Thomas jumped in and looked at Veronica and Robert and said, "Son, that was smart," and he looked back at Veronica. She had a bewildered look on her face when her dad explained, "He did it right. My mom, your grandma, was the same way." Veronica looked down, then at both men and remarked, "Ok, I am sure I will be similar in many ways."

Robert looked at her and told her, "Honey, we will tell them a week after we get married, I promise." He paused and suggested to her, "Let's focus on the wedding, and I sent emails to everyone I want at our wedding from work." Veronica smiled and asked, "How many responded so far?" Robert told her, "He didn't check his email yet because he was preparing for a trip." He told her he would do it when he returned from Naples and Tampa.

The room got quiet, and Veronica wanted to know, "Why do you have to go, and when will you be back?" Robert swallowed the last bite of his dinner and explained, "Foster and I are going to check those beach areas by FBI chopper to look for similar homes on the beaches they might want to use for future kidnapping of young girls and killing them." He then continued how they would repeat it at night and use heat sensors to see if there had been any digging going under any houses. Thomas sat there amazed at what Robert was planning on doing. I should be back in three or four days. Robert suggested to Veronica, "This will also give you time to focus on getting the wedding all setup."

Thomas declared, "That's great. Veronica and I will finish fine-toning it for the big day." Veronica asked, "Will you men have a bachelor's party?" Robert replied, "No, too busy, and I think we should have a get-together two days before everyone is here if it's ok and both families and guests can meet each other." Thomas stood up and remarked, "That's a great idea." Veronica smiled and agreed, "Dad and I will get it already."

Robert asked Veronica whether she picked out a dress yet. Veronica smiled and replied, "No, but I was thinking of going with a couple of friends tomorrow." Robert remarked, "That's good." Thomas asked Robert, "Have you got your suit yet"? Robert told him, "No, he will get it at the nearest K-Mart when he gets back," while looking at Thomas. Robert winked. Thomas looked down, trying not to laugh. Veronica stood up and told Robert, "Hell no." Robert jumped up and said, "Just joking, sweetie, let's go dancing." Thomas started laughing as he walked away from the table. Veronica stated, "I am marrying a joker."

Veronica stopped talking for a moment as she looked at Robert, then stated, "We are taking my car Mr. Comedian," and before Robert could say anything, she told him, "You drive my car. Let's go." Robert also said, "Let's go," he looked at Thomas and told him, "Thanks for dinner." Thomas, who was walking to the study, turned around, told them you kids have a good time and went into the study.

Once they left the house, he opened the Lamborghini door for Veronica, and she got in. Robert closed the door, went to the driver's side, jumped in, and started the car. Once they buckled up, they headed out. While driving, he asked Veronica where are we going? She smiled and replied, "To my club." Robert, in a surprised tone of voice, stated, "Your club?" She smiled and told him, "Yes, sir, I bought it after I got out of college and turned it around into a top-three club in the Miami-Dade area." Robert laughed and asked, "Well if I get fired as a cop, will you hire me as a bouncer?" Veronica snickered and said, "Hell no, I would have you be my personal bodyguard." Robert remarked, "I am sure the benefits are good." Veronica smiled and commented, "You would have to guard me every night." He looked at her and stated, "Sounds good to me." Veronica gave Robert the direction, and they headed to the club.

They drove up, and Veronica told Robert, "The Valet will take the car, do not worry about parking." They drove up, and a 6'5'' bouncer, about 275, stepped over and opened the door, and Veronica stepped out. The bouncer said, "Nice to see you, ma'am." Veronica looked at Robert, who stepped out, and he handed another big bouncer the car keys. He came around the car and took Veronica's hand, and they walked to the door were Robert looked and saw the huge line waiting to get a chance to get in.

Robert looked at Veronica and mentioned, "Business is good." Veronica smiled. The door bouncer pulled the rope aside, and they headed in. Robert heard a couple of people, "Say, who do those people think they are." The bouncer told them, "The owners." One other person stated, "That explains it."

When they entered, they went upstairs to the observation room, which also had an office for the manager. When Veronica entered, the manager stood up, shook her hand, and said, "Nice to see you, ma'am." Veronica introduced Robert to Jamie, who was the club's manager. She asked, "How are we doing this month?"

Jamie notified her, "About 4% better than last month." Veronica told Jamie, "That's good. Keep up the good work." Robert just watched as Jamie showed Veronica the accounting books for the month compared to the month before. When they were done, Veronica stood up from the table, smiled, and said, "Good job Jamie." She then turned to Robert and told him, "Let's go dance and have some fun." Robert smiled and replied, "Sounds good."

When they went downstairs, Veronica followed a bouncer who took her and Robert to her private table. Robert was amazed at how everything was being run. Once they sat down, she ordered drinks for both of them, and he smiled and said, "Just a Michelob for me."

Veronica said, "Honey, while the drinks are on the way, let's dance." They went out on the dance floor, which was crowded and danced, and after about 20 minutes, they stopped and went back to their table. Robert noticed their drinks were there, and they sat down, drank them, and talked about their future together.

While drinking his beer, he saw a person who was wanted for robbing a liquor store walking around. He had a beer in one hand, just moving around the club, looking like he was trying to find someone or not be found. Robert shook his head and stated, "Just my luck." Veronica asked what's wrong, Robert?

He paused and told her a guy was walking around the club who was wanted for numerous robberies, including assaults. Veronica whispered, "What are you going to do?" Robert advised her to call a bouncer over. Veronica flagged a bouncer who said, "Yes, ma'am, what can I do for you." He knew she was the big boss. Robert flashed his badge and informed him, "Get your head bouncer so I can talk to him." The bouncer responded, "Yes, sir."

A few minutes later, the head bouncer came over, and Robert again showed his badge and asked him, "Do you see the guy with the white shirt, with a red hat on his head over by the DJ's far right side?" The head bouncer stated, "Yes. Robert ordered him.

Now go find me some rope." The head bouncer looked at Veronica, who replied, "Do as he says." The head bouncer left and came back with about 8 feet of rope.

Robert smiled and said, "Perfect." Robert notified the bouncer, "Hang on to it and follow me." Robert kissed Veronica's cheek and told her, "I will be back, sweetie." Veronica smiled and said, "Be careful." Robert replied, "No problem," as he worked his way around the floor with the head bouncer about 5 feet away. Robert saw Jamie, went up to him, and explained what was happening.

Robert asked the bartender for an open beer of any type, and Robert was handed one. Robert walked by the person of interest, and the criminal saw Robert coming at him and reached inside his shirt and started to pull out his knife when Robert smashed the beer bottle over the guy's head, causing him to fall to the ground. The knife fell out of his right hand. Robert waved over the bouncer with the rope and hogged-tide, the wanted fugitive. Robert dragged him out of the club as the bouncers cleared the way.

Once outside, he called for a patrol car. Ten minutes later, two patrols and cars drove up, and when they got out of their cars and saw the fugitive hog-tied, they started laughing. Robert was grinning and said, "Cuff him. He is yours."

One officer approached Robert, requested a statement from him, and asked, "Who hog-tied him?" Robert replied, "I did. He tried to pull a knife on me, so I hit him over his head with a beer bottle." It seemed to Robert this officer did not know who he was. Robert showed his badge, and the officer stated, "Sorry, I did not know." Robert patted the officer on the shoulder and smiled.

They knew as he pointed at the other officers who were laughing. Robert asked, "Rookie?" And the officer admitted he was. Robert told him, "Don't worry about it. You did well." The fugitive was cuffed, and the rope was cut off him. He was wobbly when he was helped up. Robert asked for the sergeant, and she responded and asked, "What's up?" Robert informed her, "You might take him to be seen at the hospital before you book him." She looked at the fugitive and smiled, and concluded, "I believe you are right," as the fugitive stood there, swaying back and forth. Robert handed her the knife the fugitive had as evidence. Robert told her, "Write it up, and I will come to sign the chain of custody tomorrow and write my report." Robert then went back inside.

He walked through the crowd and finally made it back to the table where Veronica was. She took a sip of her drink and asked, "How did it go?" Robert looked at Veronica and told her, "He will have a massive headache for a long time." She looked puzzled. Robert informed her, "he pulled a knife, and I smashed an unopen beer bottle over his head." She choked on her drink and started to laugh. Robert handed her a napkin, and she wiped her mouth and the table. She smiled and commented, "You don't fight fear." He said, "No, there are no rules in a fight, and only idiots believe there are."

Veronica looked at Robert and asked, "Do you want to dance," he responded with an, "Absolutely." They got up and danced, and when 11:00 PM came, Robert informed her, "It's time to go." Veronica was a little drunk and commented, "Do we have to?" He responded and told her, "Unfortunately, I have to get a little sleep for tomorrow. It's going to be a long couple of days." He stood up and helped her, and they headed out of the club. Her Lamborghini was brought up, and she got in the passenger seat, and he took the keys, got in, and headed to Veronica's place.

While they were heading to her place Veronica who was intoxicated, asked, "What does he want from their marriage?" Robert smiled and remarked, "Two or three kids and at least one son, and I want your happiness." She smiled back, reached over, grabbed his right hand, and held it. Veronica asked Robert with a drunken slur, "What do you really want from marriage?" Robert grinned and said calmly, "I told you." She asked him, "What about your happiness?" He responded and told her, "Honey, I am a simple man. You and the kids' happiness are all I want in life now." She kissed his hand and asked, "How long will you be a cop?" Robert answered, "I do not know, but let's see what happens." Veronica smiled and replied, "Fair enough." Robert didn't bring up her dad offering him a job in his business.

When they made it to the Mansion, they got out, and Veronica was staggering, and he helped her walk, and she turned around and started kissing him all over his face telling him how much she loved him and was always waiting for a man like him. He kissed her back passionately. Veronica whispered, "Let's go to bed and make love."

Robert helped her to the door, and they walked into the house. They walked up the stairs and to her bedroom. She needed help with her clothes, and he had no problem helping her. He laid her in bed and covered her. She stated, "She loved him," and fell asleep. Robert looked at her as she was sleeping and said, "No more booze for you for a while." He then got out of his clothes, set his watch alarm, lay down, caressed her face, closed his eyes, and went to sleep.

Chapter 29

Naples and a Big Surprise

Robert got up at 4:30 am, showered and got dressed. He looked at Veronica sleeping and went over and kissed her cheek and whispered he loved her, then he went downstairs and left. Robert started his truck, and suddenly Veronica came out of the house in her bathrobe and ran to the car.

He opened the door and got out, and they embraced and kissed. Thomas looked out of his window, smiled and went back to bed. Veronica stated, "Please be careful and call me when you have a chance." Robert promised, and she asked him, "Where will he be staying?" Robert informed her, and she again told him, "I love you," with tears in her eyes. Robert got back in his truck and told her, "I will see you in a couple of days." Veronica smiled, wiping her tears and stated, "Good." She said she would get everything ready. Robert said only a few more days. He then drove off. She waved as she headed to the house.

When Robert made it to the station, he got everything ready, so when Foster arrived, they jumped into his truck and headed to Naples. Once they arrived and checked in, they went to the FBI office. After arriving, they met Agent Shults, and after small talk, they headed to the roof and got in the chopper. It took off and headed to the long beaches along the gulf. Robert and Foster looked along the beaches as they flew slowly along the beaches north to south. Robert looked and noticed none of the houses were similar in construction, size and capable of hiding them. Any tunnels would be too long and could flood by the waves coming in at night.

He told the pilot, "Let's head north and look at it one more time." Once they checked the beach line again, the pilot asked,

"Well, sir, where do you want to go now?" Robert shook his head and told himself they were not here in Naples. They might be here, but they would only pass through or lie low, not popping their heads up.

Robert asked the Pilot, "Do we have enough fuel to check the Fort Myers area?" The Pilot explained, "We can refill and fly there and look around and then refill up there and come back." Robert replied, "Let's head back and take a vehicle and see how things look from the ground." The pilot turned the chopper around and headed back to the FBI headquarters.

Once they arrived at the FBI headquarters, they went and loaded up in Robert's truck, drove to the beach, and drove up and down the beach area, checking the area out. Agent Shults claimed, "There is no way any of these houses and buildings fit what was used in other places." He looked around and remarked, "They are too far off the beach, and there are too many condos where people can see everything that goes on." They all agreed, and Robert advised everyone, "Tomorrow, we will fly to the Fort Myers area and check that out." It was 2 pm, and Robert announced, "We are done for the day." Robert took the FBI agent back to his headquarters, and Foster and Robert went back to the hotel.

Robert walked to his door and opened it up, and he was surprised as he saw Veronica napping on the bed. Robert smiled, went up to her, whispered in her ear, and said, "Hello, gorgeous." She opened her eyes and smiled. Robert asked her, "What are you doing here?" with a grin on his face. Veronica explained to Robert, "We have some unfinished business from last night." Robert smiled and remarked, "Well, you fell asleep." She replied, "Sorry, I drank too much." Robert, in an asserted tone of voice, "No more drinking, you are having a baby, and booze is not a good thing." He smiled and informed her, "A little wine here, and it is ok." Veronica agreed.

She commented, "I am hungry," and Robert replied, "Me too. What are you craving?" Did she suggest, how about fish tonight? He agreed and asked, "And by the way, where is your vehicle?" Veronica got up and explained, "I borrowed dads' jet and had a Uber pick me up and drop me off here." Robert replied, "Ok, that makes sense." They went to a seafood restaurant and had a nice meal on the outside deck over the beach.

Veronica asked Robert, "Will he be ready for next week?" Robert smiled and replied, "Absolutely." Veronica suddenly felt a little sick. Robert asked her, "Are you ok?" She advised him, "Just the feeling sick part since you got me pregnant." Veronica smiled and asked, "When we are done eating, can we walk on the beach?" Robert smiled and finished his white wine. Veronica suggested, "That's not fair." He smiled and told her, "You drank enough last night to make up for it." She laughed and commented, "Yea, my head hurt when I woke up this morning." He laughed, and she notified him, "Guess what? I think I want a cheesecake with lots of strawberries on it." Robert agreed by saying, "I will have a piece also." She changed her mind and declared, "I want two pieces." Robert snickered, waved the waiter over, and told the waiter what they wanted for dessert.

After dinner, they went and walked on the beach for over an hour, talking about getting married and plans, and Veronica was curious about the case he had been working on. She asked him, "Why are we here right now?" Robert looked at her and implied, "You mean, why am I here?" She looked at him and said, "Yes." He then explained what he was looking at and why.

He told her basically everything about the case as they walked on the beach. After doing most of the talking, he asked, "Well, what do you think?" Veronica smiled and replied, "That's a lot of information and scary." Robert looked at her and responded, "Not for me but for the victims and their families and any future victims. It's scary to them."

While they were walking back to his truck, he stopped and looked at a house on the beach. He felt like he was missing something, then remarked, "Let's go back to the hotel room. I need to check some things out." Once they arrived back at the truck, they got in and went to their hotel room. Veronica looked at Robert and told him, "We can get a hotel room on the beach if you want," and Robert replied, "No, it's all good." When they arrived back in the room, he pulled out his laptop, went on the internet, and began checking things out. Veronica watched him work nonstop without saying a thing. She was amazed at how focused he could be.

Once he was done, he grabbed his cell phone and called Foster, who was next door and requested for him to come over. A minute went by, and there was a knock on the door, and Robert opened the door. He waved for Foster to come in. Robert introduced Foster to Veronica, who remarked, "I was wondering who you left with a few hours ago." They sat down with Robert going over some thoughts with Foster. Robert concluded, "I believe we will not find anything or place similar and easy for them to commit more crimes in this area." He thought for a moment, then he announced, "I believe once they head up the coast, they will turn back to Miami because he checked the net, and there are no places similar then the Atlantic coast housing." Foster agreed and mentioned that the homes are farther back and crowded or stacked.

Foster listened and asked, "Why not just leave the state and go to Alabama because the beaches are even more different and the same with the housing." Robert shook his head and remarked, "I just feel they will do an about-face and reverse up the Atlantic coast. It's what they know". He looked at Veronica and added, "They know we will be watching all the major roads for any suspected people fitting their descriptions." Robert paused and concluded, "The closest place for them to go is Galveston, Texas, and I just do not believe they will go there, the exit points are restricted on getting off the island, compared to us."

Foster threw questions at Robert, answered them, and threw enough possibilities his way to believe it could happen. Foster asked, "Well, what do you want to do?" Robert was quiet for a moment, then commented, "Tomorrow, we take the chopper and head north and check Fort Myers, then go to Tampa to double-check there." Foster agreed. Robert announced, "Let's get an early night's sleep so we can get going in the morning." Foster looked at Veronica sitting in a chair and then back at Robert and sat, if you say so. Veronica smiled.

Once Foster left, Robert looked at Veronica as she slipped out of her dress and asked, "Are you tired, or do you want to make up for last night?" He smiled and replied, "You are the one who fell asleep." She smiled and, in a sexy tone, "I will make it up to you," as Robert turned off the bedroom light.

The next morning Robert's watch alarm went off, and he turned on the bedroom light and saw Veronica slowly moving around in bed. She rolled over and whispered, "Can we stay longer?" Robert said, "No, it's going to be a long day, and you need to get home to get everything ready." He kissed her and informed her, "Let's move it up to four days from now, and we should have our get-together in three." Veronica smiled, jumped out of bed, told him, "Outstanding," and ran to the bathroom. She closed the door, and he just lay there, then grabbed the hotel room phone, called next door, and informed Foster to be ready in an hour. Robert liked Foster. He had a good head on his shoulders, and they seemed to work together well.

Once Veronica came out of the bathroom 20 minutes later, he went in and showered. When Veronica was ready, Robert knocked on fosters room, opened the door, and stepped out. He grinned and said, "Morning," and Veronica smiled and replied, "Good morning, Foster." Veronica asked Robert, "Is he coming to the wedding?" and Foster advised her, "I wouldn't miss it for the world." Robert grinned and remarked, "Thanks," as they stepped on the elevator. Once they made it to the truck, Veronica got in the back seat, so Foster and Robert could discuss their plans for the day.

When they made it to the Executive airport, they drove up to Veronica's jet, which was already waiting for her. Robert jumped out and opened her door, and walked her to the stairs. Veronica told him, "Please be careful," as she kissed him. Robert kissed her back and whispered in her right ear, "Ok." Veronica looked down with a worried look on her face when Robert kissed her again and notified her, "I promise I will be just fine." She then went up the stairs, turned around, and asked, "When will you be home?" He told her, "Sometime tomorrow." She smiled and waved goodbye. The airport staff helped secure the door. Robert saw her looking out the window as it headed down the runway and took off.

Robert jumped into his truck, and Foster looked at Robert and advised him, "You are a lucky man, and I have no clue how you ended up with a woman like that." Robert grinned and commented back, "Neither do I, and maybe it's my outstanding personality." Foster looked at Robert and responded, "Mmmmm, that can be debated," as they headed to the FBI Government office.

When they arrived, they headed to the chopper pad on the roof, and Agent Shults was waiting for them. Once they loaded up, the pilot got them up and headed to Tampa, Sarasota, and Siesta Key areas with negative results. They observed many condos and homes, but they were extremely wealthy places on top of each other, and too many eyes would be watching everything that was happening. There were many cameras on these houses for security, which were big threats against criminals.

When they were done flying around, they landed, and everyone stepped out and headed to the FBI section of the Federal building. After they When they entered the FBI wing of the Naples U.S. government building wing, they went to the supervisor and checked in. Once the introductions were done, Supervisor Deaton asked, "How was the investigation going?" Roberts informed him, "He doesn't believe they are in Naples, Tampa or Sarasota."

Agent Shults asked, "Why and how did he come to that conclusion." Robert explained the similarities between all the older buildings up and down the coast and the similarities to being on the beach. He continued telling the FBI Agent, "There were none on the western part they have seen so far, and the condos and houses are right on top of each other, and they have cameras every place on the beaches." Agent Shults asked, "What do you need from me, Detective?" Robert informed him, "Both Foster and I are planning to head back to Naples in the morning."

The next day they loaded up and headed back to Miami. While on the way back, they discussed what they saw, and both concluded that the suspects could be on the west coast laying low and deciding what their next move would be. There are just too many places to hide. They had a list of all up-to-date stolen cars in Florida and will go through it. Foster brought up that there were few similarities between the women, except they were between 18-25 and were all in college or graduated—all racial makeups.

Once they made it back to the police station, they went to the office and went over everything. Robert told Foster, "I think they will come back this way soon due to the many places on the Atlantic side to continue targeting women and hiding." Foster commented, "None of the bodies had any DNA or fingerprint marks on them, and there was no semen in any of the victims." He stopped and added, "The autopsies documented they all had been raped because the Vaginal tracks were heavily bruised."

Robert called his boss and told him, "We need to meet with the COP, Mayor and the Governor's assistant, and I will be gone for a few weeks due to the wedding and leaving the country for two weeks." Foster sat back and stretched while Robert called around.

Chapter 30

The Wedding

Two hours later, the Mayor, COP, the COD, and the Governor showed up, which was surprising to both Robert and Foster. The door was closed, and everyone sat down. Foster looked at Robert, who told him, "Brother, you start it off." Foster smiled and replied, "Thanks, old buddy." Robert grinned and then leaned back in his chair.

Foster explained, what they had been doing over the last few days, then there was a knock on the door, and Robert yelled, "Come in." The door opened, and a couple of agents from the task force walked in. The Governor commented, "Better late than never." He informed everyone, "I asked for them to come as soon as they could so we can all be on the same page," then told Detective Foster, "Carry on, son." Foster again discussed what they had been doing over the last several days and then turned it over to Robert.

Robert stood up and started to walk around the room, and he looked at Foster, who grinned because he had no doubt Robert would hit them with some zingers. Robert looked at the Governor and declared to him, "Everyone in the room, Detective Foster and myself come to the same conclusion we believe they will be coming back this way, or they are already here." Most of the men were shocked. The Mayor looked at Robert and objected, "Detective, you claimed they are heading west and probably towards Naples." Robert replied, "Yes sir," and then went over them, monitoring stolen cars and any mysterious homicides in all of Florida.

Robert declared, "We compared many things on this case, and I am telling you, both Foster and I are telling you and everyone in this room they are either coming back or are already in the area."

One of the FBI agents stood up and stated, "Detective, we have found no evidence they are coming back this way, and we agree with your first assessment. They went to western Florida and are waiting to strike again, and we encourage everyone in this room to prepare for the next victims to be found."

Everyone in the room looked at Robert, leaning against the wall with a shit-ass grin on his face. He looked down, up, and around the room at each individual. He walked over to the Agent and asked him, "You agreed with my first assessment but not this one; why?"

The Agent sat down and looked around the room, seeing everyone was looking at him like, 'Why'? He informed the Detective, "We in the FBI respect how you do your job and all the things you did, but we in the FBI and the Taskforce, except maybe your partner, can't find one reason for them to come back this way." He paused while looking around the room and mentioned, "You mentioned houses and other things, but all those things can be manipulated to help the perps keep committing their crimes, and again why would they decide to come back here?"

Robert went over what he discovered again from the buildings, which were all similar types of places on the Atlantic coast and Pacific coast. He went into more detail about other places except Galveston and farther down Padre Island in Texas. He explained, "Those places are hard to get out of if you are on the run and need to get out quickly."

Robert continued going over his belief, "They might just pass through here and head up the coast or start over again here or do a hit and run." He took a deep breath and announced, "I do not know for sure, but I believe they will hit us because this place is too tempting with all the bikinis running around the beaches." Robert looked at the COP Mayor and Governor and informed them, "I recommend we put undercover female officers up and down the beach with undercovers watching them up and down the coast." He scratched his chin and mentioned, "The women usually, on average, disappear between 4 pm and 8 pm on average, and we need to use all our resources." He then looked at the FBI agent and told him, "You watch the west, and we will watch the east."

The FBI Agent replied, "Sounds good to me." The Governor stood up and remarked, "I agree we need to end this one way or another. I ordered the AG to have all law enforcement in all departments formulate the same plan." He looked at Foster and Robert and told them, "Good job and is that it?" Robert looked at the COD, who shook his head up and down in agreement. The Governor told everyone, "I will be here for a few days. As he looked at Detective Bench, I guess I have been invited to a wedding." Robert shook hands with everyone as they headed out. Once everyone was gone, Robert looked at Foster, asking, "What do you think?" Foster replied, "Good brother, we did good."

Robert headed to his place and grabbed some clothes and his fancy suit for the party tomorrow. After arriving at Veronica's, he knocked on the door. The butler opened the door, and Robert stepped in. Thomas was walking by, patting Robert on the back, and told the butler, "Please get Robert a copy of the house keys. He shouldn't have to knock to come in." Robert smiled and said, "Thanks."

Veronica came downstairs, went up to Robert, looked at her dad, and asked, "Dad, do you think this guy is good enough for your daughter's hand in marriage?" Thomas started scratching his head, telling her, "Maybe," as Robert stood there. Veronica looked Robert up and down and stated, "I guess he will do," as she stepped up to him, kissed him passionately, and said, "He will do." Thomas told them, "Well, I will leave you kids alone to ensure everything is ready for tomorrow."

Robert saw Thomas's assistant come out of the office and told Thomas, "It begins at 6:00 Pm. Dinner will be served at 7:00 Pm, and after dinner, the guest will go to the lawn, and the orchestra band will begin playing music." Thomas asked, "What time should we start winding it down?" The assistant replied, "I recommend about 10:00 pm," he turned to Robert and Veronica and informed them, "The wedding is at 1:00 PM at ST—Mary's church.

Robert's cell phone went off, and it was his dad. He answered it and asked, "Are you guys here yet?" His dad informed Robert, "They will be at your place in 20 minutes." Robert told his dad, "I will meet you there." Robert announced, "I have to meet my parents at my place to let them in." Thomas suggested, "Please have them come here for dinner tonight." Robert looked at Veronica, and she told her dad, "They will. Robert and I are going to go get them."

While heading to Robert's place, Veronica asked, "Did you tell them everything about my family?" Robert replied, "No, just some things, like your dad is a successful businessman and most about you." Veronica asked, "Like what?" Robert said, "I told my family you are a smart college-educated woman with a degree in engineering, a big heart and a great personality, and love children." Veronica told Robert, "Not bad." She asked Robert, "Did you tell them I can be a spoiled bitch sometimes?" He remarked, "No, that's been taken care of." Veronica asked, "What do you mean taken care of." Robert glanced at her and told her, "Your problem was no man would stand up to you." She asked, "Is that your Psychological analysis?" Robert replied, "Yes, and even your dad agrees with me." Veronica chuckled and commented, "I guess that's why I love you both. You two have your eyes wide open on how I am."

When they arrived at Robert's place, they waited, and then he saw his parent's van drive up. His family got out of the vehicle and hugged Robert, and his dad asked, "Who is this?" Robert notified everyone, "I want to introduce you to Veronica." She stepped forward and shook hands with everyone. They all talked for a minute, and after the bags were unloaded, Robert showed them his place and told them, "We are all going to Veronica's place for dinner and meet her dad." Robert's mom whispered into Robert's ear, informing him, "She is beautiful." Veronica heard and blushed. Robert smiled and replied, "She sure is." Once they went to the vehicles, both vehicles headed to Veronicas for dinner.

When they arrived at the mansion entrance, they pulled up to the house, and everyone got out. Robert's family was quiet and extremely surprised at how big the mansion was. Robert's mom asked, "Robert, honey, are you sure we are at the right place?" Robert was holding Veronica's hand and said, "Yes, let's go in." The butler opened the door, and everyone entered, and Thomas stepped forward, identified himself, and shook hands with Robert's family. He told them, "Welcome to my home, and please make yourself home." Thomas smiled and remarked, "I believe we are all going to be family." Robert's dad, Jason and Thomas shook hands, and Jason introduced everyone. Robert's mom seemed nervous about how big the house was. She looked around and saw six maids standing by.

Thomas was introduced to Robert's sister Barrie and her husband Lee and the kids, and Joseph with Elizabeth and their kids. After all the introductions, Thomas informed everyone, "Let me show you the house, please." Everyone followed Thomas as he walked everyone around the mansion. Robert and Veronica walked farther back and were snickering at the expressions on Robert's family faces during the tour. Jason looked at Thomas and remarked, "This house is amazing, and you look familiar, Thomas." Thomas smiled and told him what he had done. Robert's mom, brother and sister were amazed at what they were looking at.

Once they were done, Thomas took them to the big kitchen table, and the maids brought the dinner for everyone. Robert's parents, Jason and Shirley, while putting food on their plates, asked Robert and Veronica, "Where they met?" Shirley looked around and mentioned, "Robert never really discussed that when we talked on the phone." Veronica told everyone, "Robert has a tendency to hold his cards close." Robert looked at Veronica and stated, "Sometimes." Thomas advised everyone, "Let's have a nice dinner, then we can discuss how they met once, dinner is over. Shirley said, "Mr. Jackson, you have a beautiful home." He looked at Shirley and asked her, "Please call me Thomas." She smiled and replied, "Ok, Thomas."

When dinner was over, they went to the main living room and sat down. Robert's brother Joseph who has been quiet, said, "This is the biggest living room I have ever seen." Thomas smiled and replied, "Thank you, Joseph." Veronica sat next to Robert while Thomas reviewed the basics of the meeting. Robert and Veronica's new somethings were left out. And they needed to be left out so his parents would not worry too much about him.

After hearing the abbreviated story, Shirley told Thomas, "She was sorry about the loss of his son." Thomas said, "Thank you, and now we are going to be family and tomorrow we have a big party and the wedding." Thomas signaled the butler, who brought some red wine in for everyone. They all stood up, and while looking at Robert and Veronica, he gave a toast saying, "May you have long lives and many children, and you love each other like there is no tomorrow because love and family are more important than anything on this planet." Everyone stated loudly, "Here, here."

The next night over 200 guests arrived throughout the evening, including elected officials like the governor, congressmen and women, local elected officials, sports stars, and others. During the evening, people were assigned to the many tables on the back lawn, and dinner went with no issues. Robert hung around his parents and family, who seemed a little surprised at how many people were there and who they were. Jason and Shirley asked Robert, "Are you sure about this?" Robert smiled and replied, "Yes, Mom and Dad. It's all good." Robert's brother and sister had a constant grins on their faces when they were introduced to the Governor and both U.S Senators.

Thomas came over and told Jason and Shirley, "Please come with me so I can introduce you around, and Please do not feel uncomfortable." Jason replied, "Thank you," as they walked around the yard meeting people. Veronica was hanging around her girlfriends, who she introduced to Robert. Robert smiled and shook their hands. The orchestra began playing music, and Robert grabbed Veronica's hand and said, "May I have this dance," as he led her to the middle. They slowed dance while everyone watched. Veronica told Robert, "I will always be there for you." Robert stopped and looked at his future wife and touched her face, and whispered, "I will always be there for you and more." Veronica leaned in and kissed Robert and told him, "I love you." Robert dipped Veronica, who was smiling, and said, "I love you too." They then went back to slow dancing while everyone clapped. Two of Thomas's business partners standing with him asked him, "Do you trust him?" Thomas replied, "He would die for her."

The evening went without a hitch, and when it was over, Robert left with his family. Veronica asked, "Why" before they left. He informed her, "I will see you at the altar," and kissed her. She smiled and held her dad's hand. Thomas looked at Robert, tapped his head with his finger, and said, "Smart," then said, "We will see you tomorrow, don't be late." Everyone laughed as they laughed. Thomas shook Robert's parents' hands and commented, "I will see you guys tomorrow."

The wedding started at 11:30 AM, with everyone in their seats. The church was full, with all the elected officials and family from both sides up front. Robert walked up and down the church shaking hands and talking with people. He finally made it up front where Foster, his best man, was standing with Robert's brother Joseph.

At exactly noon, the music began, and Thomas Jackson walked down the aisle with Veronica holding her dad tight. She wore a white dress with a short train. Her friends were the maid of honor and walked up front first. Everyone was quiet as Thomas walked Veronica to the alter. When they arrived, Thomas handed Veronica off to Robert. Both Veronica and Robert held each other's hands, and the ceremony began.

By 12:45 pm, the final words were spoken when both parties said I do, and the priest informed Robert, "You may kiss the bride." Robert leaned in and held on to Veronica, and they kissed. Veronica had tears coming from her eyes as The priest turned the new couple around and announced, "Ladies and gentlemen, I present Mr. and Mrs. Robert and Veronica Bench." Everyone clapped as the new couple headed down the aisle to the exit door.

While standing at the entrance, everyone came out the door and shook hands and talked with everyone. When Robert's family came out, they hugged him and Veronica. Thomas shook hands with Robert's parents, brother, and sister. The limo drove up, and Robert told his parents they were heading to the house and then heading to the airport. Robert's mom was crying and informed him, "It was a nice wedding, and hopefully, there will be kids coming." Both Veronica and Robert looked at each other, and Veronica kissed Robert's mom and asked, "Can I call you mom?" Shirley said, "Absolutely." Veronica told her mother-in-law, "We plan to have two or three kids." Everyone clapped, and Robert hugged his brother and sister and their spouses and told them, "We have to go," then Robert and Veronica headed to the limo with rice being thrown in the air. They got in and waved as the limo drove off with just married painted on the limo.

Chapter 31

From a Good Time to Bad

Once they arrived at the mansion, they got out, and he carried them through the door and up the stairs. Veronica said, "How much time do we have, my husband?" Robert said three and a half hours. Veronica provocatively stripped out of the wedding dress and stated, "Honey, come and get it." Robert got out of his clothes, and they made love for the first time as husband and wife.

While flying to Barcelona, Spain, in a Gulfstream Global 7500, they sat and talked about their future together and if the baby was a boy or girl. They were looking forward to their honeymoon on the cruise ship going around the Mediterranean. They napped here and there, and when Robert sat there thinking about work, Veronica would smile. She would say, "Baby, please don't, this is our time, and you will catch them, but let's enjoy this time because our honeymoon only comes once." He smiled and informed her, "If I look like I am thinking about it, pull me back." She agreed.

With Robert gone for two weeks, Foster was in charge of the investigation, and he moved over to Robert's work area and went through everything. After looking through all of Robert's notes and evidence gathered, he knew Robert and he were right. These people would come back and either come here or go up farther north of the Miami area. Foster met with the Chief of Detectives, Gomez and reviewed the notes and evidence Robert mentioned. The COD agreed with Foster it should be happening again at any time.

The COD notified Foster he was going to brief the COP and the Mayor on preparing for a possible nightmare scenario. The COD also mentioned, "He will get with the FBI to start using drones to monitor the beaches and have a standby evidence team ready at a moment's call." Foster suggested an increase in the beaches of foot patrols. The COD remarked, "He will request from the COP to notify the other departments farther up the coast to do the same thing." He paused and asked Foster, "Why would they come back this way?" Foster shared what Robert said to him, "Narcissism."

Two weeks went by, and Robert and Veronica flew home and were picked up at the Miami airport by Thomas and the chauffeur. When they walked out, they saw her dad. She waved at him. Veronica had a glow on her face, and Robert looked relaxed for the first time he had ever seen him. Veronica ran up and kissed her dad, "Telling him they had a great time." Thomas smiled and replied, "Great." The chauffeur grabbed the bags from Robert and put them in the trunk. When Robert advised him, "I got it," the chauffeur helped him anyway. Once the bags were loaded and everyone was inside the vehicle, the chauffeur took off for their home.

Thomas asked Robert how it was/ Robert smiled and said thank you, sir, it was great, and I had super company. Robert asked how things were going on here. Thomas said nothing special, same old stuff. Veronica then went into where they went and all the pictures and videos they had taken.

Thomas looked at his daughter and asked, "How is the baby?" She told him, "Fine, no problems, and I have been getting the munchies a lot lately." Robert commented, "She has been eating good and healthy with a side order of cookies." Thomas laughed and remarked, "Nothing wrong with that."

Veronica then looked at Robert and asked, "When do you have to go back to work?" She didn't want to ask while they were on the honeymoon, but she needed to know. Robert advised her, "In one week, but I need to check in when we get home, and we have the whole week to do what we want." She smiled and replied, "Good," as she leaned on Robert. Veronica fell asleep on Robert due to the long flight home. Once they made it home, she woke up, looked around, and told everyone, "I am exhausted." Thomas said,

"We understand." Robert recommended, "How about I help you upstairs and you nap before dinner." She stated, "Ok." Robert took her upstairs, and when she lay down, she kissed Robert and informed him, "I had a great time, did you?" Roberts whispered, "It was great, and I had the best company," and he kissed her as she closed her eyes and fell asleep with a smile on her face. He kissed her forehead, and he went downstairs.

The chauffeur was at the door with the bags, and Robert informed him, "Thanks, I will take them." He then put them in the corner of the room and went downstairs. Thomas was downstairs waiting for him and asked, "Well, Robert, how is she been doing?" Robert replied, "She has been doing good."

Robert explained, "She gets a little tired here and there, but I think she is maybe a little farther along than she thinks." He paused and informed Thomas, "We have a doctor's appointment tomorrow, so that we will find out for sure." Thomas remarked, "Great," and asked, "How about we sit down and talk." Robert remarked, "How about we walk? I have been sitting for too many hours." Thomas chuckled and replied, "Do you play golf?" Robert implied, "He did." Thomas announced, "There is still enough sunlight to play nine holes, and I always have a slot always open in an hour at a local course." Robert told Thomas, "Let's go, and we can take my truck." Thomas thought for a minute and then agreed.

Once the gulf bags were loaded up, they jumped in and headed out to the golf course with two bodyguards following them. Robert asked, "What happens if I lose them." When Thomas notified Robert, "It would never happen." Robert snickered and responded, "What? I have a tracker on my truck." Thomas described how and where it is on his vehicle, and he informed Robert, "He had it put on once you proposed to Veronica." Robert looked at him, and Thomas shrugged his shoulders and advised him, "I have to protect her at all costs, and I hope you are not pissed off about it?" Robert laughed, saying, "No, I am not, she is your daughter and my wife, and I want nothing more." Thomas replied, "Thanks."

Thomas was a little puzzled about how his son-in-law takes things when he finally asked Robert, "Why are you so easygoing? Robert got quiet for a minute and suggested it was having good parents, a good family, my time in the military and what I do." Thomas stated, "That makes sense, and Veronica is lucky to have a good man as a husband." Robert laughed and commented, "Only time will tell." Thomas remarked, "I think you two will be fine." They spent the day golfing, and they agreed not to keep score.

Throughout the day, they talked about family and Robert's career plans. Thomas immediately confronted Robert and informed him, "I really want you to come and work for me. It would make things easier for you and Veronica and the baby." Robert chuckled and responded while walking to his truck, "I know you two will keep bringing it up, so when I get to my ten years in the police department, I will look at everything and see how it's going." Thomas replied, "Fair enough." Robert got quiet and asked, "What would I do?" Thomas suggested, "Maybe train you in all areas of the business." Robert laughed but didn't say anything.

When they made it home, Veronica was sitting on the couch reading a book on understanding the criminal mind. The door opened, and Thomas and Robert walked in. Veronica got up, went up to both men, kissed them, and asked, "Where did they go?" Robert mentioned, "We went golfing." She smiled and remarked, "Who won?" Thomas told her, "Nobody, we didn't keep score, Just having a good time and talking."

It was time to head back to work, and Robert got up at 5:30 am, and as he was getting dressed to go run, Veronica woke up and asked, "Where are you going?" He replied, "Running on the beach, I have to get back into my routine." He put on his running shoes and suggested that she come and run. She smiled and told him, "No, but how about I just walk and watch you run since the baby is bigger than I thought." He smiled and told her, "Sounds good." She got up and dressed in some sweats.

When they arrived at the beach, they started walking, and Robert took off after about 100 yards of walking. Veronica yelled, "Have fun," and he laughed. It was 6:25 am, and he was about a half mile out when he thought he saw a clump of clothes in the water, and then he saw another clump as he slowed down and started to walk towards them. He got a chill up his spine and went into the water and saw both women dead in the water. He pulled them out of the water on the shore and called 911. He identified himself, and he told the 911 operator what he needed. Then he hung up and called the COD, who answered, and Robert filled him in.

Robert looked around, and there were rich fancy houses far away from the beach, and he was puzzled. He realized they were back, but this did not fit their regular pattern. He looked around and saw Veronica walking towards him about 50 yards out. He yelled at her, "Stay where she was." Veronica saw the two bodies and covered her mouth, and turned around.

Robert called Thomas and, in an asserted tone, "I need a bid favor," he gave his location. He told him, "I need you to come and get Veronica immediately because I found two more bodies, and she is extremely upset." Thomas remarked, "He was on his way." Robert ran up to Veronica and held her while telling her, "I want you to stay right here because I have my work to do." She was crying and extremely upset when Robert stated, "It will be ok."

Within 20 minutes, police and FNI evidence teams had arrived and cornered off the section of the beach. Before anyone arrived, he looked for tracks but did not find any.

Veronica sat in the sand while Robert was doing his job. She saw her dad running up, and she got up and ran to him. Robert saw Thomas and went up to him and Veronica and told his father-in-law, "I need you to take her home immediately." Robert turned and saw Foster walk up to him, and he informed him, "I will be right back." Thomas, Veronica, and Robert walked to the limo, and Robert kissed her and insisted she not go anyplace without her dad. He pointed at the two people in another car because something was not right about this. Robert kissed Veronica again and told her, "I will be home in a little while to get out of these clothes," and he headed back to the crime scene. Tomas looked at Robert, saying, "Son," as Robert turned, "Be careful." Robert smiled, replied, "It's all good," and returned to the crime scene. Thomas told the chauffeur, "Let's go home."

Robert stopped for a minute and flagged down a police officer who came up and said, "Yes, sir." Robert informed him, "I need you to find a video camera without telling anyone. Go find a high spot and film everyone in the crowd over there and anyone who comes this way to watch." The young officer commented, "Yes sir," and went to his car, grabbed a camera out of the car trunk, where he found a high spot and began filming all faces.

Within 30 minutes, the Mayor and the Police chief also arrived with numerous media stations who put up their recording systems and began filming. The media tried to get close, but there were enough police to keep them and gawkers far away. The usual media statements came out, freedom of the press and so on, trying to manipulate and intimidate the Police Officers. The Mayor and COP yelled out to Robert. He knew all eyes would be on him, including the press.

He walked up and said, "Morning." The Mayor looked at Robert and asked, "Is this them." Robert remarked, "Let's go to your vehicle while the FBI evidence team does their job, and out of sight of the press," and he claimed, "No, this is not them." He suggested, "This is a copycat, which could be a bigger mess." The COP remarked, "What do you mean bigger mess?" Robert told them, "The real ones might get jealous and try to up the other guy, and we have a nightmare scenario." He looked at both men and suggested, "They lay low and let this person keep going till he gets caught, and then they continue." Robert shook his head and mentioned, "They do our job and kill him or them for taking all their credit."

The Mayor looked at the COP and said amazing, all good points, so Robert, what should we do? The COP looked at Robert, who said we hang the copycat out to dry first. The COP smiled and said what makes you think the other killers will target him. Robert smiled and said nobody likes to see other people get their credit. I think we should tell the press we have a copycat and make up some BS about him trying to take credit for other crimes.

The COP told the Mayor, "This is one big mess." The Mayor and COP had a conversation about how this will look politically. Robert interrupted and explained what they should do by saying, "We should tell them the suspect was abused by his mommy and is looking for stardom and being a star, and he believes if he acts like the others, he will be famous also." The Mayor had a concerned look on his face but claimed, "Detective, that's a hell of a risk," when the COP jumped in and implied, "The odds are the bad guys and us both hunting this guy, he feels the pressure where he will make a mistake and either we catch him or the others do." The Mayor grinned, declaring, "This can save lives in the long run." The COP advised the Mayor, "So far, the originals have not struck yet, and we have nothing to lose except our careers."

Robert leaned back and advised them, "Gentleman, we need to flood the beaches with undercovers and drones during the day and night." He rubbed his chin and informed them, "I believe we have a better chance at catching this copycat quicker than the others." He then looked at the Mayor and suggested, "I encourage you to go and talk to the media and discuss some of what we agree on because this will cool some panic and let the business community know we are on it." They exited the car, and the Mayor said, "You would make a good politician." Robert laughed and responded while laughing, "No, I just like being a cop." The COP looked at Robert and informed him, "We are playing a dangerous game, you know." Robert replied, "Yea, and it's getting worse as time passes."

The COP, the Mayor, and the mayor's executive assistant, who was not in the car, walked to the media and gave questioning and answer interviews with the press. One would talk, and then the other. After ten minutes of the press questioning, they left. Before they left the COP, the Mayor informed the press, "We have no doubt this copycat will be caught soon."

Chapter 32

Business

Robert went back to the crime scene and discussed with Foster, who flagged down Agent Fox of the FBI and requested, "We need your help to get all video from those businesses and condos over the last 36 hours." He agreed and notified Foster, "We will get the judge's signatures to get it all." They turned around, headed away from the crime scene, and left in their vehicle.

Robert and Foster walked down the beach and looked around. A reporter came up to them with a video running. She asked Robert detective, "You have a great history of solving crimes. Why is this one taking so long?" He looked into the camera and informed her, "Every case is difficult, this is real and not a 60-minute tv show or a two-hour movie and resolving all questions and the criminal is behind bars." Foster jumped into the conversation, declaring, "This takes time, and a solid joint law enforcement working together will end this nightmare."

The reporter looked at Foster and asked, "Detective do you agree with Detective Bench?" Foster patted Robert on the back and replied, "100% he is absolutely right, and I encourage everyone watching this to look out for each other and report anything that does not look right. Thank you. We got work to do." The reporter stated, "Thank you," as the two detectives walked down the beach, looking around.

After about 100 yards, they stopped, and Robert informed Foster how he had an officer filming everyone who was on the beach watching us, and maybe this copycat will want to watch us and see what we do and are doing. Robert suggested to Foster, "Get someone else to get a video of all vehicles and license plates of all vehicles in parking lots by the beach within a 200-yard radius." He felt there was always a chance the copycat might want to watch. He was aware sometimes murderers like to watch what we are doing instead of fleeing. In some cases, they are like some arsonist who likes to watch the fires they started. Robert believed; Police should always use video when they have a chance. You just never know.

Once they were done with the crime scene, Foster and Robert headed to the truck when some reporters with cameras and notepads surrounded both and began yelling questions. Foster stopped and looked at Robert and smiled. Robert stopped and said, "Shoot." One lady reporter asked, "Are these murders the same as the others?" Robert replied, "A copycat does these." Foster whispered into Robert's ear and commented, "Do we really want to do this?" Robert grinned and remarked, "Next question." A tv reporter stepped up and asked, "Why are these different?" Robert declared, "Wrong question next." Another reporter mentioned the similarities of these murders, for example, the beach and the two females. Robert stated, "One more question." A person stepped up and sarcastically said, "Detective, what makes you so sure about these crimes not being similar?" Robert laughed and informed him, "Because I know," and they walked away.

Robert stood away from everyone and watched the crowd coming and going. He watched the press constantly filming and talking to people in the crowd when he saw the COD approaching him. Once Gomez stepped up to Robert, he asked him, "How are you doing, and how was your vacation?" Robert grinned and replied, "I wish it were longer, but a lousy first day back, and it's not even noon yet." They went over things, and Robert informed him, "He was going home to get cleaned up." Gomez replied, "Fine, I will see you at the office."

After Robert got home, he noticed Veronica was asleep on the couch, and Thomas came out of his office and waved for Robert to come into his office. They went in, and Robert quietly closed the door. Robert asked, "What's up?" Thomas told Robert, "Veronica was so upset she cried herself to sleep." He asked, "How did it go?" Robert informed him, "It was a copycat, and we will get him one way or another." Thomas informed Robert, "I will have the cook warm you up something." Robert suggested, "Just a sandwich would be fine." Thomas remarked, "Ok," as Robert walked out of the office.

Two hours later, Robert was back at the crime scene and asked Foster, "Is there anything new going on?" Foster commented, "No, we are just cleaning up right now." Once they were done with the crime scene Foster and Robert went over everything Robert missed while he was gone getting cleaned up. Robert, who liked working alone since his regular partner retired, looked at Foster and suggested, "We work pretty good together don't you think?" Foster smiled and agreed. Reading Robert's mind, he mentioned, "Yes, it's a good idea to become partners." Robert chuckled and replied, "See, we already know what we are each thinking, so I will let the boss know."

Robert went into a spill about how he can work for hours without stopping, and if it's a problem, you do not always have to drop your family life. He told Foster, "I know you have two kids; dads are very important." Foster immediately interrupted him, "Stop, you sound like my wife, and I will head home when I have to." Robert smiled and stated, "Fair enough."

Foster asked Robert, "By the way, how long has she been pregnant?" Robert looked at Foster and replied, "How did you know?" Foster smiled and notified him, "My wife told me, remember she is a nurse." Robert listened as Foster informed him, "While at the wedding, she whispered it in my ear, and I asked how did she know?" Foster glanced around to make sure no one else had walked up, and he told Robert, "She has a certain glow woman can sense from another woman when there is a pregnancy." Robert chuckled and commented on who has the brains in your family.

When they arrived at the station, he dropped Foster off and notified him, "See you in the morning." Foster waved and walked to the building, and Robert headed home. While driving, he called Gomez and declared, "Both Foster and he want to work as partners." The COD laughed on the phone and remarked, "I will make it official tomorrow." Robert responded, saying, "I know what you are thinking, and things change." Gomez laughed on the phone and hung up.

Once Robert made it home, he opened the door and walked in and noticed Veronica and her dad were not there. He asked one of the maids where they were, and she replied, "At the Tower." Robert went and jumped into his truck and headed to the downtown Tower, and after parking, he went inside.

Robert was amazed at how big it was and all the suits walking around. A few people looked at him but kept walking. He stepped up to the information desk and asked the security officer, "Where is Veronica Bench's office?" The security officer was reading a paper and ignored him. Robert repeated himself and asked, "Sir can you tell me how to get to Veronica Bench's office?" The security officer put the paper down and informed him, "There is no Veronica Bench that works here, and I know everyone who works in this building," he then picked up a phone and talked to an unknown person.

Robert took a deep breath, leaned over the counter, and informed him her Maiden name was Jackson. The security officer asked, "Ms. Jackson?" Robert replied, "Yes can you tell me how to get to her office?" The security officer stood up, and his 6'5'' height and 275 pounds looked down on Robert and remarked, "Why do you need to see her?" In a pissed-off tone, Robert smiled and told him, "We can do this the easy way or hard way," as he showed his badge and his 45. The security officer snapped back, saying, "So what, why do you need to see her?" Robert again leaned forward and replied, "Because I am her husband, you dolt." The security officer immediately sat down, apologized, and informed the Detective, "Let me escort you there, sir."

Robert looked at the security officer and informed him, "No, just tell me how to get there." The security officer stood up again and pointed in the direction of the private elevator and the proper floor. Robert stepped up to the officer and whispered, "Do not fuck with me. Wife is nothing compared to how far I will go, do you understand?" The security officer said, "Yes, sir, it will never happen again." Robert smiled and commented, "Good We will say it never happened," as he walked to the elevator. The security officer sat down, wiped his forehead, and breathed deeply.

Robert found the elevator and took it up to the 24th floor. When the door opened, he walked out and stopped. He observed People in a lot of their cubicles working. H began to walk around and saw a huge meeting room with people around a huge, long table and noticed Thomas at the head listening to his daughter walking around and talking about something. All the people in the room were listening. Thomas saw Robert stand up and waved for him to come in.

Robert opened the door and stuck his head in. Veronica saw Robert, smiled, walked over to him, and steered him into the room. She announced, "For those who do not know, this is my husband, Detective Robert Bench." Veronica grabbed Robert's hand and walked him to another chair, and before he could sit down, Thomas requested that he pull his chair next to him and Veronica's chair.

Thomas mentioned, "Well, you can see the last few minutes of our meeting." One man over-marketing raised his hand and asked, "Should he be here, sir?" Veronica started to speak when her dad interrupted and informed everyone in the room, "This is my son-in-law, and he is always welcome to sit in any meeting he chooses." Veronica also commented, "He is my husband, and I asked him if he wanted to be part of this business, which means he would be higher than anyone one of you." She stopped talking and let that sink into everyone's heads in the room. She said, "However, he turned it down to remain a detective for now."

Veronica smiled, looked at Robert, and asked, "Is that still true right now?" Robert smiled and replied, "Absolutely, for now." Veronica then went back to finishing up the meeting. Veronica liked what Robert said and knew there would be a chance to get him out of his dangerous job to help her run the business once her dad stepped down. She wants their children not to have to worry about him like she does.

Once the meeting was over, Veronica looked at Robert and asked, "Why are you here, honey?" Robert notified her, "I have some free time, and I wanted to take my beautiful wife and the mother of my child to dinner with my father-in-law." Thomas and Veronica agreed, and Robert told them, "Red Lobster at 7:00 PM, and I will meet you."

Veronica told him, "Hell no, let me show you the big office I work in." Robert smiled, saying, "Show me." Veronica grabbed his hand, and they walked down the work aisle to this huge office with two big desks. One was in a far corner, and one was in the middle. Robert looked around and was stunned at how big it was, the TVs showing stock telephones on a big table.

Robert went and looked out the window and observed the great view over the water. Thomas walked in and asked him, "What do you think?" Robert was amazed and told Thomas, "This whole building is nice, and this office is super." Thomas went to his desk and informed Robert, "When you are ready to give up the badge, you will always have a job here." Veronica stepped up to Robert, kissed him, and commented, "No pressure, right, Daddy?" Thomas just smiled and informed them both, "I have to go talk to some people, and I will be back in about 45 minutes," as he headed out the door.

Veronica walked up to Robert and whispered, "This is a beautiful view, isn't it?" Robert grabbed her and smiled while saying, "Sneaky, just sneaky." She kissed him and replied, "I just want the father of our child to be safe." Robert told her, "Fair enough," and he went and sat on the couch. She went to her desk and looked at Robert as she sat down. She watched him lean his head back and close his eyes. In a minute, he was asleep.

Approximately 45 minutes later, Thomas walked back in and observed Robert pass out on the couch while Veronica was working. She was on the phone discussing some purchasing deal when she put her finger to her lips so her dad would be quiet and let Robert sleep. Thomas shook his head in acknowledgment, went to his desk, and did some work, trying not to make any loud noises.

Approximately an hour later, Robert woke up and stood up and stretched. Both Thomas and Veronica were on their phones. Robert walked over, kissed Veronica on her head, and waved to his father-in-law as he headed out the door. Thomas waved back as the door closed. He went to his truck and made some phone calls to Foster and his boss about the cases. Foster notified Robert, "They received a phone call two hours ago from a family fishing early in the morning. The last two bodies were discovered on the beach." Robert responded, "It sounds interesting." Foster replied and told Robert, "You might want to come in and look at the video they recorded."

Robert headed back to work and made his way through the heavy Miami rush hour traffic. After parking, he ran to his office due to his Police gut telling him things were going to get better. He saw his boss, who was talking to a man who had his three sons with him. The Chief of Detectives introduced Robert to the family, and the father handed over his digital camera to the COD, who asked them to "Please wait here." The father requested, "Please be careful of the camera. It's the only one they have". Robert smiled and informed him, "Sir, if we break it, we will buy you a brand new one." The father advised them, "Fair enough, and I think you gentlemen will see something that looks extremely suspicious around the 20-minute time frame."

After they went to the video room, they hooked up the camera and began watching it. The first twenty-minute video showed them fishing in the moonlight and just having fun—typical dad with three sons going out before the sun rises and just trying to catch fish. One of the kids can be heard asking his dad, "What's that over there?" The Detectives believed It was the youngest. The camera was turned in the direction the child was pointing, and it showed a boat about a 20-footer heading close to the beach, and there was a white male on the boat with a head cover and a black jacket. The camera focused in and out, trying to see what he was doing. The dad told his boys, "Not a sound." And you can hear the dad whisper to his oldest son, "What is he carrying to the front of the boat?" The father saw the person dump what could have been possibly a body over the deck. Then he dragged another suspected body again to the front of the boat and pushed it over into the water near the beach.

The unknown man jumped into the water and pushed the boat off the sand back into the deeper water. Robert and Gomez looked at each other. Then Gomez hit pause, and it showed the name of the boat. The name was The Flying Dove. They burnt a disk from the camera and downloaded it into their computer drives for evidence.

They walked outside and informed the dad they had to hold on to the camera as evidence, and he needed to sign some papers so we could return them once the DA allowed us to. The father looked at his sons and back at the two detectives and stated, "I hope this helps. My wife and I raise our sons to do the right thing." Robert shook the father's hand, looked at the kids, and notified them, "Your dad just saved some people's lives, and you should be proud of him." The kids smiled and replied, "We are." Robert and the COD went to the Roberts office and called the coast guard since the DMV was closed to verify who the owner of the boat was. Once they received it and where this person lived, they called the District Attorney's office and had people on standby to file an emergency search warrant once they got a judge to sign it.

Chapter 33

Problem Solved

One hour later, the DA assistant was at the office door with the search warrant, and Chief of Detectives Gomez grabbed it, telling Robert, "Call SWAT and have them get there and stand by till we arrive." Robert called Foster and informed him of what was up and to meet him there. Once Robert hung up, he headed to the suspect's location. While driving, he called Veronica and informed her, "He won't make it and to go home with her dad." She asked, "What's going on?" Robert told her to watch the local news. Love you," as he disconnected the call.

The old house was on SW 24th Street and SW 48th Ave. He parked down the street about 150 yards from the house when he arrived. The SWAT team encircled the house, getting men stagged for the assault. The team snipers and spotters were preparing to cover from high rooftops covering all entry and exit points from their locations.

Robert worked his way up to where the entry team was preparing to enter. He looked at his watch and saw his partner heading his way when suddenly someone started shooting at Foster from an upstairs window. Foster leaped to the ground and fired at the upper side window. Robert looked at the SWAT LT and yelled, "Go, go, go." The door was busted down from the front and back by entry teams. The men peeled off throughout the building once the two five-man teams entered the house. With Robert coming up behind them, two team members went up the stairs, and numerous shots whizzed by the two SWAT team members causing them to backtrack back down the stairs.

The suspect yelled out, "I know why they were there, and I promise to kill as many of you as possible." Robert whispered, "Step back a step and follow me." They went to the front, and Robert pointed to an old type latter on the far side of the house. They ran and climbed up the wooden stairs to the front cover and jumped through the open window. Robert was the second one through the window, and shots rang out from the upper hallway into the room.

The first man was struck in the chest and collapsed to the ground. He was just dazed due to the vest protecting him. Robert fired his 45 as fast as he could squeeze the trigger into the man still shooting from the doorway. The man fell to the ground and died immediately. Robert and the second SWAT member, behind him when they entered, moved through the upper rooms. They yelled out, "Clear." The first SWAT member staggered behind them and notified them on the radio, "All clear." Everyone heard the Lieutenant tell his teams to conduct a secondary search in case others hid.

While Robert crouched and looked at the dead suspect, he heard a SWAT member yell, "Hey, Detective, come up to the attic." Robert heard Foster call up the stairs, "Hey Robert, where the hell are you?" Robert replied, "Up here and call the boss and tell him we got our copycat."

Robert looked up and asked Foster, who came around the corner, "Are you ok?" Foster replied, "Yea, that was a close one." Robert grinned, saying, "Yea, it was," looking at the dead suspect. He told Foster, "Let's go to the attic." When they arrived in the attic, their jaws opened. There were copies of all the local media reports of all the killings on the walls. Robert yelled out, "Lieutenant."

A minute later, the SWAT LT came up and remarked, "Wooh," when he saw all the paper cutouts. Robert told the LT, "Go ahead and get your people out of here and file your paperwork once this house is taped off." Robert got on his cell phone and called his boss, who informed Robert, "The Mayor and COP were with him and headed his way." Robert looked out the attic window and saw Reporters all over the place, including a couple of news choppers in the sky.

Veronica and Thomas arrived home, went to the TV, turned it on the local television channel, and waited to see what was happening. After about 20 minutes, the news channel reported the Police SWAT Team conducted a raid that ended up killing the suspect. The Video showed Robert and Foster coming out of the house with SWAT members and FBI evidence team personnel heading in. Robert and Foster could be seen talking to each other when a vehicle drove up with the Mayor and COP, and COD. They exited the vehicle and were briefed on what happened by Robert, Foster and the SWAT LT.

The Mayor looked at Robert and Foster and told them, "Good job." The SWAT LT came over and shook the hands of the Mayor. COP and the Mayor patted the LT on the back and told him, "Your teams did a super job." The Lieutenant informed the Mayor, "The team member who was shot is being taken to the hospital by the team medic to get checked out." The COP told the LT, "Please tell your team I said they did a great job today," and the LT replied, "He would," and he left. The Mayor fixed his tie and announced, "Gentlemen, let's go talk to the press." Robert and Foster started walking away when the Mayor said, "Oh no, you two come with me."

Robert and Foster looked at each other, shrugged their shoulders, and followed the Mayor COP and COD to the press conference. The Mayor started the conference with, "Ladies and gentlemen of the press, we will try and give you some answers on what happened here tonight, but I first want to say all law enforcement did a super job in this investigation." He looked around at all the reporters and continued discussing the case by mentioning how "Detective Bench and Detective Foster were the ones who put the final pieces together to end the suspect's terror of women."

The Mayor then turned it over to the Chief of Police, who discussed how the evidence was gathered, a warrant was used and how law enforcement attempted to capture this murderer. The COP then explained in more detail, "How unfortunately he resisted by trying to shoot police officers, and one was shoot, but his vest saved his life." He had the COD Gomez step up and continue the news conference. Gomez reviewed how evidence was gathered, except he left out the part about the video. He credited old fashion police work and Detectives Bench and Foster's great job. Once he was done, he had Detective Bench step up to discuss the investigation that was conducted.

Robert stepped forward and gave an abbreviated description of what happened and how unfortunate they had to shoot the suspect multiple times during the exchange of gunfire. He paused and announced, "The suspect died on the scene." Robert, in a firm tone of voice, "I would also like to add this person was the copycat killer of those two women from the other day and not the perpetrator of all the other homicides up and down the coast."

He informed the press, "Detective Foster and I are spending as much time as possible working with the FBI task force to catch the criminals, so please stay vigilant and be mindful of your surroundings." Robert looked at Detective Foster and asked, "Would you like to add to this?" Foster stepped forward and informed them, "All information is helpful, and all it takes is one person to give us the needed information to assemble the puzzle." He looked at Robert, turned back to the press, and said, "That was key in ending this person's criminal behavior. Thank you." The press started yelling questions, but Robert and Foster walked away.

The Mayor and the COP stepped up and began answering questions they could ask. Robert and Foster walked to their cars and headed back to the Police station. Veronica and Thomas looked at each on how Robert and Foster presented themselves. Veronica looked worried. Thomas told her, "Honey, he is ok, that's what matters, and We both want him to come and work in the business, but it's up to him, not you or me, to decide that." Veronica halfhearted smiled and informed her dad, "I am so worried about him, he takes the risk that most people never do, and it doesn't bother him." Thomas got up and stepped over to Veronica and put his hand out, and she got up, and they went and ate dinner.

Robert and Foster were heading back to the station, talking about what had happened, when Robert pulled over and said we both agree they are coming, back-right? Foster responded and said, unfortunately, yes. The fisherman and his kids were out on a boat when this piece of crap was filmed. How about we do the same thing? We use the coast guard, all police boats, sheriffs, and drones during the night to patrol up and down the beaches. Foster smiled and agreed.

When he answered, Robert and I had an idea. Foster called the cod and said, "We should try and draw this or these people out beside all the decoys and heavy patrols during the day and while there is light. We need to meet with everyone in the FBI task force room tomorrow morning at 8:00 AM," and then Foster hung up. Foster then realized he left his car back at the scene. Robert laughed and said let's get it. He turned around, and they went back to retrieve Foster's car.

Robert made it home at about 11:00 PM and walked in and saw some cold food on the table. He sat down and ate. Ten minutes later, Veronica came down and sat next to Robert in a see-through nighty. She was beginning to show her pregnancy. Robert kept on eating.

Veronica sat there and finally asked, "Are you ok?" Robert replied, "Yes, one bad guy down." She asked him, "Did you have a vest on?" He lied, saying, "Both Foster and he wore one." Veronica asked, "Did you kill him or did SWAT?" He informed her, "I did. The SWAT officer in front of me caught the rounds, and so I put about five rounds into his chest with extreme prejudice." She commented, "Good," got up, and started to walk away when she turned her head and told Robert, "I love you. We do not want anything to happen to you." Robert put his food down and stated, "I know. Besides that, how are you?" She looked at Robert and suggested to him, "Come upstairs, and I will show you how I feel." He pushed himself away from the table and replied, "I guess that's what they call a dessert." She smiled, and they walked upstairs and went to bed.

The meeting started at exactly 8:00 AM, and everyone was there, including the Mayor. Robert looked at Foster, who smiled and commented, "No, you go ahead." Robert looked around the crowded room and ensured no one could let slip what they were planning. He announced, "This is going to be tough on everyone here and others." He had a serious look on his face and informed everyone, "This information is not to go outside this room at all, and I do not want any leaks or even hints to the wrong people." Robert looked at the FBI agents, U.S. Marshals, and DEA and explained, "Washington is not to be in the loop until I say so because they have the biggest mouths on the planet." Everyone in the room agreed with his words.

Suddenly, the door opened and in walked the Governor. He informed the Detective, "Please do not stop." Robert notified the Governor, "Your aids have to leave." The Governor turned around and had his aids and State troopers step out. When the door closed, Robert explained, "Governor, this is 100% need to know," and the Governor replied, "I understand." Robert announced, "There are 16 people in this room. If this information comes out as he looked at the Governor, I want the leaker prosecuted and his balls cut off." The Governor looked at everyone in the room and commented, "I will make sure that happens personally."

Robert described how this would go from when it gets dark to before the sun comes up seven days a week, including using the coast guard and all boats with night vision to watch the shores far out so nobody sees us. Robert insisted No smokers are allowed to be selected because they are more likely to try and take a puff to get their nicotine fix. The plan was to be done seven days a week. The

Governor raised his hand and asked Robert, "What are we watching for." Robert replied, "The beach murderers." He looked around the room and informed them, "I believe they are back someplace along the Atlantic coastline, more likely in our area."

He walked around the room, saying, "The people in the boats will be selected and only told to watch for suspicious activity and drug smuggling." He stopped, leaned on the wall, and recommended, "To use the fasted boats to catch drug running." Robert insisted, "We cannot have loose lips to the press." Then Robert looked at the Governor and asked, "Well, sir, yes or no?" The Governor smiled, looked around the room, and commented, "Let's find these bastards and end this." Then he looked at Robert and asked, "When do we start?" Robert replied, "Immediately tonight." The governor said, "He will make phone calls with the Mayor and Police chief."

Robert looked at Foster and commented, "Well, what do you think, compadre?" Foster remarked, "We will see, Paleface." The Mayor stepped up to Robert and asked, "What are the odds of catching them?" Robert looked around and stated, "4 to one." The Mayor replied, " I will take those odds," as he walked over to the Governor.

The task force began making phone calls and gathering people to be used that could be trusted. Robert pulled the COD over and informed him, "We need to use drones also to cover more territory." Gomez looked at Robert and asked him, "You are acting as if we can catch them." Robert advised him, "They have not struck, and there have been no kidnappings lately, so we need to rent one of those houses and get undercovers dressed up as college kids partying all the time."

Gomez smiled and remarked, "Let me guess, no badges or guns on the women, but eyes on them on the beach when they walk around?" Robert informed Gomez that absolutely thin clothing would show guns and badges, but they could have a small gun between their thighs if they wore dresses. Gomez laughed as he walked away. Robert replied, "Just make the undercovers look real."

Once they were done discussing everything with the COP, Robert informed him, "I am going home to get some sleep, so let's meet here at 6 PM," as he walked out the door.

An hour later, Robert was in bed and fell asleep immediately and slept until he was woken up by a maid knocking on the door at 4:30 pm. He asked, "Who is it?" One of the maids informed him, "Your wife called and said she will be home soon." He replied, "Thank You," as he slowly got out of bed. He went and took a shower and changed into dark clothes for the night. After getting dressed, he reached under the bed, pulled out a black bag, and pulled out a Glock 19 to carry as an extra weapon and, of course, his two knives. He placed one in his boot and the other small in his belt and headed downstairs.

Robert went to the kitchen to make himself a sandwich when the cook came in and informed him he would do it for him. Robert waved him off and replied, "I got it." Once the sandwich was made, he grabbed some orange juice and sat down at the kitchen table.

Veronica and Thomas arrived a few minutes later, and she remarked, "Hungry?" Robert informed them, "I will be gone all night and won't be back until morning." With concern in her eyes, she asked, "Why?" He informed her, "I will be working nights until we get the murderers." Thomas remarked, "Is this your plan?" He smiled and told him, "Basically, this needs to end, and they have not struck, and I feel it will be soon here in this area."

Veronica smiled, sat down, looked at Robert, and asked, "Can I have a bite?" Robert laughed as he handed her his sandwich, telling her, "Go ahead. I am done. I do not want a full stomach because it will make me want to nap when I should be watching." She finished the sandwich and asked him, "So you will be home now during the day for a while?" Robert replied, "Yes." Veronica looked at her dad and informed him, "I will be staying home for a while with Robert." Thomas looked at his daughter and remarked, "Sounds good sweetie," he looked at the cook, who walked in and informed him, "Dinner for two," and the cook went back into the kitchen.

Robert went upstairs, brushed his teeth again and came back downstairs. He looked at Veronica and commented, "This will end soon, I promise." Veronica smiled and took his hand and put it and her hand on her stomach, which was getting bigger. Robert kissed her and headed back to work. Thomas looked at Veronica and told her, "He will be fine." She looked at her dad and asked, "You promise," and he replied, "Yes, I have no doubt he will be ok."

Thomas informed her, "My sources told me he will have an army with him." She looked at him and asked, "Who?" He replied, "The Governor." Thomas declared, "When this is over, I will sit Robert down again and make an offer. As they say, he can't refuse". Thomas commented, "You just take care of my grandson, and did you tell Robert yet?" She replied, "No," while looking down. He said, "Honey text him in about 30 minutes so he will know." Veronica smiled and agreed. She remarked, "I am hungry. Is it dinner time yet?" Thomas walked with her, and they ate at the table.

Robert made it to his assigned boat, jumped in, and Foster was already there. He had a couple of fold-up chairs, and Foster leaned them against the big light holder. Robert signaled to the other boats to head out to their designated area. Robert then received a text from Veronica saying it was a boy. Robert smiled, and Foster asked, "What's with the smile? I have never seen you have a smile like that before." Robert looked at Foster and informed him, "I have a son." Foster said, "Congratulations." Foster chuckled, "Wow, another Robert Bench, scary, and by the way, what are you going to name it?" Robert notified him, "Davis Thomas Bench after his grandfathers." Foster smiled and replied, "That's nice." Robert text Veronica with an emoji smile. She responded with a heart back. He sent one back with an eye, heart and you. Then he texted, got to go.

Chapter 34

Long Nights and Dangerous Moments

They arrived at their spot, and the boat engines went off while they just watched the beach areas with their heat sensor scopes. They also saw the house with the fake party going on. The first night was a long one. However, farther south, a Police boat chased a smuggler's craft and caught them before they could get a shore. Foster heard at least 50 kilos of cocaine was confiscated. Robert chuckled due to it being a little surprise for the smugglers.

Around 5:00 AM, Foster looked at Robert, and they both agreed it was time to head in. Foster got on the radio and notified everyone to go ahead and head on in before the sun came up. Once they arrived at the pier, Foster jumped off first, followed by Robert. The crew stayed and cleaned up. Foster and Robert headed to their vehicles when Robert informed Foster, "I will call the boss and check-in." Foster smiled and stated, "See you tonight." Robert waved as he jumped into his truck to head home.

While driving home using his Bluetooth, he called his boss, and they went over what occurred during the night and what the other observers saw. They both agreed it was a good night since 50 kilos of coke was caught. Gomez mentioned, "At least the Mayor and Police Chief can use this as a good smoke screen if it gets leaked out on what we are doing." Robert agreed and informed Gomez, "I just drove up to the house, and I will talk to you tomorrow," as each hung up. Robert got out of his truck and walked to the door. He stopped, sat down on the porch chair by the door, and sat there for a few minutes, thinking about the night. Robert smiled, thinking about having a son. He called his family, talked to them for a while, and let them know how it was going. Everyone was happy, and of course, his brother and sister ribbed him, but it was all in fun. He got up and opened the door, and walked in.

Robert walked in and went straight to the dinner table, where he saw Veronica and Thomas eating breakfast. She got up, and Robert hugged her and kissed her, and asked, "How's our son doing?" Veronica told him, "He is eating a lot." Robert sat next to Veronica, and she asked him, "What would you like to eat?" He replied a vegetable omelet. The cook stated, "Give me 5 minutes, and it will be ready." Once it arrived, Robert ate without saying anything. Veronica and her dad discussed work, and after swallowing the last bite, Robert asked her, "When did you find out?" She remarked, "Yesterday morning." Robert asked her, "Let's go for a walk before I crash." Veronica got up, and they went outside and walked around the property.

As time passed, Veronica started to show her pregnancy and ended up not going to work due to the stress she was dealing with at her dad's office. Thomas agreed and had no problem taking over more so she could be relaxed at home. Robert went weeks working every night and, during the day, would stay up for a couple of hours and then sleep. Veronica began getting up early so she could sleep when Robert slept. Due to the job, she worried about Robert and ensured breakfast was there when he arrived home. Veronica also had him out running on the beach when he woke up.

Time went by, and a few more smugglers were caught with over a total of 200 kilos of cocaine, 100 kilos of meth, and 1 kilo of Marijuana confiscated. The evidence and individuals were handed over to the feds for prosecution. The nights were long and drawn out, with nothing showing to help them locate their pray.

Then one night at about 10:25 PM, a young 21-year-old girl was taking a shortcut across the beach. A large man attempted to kidnap her on the beach, but two Navy personnel who were up from Key West were drinking on the beach, heard a scream and ran to help her. The man who was trying to drag the girl off the beach saw the two men running toward him, and he let her go and took off running. They stopped to see if she was ok, and she was in shock. They called 911, and police arrived 10 minutes later. The two navy men described the man as a white male, bald, about 6'ft 4 or 5, about 270 pounds with a goatee. He had a black T-shirt on with blue jeans. They gave the location he ran, which was towards a dock. More police showed up, and they headed in that direction to see if they could find anything.

Robert was called on the radio and was told of what had happened. He signaled the Captain to take him to shore immediately. Foster asked what was happening, and Robert told him what had occurred, how this girl was lucky those two Navy guys were close by, or they would have another dead girl. Robert called his boss and told him what had happened and the general area. Gomez informed Robert, "I will call the Chief and let him know so he can fill in the Mayor." Then Gomez told Robert, "You were right on with this. We need to meet in the morning to narrow this down." Robert agreed and requested by saying, "Let's get the Taskforce together," and Gomez agreed.

Once the boat Robert and Foster were on made it to the dock, they got in their cars and headed to the attempted kidnapping spot. After following each other, they parked and walked out to the beach and talked to the investigator and police officers, who were looking for other witnesses, video, or anything to identify who the person was. Robert asked, "Where is the lady?" The Police officer replied, "She was taken to the hospital for her bruises and the trauma of narrowing escaping a dangerous situation." Foster asked, "Where are the two sailors?" The officer pointed the two guys out. Robert and Foster walked up to the men when Foster identified themselves, and they remarked, "Good job, guys." Both men smiled and stated, "Thanks." Foster requested they go over everything they saw, heard, and did. One of the men remarked, "I didn't say this before, but the guy had a smile on his face when she was trying to fight him." He paused and commented, "The guy seemed to like her fighting him." Robert requested them to tell him, "Which direction the guy went and like he was running trying to figure out which way to run away from you guys?" One commented, "He seemed to know where he was running to like he was familiar to the whole layout."

Robert thanked them after he received their information. He told them, "Thanks. I want to call your boss so they know what you two did to save that girl's life." One of the sailors remarked, "That's ok, it's all right, just doing the right thing." Foster responded, saying, "Hell no, what you two did was big. It helped with our investigation." They all shook hands, and Robert and Foster walked away. Robert commented, "Let's call it a night. But first, let's get everyone to start overloading this area at night since they are in this area." Foster made the calls, and they called it a night and headed home since the Police were walking the beaches.

Robert made it home at about 1 am, walked up the stairs, and entered the bedroom with Veronica sleeping on her side. Her stomach was big, and she was in a nightgown. He went into the bathroom, cleaned up, and then quietly crawled into bed, not wanting to wake her. He fell asleep and woke up at about 6 am when Veronica woke up smiling, saying, "When did you get home?" Robert replied, "About 1 am this morning, and I did not want you to wake up." She kept smiling and informed him, "I wish you did?" He laughed as he jumped out of bed into the shower. Once he was done, he got dressed, kissed Veronica on the lips, and told her, "I will be home late in the afternoon." She replied, "What is going on?" He told her what happened last night and knew they were getting closer. He kissed her again and grabbed an apple, and headed out.

Once he arrived at work, he went to the meeting room and waited for everyone to arrive, and they all slowly came in, including Foster, who arrived ten minutes later. They both agreed that once they were done in the meeting, they would head to where they believed the suspect could be and check it out.

During the meeting, everyone discussed what had happened the night before and where the incident occurred. Robert suggested how they needed to target where the attempted kidnapping happened and load it up with vehicle patrols and foot patrols on the beaches. The Police Chief interrupted and asked him, "How close do you think we are to end this crap, detective?" Robert looked at the Chief and advised him, "Hopefully, with some more luck soon." Once the meeting was over, Robert and Foster headed to last night's attempted abduction area and walked the streets for hours.

After walking around, Foster stopped, looked at Robert, and announced, "We need to increase the drone flights over this area during the day and night." Robert stated, "I agree," and he smiled and replied, "Hang on," he called the Governor's office and requested Air National Guard to fly over this area to assist law enforcement during the night hours using their high night vision technology. The governor agreed, and it was worked out. Robert told Foster, "Tonight I am going fishing on the dock while you are in a chopper with their high heat sensors." Foster smiled and chuckled, "So you get to fish while I get to fly around." Robert laughed also and mentioned, "It's time to call it a day."

When Robert arrived home, he noticed Veronica was napping on the couch. Later, she woke him up, and they walked around the property grounds. Veronica had that glow around her that many pregnant women have. She was getting closer to delivery, and it was a big worry with him being at work at night. Robert told her, "He was going back to the day shift after a couple more days." He shared with her, "Two Navy sailors saved a girl during the night from the kidnapper, and we know the area he is at, so it's just a matter of time." Veronica remarked, "Great, then we can spend more time together." He chuckled and stated, "Absolutely." Robert commented, "I am hungry. How about you?" She laughed and reminded him," I am eating for two," and they went and had dinner together.

After eating dinner, Robert headed to work with his fishing equipment and went to a dock he believed was in the right area. He fished for a couple of hours, and when he caught a fish, he threw it back in the water and kept fishing, listening to the radio. During the night, he heard a few planes fly over, and he used his radio system and called Foster and asked, "How was it going?" Foster advised him, "We haven't seen anything out of the norm, and all the places had three or more people in the homes, either eating, watching tv or sleeping." He looked down at the beach they were flying over and informed Robert, "No hidden areas observed, out."

When it got to midnight, Robert felt nothing was going to happen, and it was time to call it a night. He gathered all his fishing gear and went to his truck. Robert called his boss, and they discussed what did not happen, and both agreed to gather the Taskforce and go over some things in the morning. Gomez asked, "What time?" Robert informed him, "10:00 am." Gomez agreed, and they each hung up. Robert called Foster and went over what he told Gomez as he headed home.

He finally made it home around 1:30 am, stepped into the bedroom, and saw Veronica sitting up and turned on the small light by the bed. She said glad you are home, sweetie. She got out of bed, stepped up to Robert, hugged him, and started kissing him. She stepped back, dropped her nightie, stood there naked, and made love to me. Robert smiled, and they made love and fell asleep.

Robert woke up around 8 am and noticed Veronica was not in bed, and after he showered, he went downstairs, had a nice breakfast, and headed to work. He was informed Veronica went to work with her dad. After eating, he went to work, and while driving, he put his thoughts together on what he believed the next step was to flush out this individual. Once he arrived at the office, he wrote some notes down, and people started to come in and sit at the big table. After everyone arrived, Robert went over everything and looked at the Chief of Detectives, saying, "We need to start pounding on doors in this area on the beach, and we need to start rattling all cages possible." He looked around the table and advised everyone, "They need to see us getting close, and also, we need to have drones flying in this area and checking all parked vehicles to see if they match stolen vehicles." Robert sat down and told the men in the room, "This includes putting uniforms walking on the beaches and streets because they are here, and we need to be ready to force them to make mistakes." Robert looked at Foster, who informed everyone, "We, we need to pass out on tv, YouTube, TikTok, Facebook, on cars, every place on their description."

After the meeting, Robert and Foster headed out to the suspected area and began knocking on doors with pictures and interviewing people. Robert and Foster split up and agreed this needed to be done so they could cover more ground. While knocking on doors, they observed other detectives knocking on doors on the opposite side of the street. Most of the people they interviewed knew nothing, but one old man remarked, "The picture of the man looked familiar, but he could remember where he believed he saw the person." After knocking on doors all day, they stopped around 4 PM, and Robert and Foster called it a day.

They leaned against Robert's truck and talked and compared notes when Robert received a phone call from a person calling about the drawing. They jumped in Robert's truck and headed over to meet with this person. When they got there at a small pizza restaurant, they walked in and met the owner. They were informed, "One of the drivers has seen this person." Foster asked in an insistent tone of voice, "Where is the driver?" The manager apologized and told both Detectives, "The driver should be back in about ten minutes." They were offered a pizza, but they declined and sat there watching everyone walk up and down the street.

Approximately 10 minutes later, the driver returned and walked into the restaurant's front entrance when Foster and Robert stood up and walked over to him with the manager. Foster explained, "Why were they there," and the driver claimed, "I believe I saw that man on the drawings when I delivered him some pizzas." Both Robert and Foster looked at each other, and Robert asked, "When and where did he deliver the pizza." The driver explained, "He believes it was two pizzas, and the guy was a big guy, about 6 feet 4 or 5, and Bald." Robert showed him the drawing. The driver remarked, "Yea, that's him, and we should still have the address on file."

They went to the office, and the manager shot up the list of addresses from a couple of days ago, and the driver pointed and stated, "That's it." Robert pulled out his cell phone, and before he called the COD, he notified the Manager to print that out. Once Gomez answered, Robert claimed, "We got him. Get SWAT and all available officers to surround this cottage right now." Robert gave his boss the address and hung up, and both Detectives ran out of the Restaurant to Robert's truck.

When they arrived at the address, Robert and Foster headed down the street in Robert's truck. They parked at the front left side, jumped out, and called in their location. Robert and Foster pulled their weapons out and slowly walked to the house when they received gunfire from a window on the first floor. Foster was hit twice, and Robert ran over and dragged Foster behind a car. Foster was hit in the vest by one shot and one in the leg. Robert pulled off his belt and wrapped it around his partner's left leg to stop the bleeding bullet wound, when Foster, in an angry tone, stated, "Damn, I can't believe this shit." Robert told him, "Shut up and be happy you had your vest on." Robert was pissed off and asked, "Are you ok?" Foster replied, "Yea, what are we going to do now?" Robert remarked, "Hang on," as he reached down, threw Foster over his left shoulder, and carried him behind his truck as fast as he could. Once they got behind his big truck, he laid Foster down. Four more shots were fired when they were moving to the truck with them missing. He knew it was a handgun coming from one person when Robert got on his radio and stated Officer down and their location, and the suspect was armed. The Dispatcher announced the officer's down-location on all channels, and the murder suspect was armed.

Chapter 35

The City takes a Deep Breath.

Foster yelled at Robert, "I will watch the front door. He might go out the back." Suddenly, Robert saw a flash of a large man bald white male running down the beach, looking behind him as he ran. Robert took off running after the suspect while Foster called for help and an ambulance. Within minutes SWAT arrived with all available officers arriving. Foster was taken to an ambulance, and he yelled at the SWAT Lieutenant, "Hit the cottage now," and he pointed in the direction Detective Bench was heading. Some SWAT officers took off running to assist the Detective in foot pursuit. Lieutenant Jacobs told his team to hit the cottage, and he called the choppers to head in the direction to put eyes on the foot pursuit. The news media picked up the chatter about what was happening on their radios and headed to the area.

While sprinting on the beach after the suspect, Robert slowly gained distance from the suspect. While running, he heard sirens all over the place, and he saw choppers flying over him. The suspect ran through crowds on the beach, knocking some to the grown as they kept running to get away. Robert was amazed at how such a big man could still be running this far without slowing down for air. Then suddenly, Robert observed the suspect running towards another condo area.

Robert was glad he ran almost daily, or he would have quite a while back. He finally noticed the suspect was tiring, and he was getting even closer. He was about 20 yards away when both men entered a huge parking lot. Robert noticed a tv channel chopper was above him with two police choppers following the foot pursuit. He had no doubt the news crew was showing it live all over Florida. He was sure the Police chopper was giving directions to the other officers on the ground to assist the detective.

While running towards a busy intersection, Robert saw the big man start vomiting while he was running, and he was only 10 yards away as he dodged vehicles trying to get the suspect. He was almost ready to lunge after the suspect when a truck hit the big man at about 55 miles per hour. The big man bounced off the front of the vehicle, and his head smashed against the pavement. Robert stopped and was coughing and gasping from the run as he stood over the suspect.

He looked around as he stood over the big man whose head was smashed open from the pavement. Robert reached down and checked to see if the suspect had a pulse, and there was none. He put the dead man in cuffs and walked over to the driver, who was still in the driver's seat. Robert asked the driver, "Are you ok?" The driver replied, "I didn't see him." Robert responded, "Sir, it's all good. You just saved the state a whole lotta money." Then Robert asked, "If he had any injuries?" The driver answered back, "My neck and ankle." Robert pulled out his phone and called for an ambulance for the driver and his boss.

Gomez answered, informing Robert, "They are only two minutes out." Robert heard the sirens and notified him, "I need an ambulance and the morgue. The piece of shit is 100% dead." His boss asked, "Did you shoot him?" Robert laughed and said, "No, a good Samaritan hit him hard with his big truck." Gomez started laughing and remarked, "Outstanding," while he was laughing, he asked Robert, "Are you ok?" Robert took a deep breath, and he was quiet for a moment. Gomez asked again with concern, "Robert, are you ok?" The Detective responded by saying, "Yea, I am all right, and boss, how is Foster?" Gomez told his Detective, "Foster is fine and already in surgery." Then police began arriving from all directions. The intersection was a big mess, with vehicles all over the place. Rubber knickers didn't help.

Veronica and her dad were working when the chase came over the television. Thomas turned up the volume and watched the foot chase as he glanced at Veronica and informed her, "It looks like that's Robert chasing someone." Veronica jumped out from her desk, stepped up to a few feet from the large tv, and watched.

She commented, "It is Robert, as she held her baby in her womb and gasped a couple of times when he almost got hit by a couple of vehicles." Thomas looked at his daughter, asking, "Are you ok?" She nodded her head. They saw the person he was chasing hit hard by a large truck, and Robert stood over the suspect. She went to her cell phone and called Robert, and it went to a recording. She called again with no answer.

Robert ignored the cell phone, and then he finally answered it hearing Veronica, with concern in her voice, ask him, "Are you ok?" He commented, "I am fine, and we got the SOB." Robert paused for a second and told her, "Foster got shot twice, and he is in surgery." He looked around and continued telling her, "Foster got hit in the vest and leg, but he is doing good." Veronica said the only thing that matters is his being ok. Robert stated, "Foster got shot twice, but he is doing ok." Veronica got quiet and began crying, and Robert replied, "He is ok, and so am I. That's all that matters."

Robert paused and watched his boss drive up, and he told Veronica, "I have to go to the hospital and see his wife and kids." Veronica remarked, "She will meet him there." Robert said, "Sure, honey." Veronica told him, "I love you, and Robert replied, "Love you too, sweetie." Once they hung up, Veronica informed her dad, "Foster was shot, and she is going to the hospital to meet Robert there." Thomas informed his daughter, "I will go with you," as he picked up the phone and told the other person on the line to get his vehicle ready and that they were coming down.

Robert arrived at the hospital and made it to the floor where everyone was waiting for Foster to come out of surgery, and there were police everywhere. When Robert walked in, everyone started to clap and pat him on the back. Veronica and Thomas were sitting down when he walked in. They stood, and she ran to him and hugged him. Thomas shook Roberts's hand and remarked, "Congratulations." Robert and Veronica walked down the hallway and found Foster's wife and kids. Janet hugged Robert and kissed him, saying, "My Foster told me you saved his life, and our family is so grateful." Robert informed her, "Not really. I just got him out of the line of fire and treated his leg." Janet stated, "That is saving his life," and she kissed him again.

Janet hugged Veronica and asked, "How are you doing?" Veronica smiled and remarked, "Anytime." They talked and went and sat down. At the same time, Thomas stepped over to Robert, stating, "I will be over there if you need me." Robert shook his hand again, answering back, saying, "Thanks." Robert went over and talked to Foster's kids and informed them, "Your daddy is going to be fine. He did a great job. He saved a lot of lives." He looked up at Veronica, who was smiling, talking to Janet and advised them, "You kids should be proud of your daddy. He is a hero." The 8-year-old looked up and asked, "Sir, do you promise my daddy will be ok?" Robert smiled and told her, "Yes."

Then the surgeon came out and went to Foster's wife and explained to her that her husband was doing fine with no issues from the surgery. The doctor informed Janet and the kids, "I will have someone take you and your kids to his room." He waved to an orderly who came over, and they followed him. Robert asked, "When can he have guests?" The doctor informed him, "Only family tonight but maybe tomorrow for everyone else. Tomorrow should be good." Robert shook his hand and yelled, "Foster is doing fine the surgery went good." Everyone clapped. Then the Mayor, COP and the COD walked into the waiting room area with FBI agent Fox.

They went to an area away from the other officers and discussed what happened. The Mayor told Robert the Governor would be here tomorrow, and we pushed back the conference to 10:00 am tomorrow. While looking around and talking, he saw

Thomas Jackson with his daughter sitting down, watching Robert. The Mayor said, "Excuse me, I need to talk to someone." He went over to Mr. Jackson, who stood up, shook hands, and talked.

The COP looked at Robert and told him, "You and Foster did a great job ending this nightmare." Robert replied, "Yea, unfortunately, Foster got hurt." The COP remarked, "He will be taken care of, Lieutenant." The Chief of Detectives smiled and declared, "I forgot about that." Robert shook their hands and insisted, "I want Foster to get his Sargent and gold shield immediately." The COP commented, "Absolutely. I will announce this tomorrow after we see him in the morning."

Robert looked at Veronica, and she didn't look well; she waved and smiled at him. He said, "Excuse me," as he walked over to her, and she looked like she was having some pain. Thomas didn't see it because he was talking to the Mayor. Robert asked her, "Honey, are you ok" and she shook her head and whispered, "No, I think my water just broke." He saw the chair she was sitting in was wet. Robert yelled at a nurse who was walking by and said, "My wife s water just broke, and she needs help." Everyone in the waiting room got quiet as the nurse ran over to the desk and grabbed the phone, and announced she needed assistance in the waiting room as a woman was having a baby.

A couple of other nurses ran out of a door with a bed and helped her onto it. The head nurse asked, "Who is family?" Robert replied, "I am the husband," and he pointed at Thomas, saying, "He is her father." She informed both men to come with her as they pushed Veronica to the elevator. They crammed in there as Veronica started to yell, "The baby is coming." One nurse talked to her calmly and helped her get her breathing steady when the elevator door opened, and they pushed Veronica to the delivery room with Thomas and Robert following behind. When they got to the room, Veronica started screaming, "The baby is coming." One nurse proclaimed, "Only one of you can come in." Thomas said, "He is the husband," and Robert went in. Thomas took a deep breath and sat outside the delivery room. He called his assistant to tell him what was going on and told him, "Watch the store while he is away." A couple of minutes later, the Mayor, COP, COD, and a few other officers came down to see what was going on.

The Mayor and Thomas sat and talked about being a grandfather and other things. Robert held Veronica's hand as she screamed in pain, and the baby came out fast. There was no time to give Veronica an epidural shot to help with the delivery, and the doctor was not there yet, so the head nurse delivered the baby with help from the other nurses. When the baby was delivered, Robert cut the cord, and Veronica was handed the baby after getting cleaned up. She held the baby and looked at him, and Robert smiled, saying, "Our son, Robert, our son." Robert smiled and kissed his wife, telling her, "You did a great job, sweetie." He was told by a nurse the baby weighed 7 pounds 8oz. Robert asked, "What are we calling him?" Veronica remarked, "What we discussed, Robert Thomas Bench." Robert told Veronica, "Great, I will get your dad and be right back."

He stepped out, and Thomas stood up, and Robert hugged Thomas and said you are the grandfather of a 7-pound 8 oz baby boy. He announced, "The name is Robert Thomas Bench." There were congratulations going around the corridor. Robert looked at the COD and informed him, "After tomorrow, I will be taking some time off." The COP chuckled and stated, "It's well-earned, LT." Then Robert and Thomas went into the room. Veronica smiled and said Daddy, here is your grandson, Robert Thomas Bench. She handed the baby off to Robert, who held him, then he let Thomas hold the baby, and he then handed the baby back to Veronica, who would not let him go.

Even when the nurse said he would be cared for, Veronica refused to hand the baby over. The nurse refused to argue with the new mom knowing who she was and her father. After an hour, Veronica allowed the child to be taken so a 'tag' would be put on the baby and the baby footprinted. Veronica was given a wrapping tag so there was a match so there were no mistakes on who the mother was. Thomas stepped out and called his security, and 30 minutes later, two men showed up, and they were informed once Veronica was moved to her room, they were to stand outside the room, and if the baby left the room, they were to go were ever it went. If the baby leaves the room and with who, a text is sent to me immediately. Their job was to protect the baby if anybody thought of kidnapping his grandson. He then returned to the room, and pictures were taken with the baby. Veronica and Robert were all smiles. Robert went and sat in a chair and sent email photos of the new baby to his family.

Later on, Veronica was moved to her room with the baby. The hospital administrator showed up due to nurses wanted to take the baby and put it in the room to be watched by staff with the other babies. Thomas resisted, and the administrator showed up to resolve the issue. Thomas and the administrator had a one-way discussion with Thomas not having it, and she understood this was not a man to say no to. The administrator told the nurses, "Take whatever is needed to the assigned room," and she walked away. She was well aware he was a big donor to the hospital, and it would not be a good idea for him to get pissed off.

Later on, when Veronica and the child were in their assigned room with Robert and her dad, she would not let the child go, and then the baby started to cry when a nurse who walked in remarked, "The baby must be hungry." Thomas smiled and responded, "I will step out." A little while later, he came back in. The baby was lying on its side asleep, and so was Veronica. Robert was standing over Veronica, watching her sleep. Thomas looked at Robert and asked him to step outside so they could talk.

When they were outside, they went to an area away from the staff walking around. They watched the two security men standing at Veronica's room door. Robert looked at Thomas and asked, "What's up?" Thomas informed Robert, "I want to thank you for being the man she needed to make her happy, and she has never been so happy." Robert was appreciative of what he was told and commented back, "Thanks, I am the lucky one." Thomas smiled and said, "No, she is." Robert looked at his father-in-law and said, "What do you want to talk about?" Thomas mentioned, "I watched how stressed she was over the last few weeks, and it made me think how much she worries about you."

Robert replied, "I know." Thomas then got to the point. He explained, "I want you to come and work with me as a special assistant, and I will teach you the nuts and bolts of my company, and over time you can help Veronica run it when I am long gone." He looked around the area and continued, saying, "She will need you to be her Rock when things are tough." Robert replied, "Thanks." Thomas informed Robert, "I will pay you well, and I will let Veronica decide on the pay, and working for me, you will be with your wife and child more than you would be as a cop." Thomas stepped up to Robert and said, "I am not your dad, but I need to tell you this: You are a hardworking man that takes care of business as a detective. Now it's time to be a father because everything changes, your goals, agendas and happiness." Thomas walked over to the drink machine, put in some money, got a soda, and looked back at his son-in-law, waiting for a response.

Robert looked at his father-in-law, then out the window, and back at Thomas, informing him, "I will need some time to think about it, sir, but I want you to know that I agree with everything you said." Robert turned around, leaned on the window, and told him, "Give me a couple of days to finish tying up this case, and I will give you an answer." Thomas smiled, saying, "That's fair enough, and if you say no, it will not change anything between you and me."

The next day after going in early to see Veronica and the baby and visiting Foster and his family, he went to work and started to write up his reports when suddenly the COP came in. Robert looked at the COP and stood up, and they shook hands. The COP again complimented Robert and Foster on their performance in this case and then said, "I will be headed to the hospital to see Foster and give him the good news of his promotion and gold shield." Robert informed the COP, "I saw him this morning, and he is doing good." Then the COP ordered him, "Meet me out front in 10 minutes for the news conference." Robert stated, "Ok," and the COP left.

Chapter 36

New Life meets old Enemies.

The Police executive started the news conference and went over the basic part of what had happened and where the crimes occurred up and down the coast. She stepped back after introducing the Mayor, who congratulated all law enforcement and the newly promoted Lieutenant Robert Bench and Sargent Foster for a job well done. Once he was done, the COP stepped forward and congratulated the local police and the FBI, who assisted in this case. He added that LT Bench and SGT Foster will receive the department's highest medals, and the governor will appoint the state's highest medals to these two men. He asked LT Detective Bench, "Please come up and say a few things."

Once Robert stepped up and discussed how they put the case together, they solved and ended these crimes. Once he was finished, he told the press he was ready for questions. The press asked, "Are you sure this is the guy?" Robert replied, "Yes, he was involved with all those homicides." He answered some other questions about his partner and himself when one reporter asked him, "So, Detective, what are your future goals?" Robert answered, "I will have to see. Right now, I am an LT detective and enjoy my job. Next question." Another reporter said, "LT, we were told you are a new father from the daughter of the richest man in Florida. How does that feel?" Robert paused for a second before continuing and stated, "Being a father changes everything," and he stepped away from the mike.

The police executive answered some more questions, and the news conference ended. Robert headed into the police building and went and finished his paperwork. His boss came in and told him, "Get out of here and go take a vacation. See you in a month, and by the way, congratulations on being a new daddy." Robert reached into a box and handed Gomez a cigar with a wrap that stated it was a boy. Gomez said, "Thanks," and he walked out. Robert walked out, locked up the room, and handed out cigars to everyone.

A week later, Veronica and Robert were walking on the beach when he turned and looked at Veronica. The baby, who was in a daddy, carried a sling and said, "Honey, I know you want me to quit my job, and I have thought a lot about it and how my job could hinder my relationship with you and our child." Veronica put her hand on his cheek and kissed him, informing him, "I will support you in whatever you do because I love you." Robert grinned and said, " I will take your dad's offer. I love my job, but you and the baby mean more to me, and I hate being away from you two." Veronica hugged, smiled, and kissed him, replying, "I love you, and are you sure?" He looked into her eyes full of love telling her, "Yes."

He turned around, pointed at the two bodyguards following them about 50 yards away, and commented, "It would make their jobs easier for them." She took his arm, leaned on him, and told him, "You will do good, and by the way, what did my dad say he will pay you?" Robert repeated what her dad had said, and she stopped walking and looked at him with a smile on her face. She asked, "What do you want?" Robert replied, "Just watch what I make as a Detective, and it will be fine." Veronica looked at him and remarked, "Are you serious?" He stated, "Yea, I need to make something to contribute to this family." She laughed and said, "Hell no, you need to make more."

He looked at the baby and told Veronica, "I am good with it." Veronica claimed, "That is ridiculous. What did my dad say a long time ago?" Robert laughed and shrugged his shoulders. He was getting a kick watching Veronica wanting him to make more money. She commented, "I believe a million was the offer, not what you are making." Robert smiled. He knew he was just playing. She smiled, "That's your pay." Robert replied, "No, that's too much.

How about we start simple, like $200,000, to be fair." Veronica stated, "OK, OK," as they walked down the beach.

Robert saw his boss the next day, and he gave in his two weeks' notice, shocking his boss and coworkers. Gomez looked at Robert and asked, "Why?" Robert told him, "Family opportunity and a pay increase." Gomez tried to talk him out of it, but Robert remarked, "It's a done deal." He further added, "It's a new challenge, and I have a kid now, and that changed everything." Gomez Smiled, telling him, "I wish you luck, and I hope I get free tickets to the games." Robert smiled and told Gomez, "Just call, and by the way, you have my number." Gomez smiled, and they shook hands and walked out of the Police station.

Everyone was surprised when it was announced he was leaving the force, including the COP and Mayor. The Mayor asked, "Is there anything we can do to get him to stay?" The COP replied, "No." The Mayor laughed and commented, "Well, I hope you give him a good sendoff." The COP declared we would give him a huge one. He made this city better." The Mayor added, "I am sure Jackson gave him a good offer." The COP smiled and agreed with the Mayor.

Thomas Jackson had another desk in his office on the opposite side of Veronica's desk. Robert's first assignment was auditing all security matters with the business, including the stadiums and teams. It took him a while to get used to his new job, but he would sometimes admit to Veronica he missed his old one, but he was not sorry he quit.

In the middle of the floor was a large mat where the baby could crawl around and play with toys. It had a two-foot siding to keep the baby in a set area. There was also a blanket on the mat. Thomas as a grandfather, was extremely protective of little Robert, and nobody was allowed to walk in without approval so the baby could crawl around without being stepped on. All three adults always had an eye on the baby. Most of the time, one of the adults was always playing with the baby. When it was breastfeeding time,

Thomas would step out and use that time to take care of things outside the office.

Working together made both Veronica and Robert closer and tighter. They would take their lunch hour together, and he began teaching Veronica self-defense again. They would run on the beach together first thing every morning. She also had a yoga room set up and a yoga instructor to teach women who wanted to learn. Thomas added a large weight room in the building and a childcare center for parents to have their children at work near them. Veronica insisted on it, and Thomas signed off on it. He did notice employee morale improved with these changes. Robert Jr. stayed with the family and did not go to the childcare area. Thomas was insistent on it because he was always concerned with the risk of kidnapping. Robert and Veronica, and the baby always had bodyguards around them. He changed it from two to four men, all with special operations training and armed to the teeth.

One day Robert was going through paperwork when he overheard Veronica arguing with one of the executive staff over a business transaction. He heard the man say, "I don't care who you are, I run this section, and I don't need some spoiled rich bitch telling me what I need to do," and he hung up.

Veronica got a little upset, and she looked up and saw Robert with a pissed-off look on his face. He looked at her and asked, "Who was that?" She told him, "Don't worry about it. I will let my dad handle that guy." Robert's voice went a little louder, demanding to know who that person was. She refused, and his eyes looked black with rage, and she had never seen him look that way since she saw him shoot her brother's killer. It gave her goosebumps, and fear went down her spine. She suggested, "Honey, I will take care of it." Robert stated one more time, "Who the hell was it?" She knew he was pissed off and informed him, "It was Newman, president of the purchasing section, and he has been with my dad for 20 years." Robert turned and left the office. Veronica got up and yelled to Robert, "Don't," but he was gone. She couldn't chase after him because of the baby in the crib. A minute later, her dad walked in, asking, "What is Robert doing?" After she told him, he replied crap and went to where Robert was heading.

Robert walked out of the elevator and headed straight to the conference room, where a meeting was going on with Newman standing and talking to the group around the large table. The door flew open, and Robert walked in and grabbed Newman by his collar and slammed him against the wall and threatened him by saying, "If you ever talk to my wife like that, I will throw you off the roof." Newman pissed on himself while some in the room started to snicker. Robert then told Newman, "You owe my wife an apology, you little weasel."

Thomas entered the room and ordered Robert to let go of him. Robert looked at Thomas and suggested, "You fix this, or I do." Thomas could tell Robert was furious, and he said calmly, "Robert, please let him go." Robert released Newman as people in their chairs stood up and stepped away from the table. Thomas walked up to Newman and declared, "We have known each other for 20 years, and you do this?" Newman responded and stated, "She was sticking her nose in my business." Thomas looked at Newman, not saying anything. Newman continued, saying, "Thomas, I do not need a woman telling me what to do." Thomas informed him, "That woman is going to run this entire place like you have been told in the past." Newman declared, "I will fight you on this, and I bet the board will agree with me." Thomas laughed, stating, "We are not a stock business. I own 100% of this company. The board works for me," and he looked at Robert and told him, "Call security and have them come up." Robert stepped out and called security by phone. A few minutes later, they showed up. Thomas informed Newman, "You have two choices get fired or resign." Newman laughed and replied, "I am not quitting." Thomas told him, "You are fired," and he looked at security and ordered them to get this piece of shit out of here, and Newman, we will mail you your crap in your office. Newman declared, "He was not leaving." Thomas looked at security and informed them, "Get him out of here one way or the other." They stepped up, and Newman got nervous, and he was escorted out of the building soaked in his own urine.

Thomas looked around the room and informed Robert, "You now run this section. It's all yours." Robert looked at Thomas face to face and said stated, "Thanks, my way?" Thomas smiled, saying, "Your way," and he left. Robert went and sat down at the head of the conference table and asked everyone to please sit down. They all looked at each other and then sat down, unaware of what would He told them, "I know nothing about this department," and allowed everyone to discuss what they did and what should be the department's goals.

They were impressed because their former boss never asked them that or cared what they thought. Once everyone was done, he remarked, "All I ask is to do your job, and if you make me look good, I will do the same for you, but if you are a lazy worker, you will be gone." He looked at the person on his left and asked her what her name was again, and she replied, "Barrie." He requested for her to "Please have name list in front of everyone so I can learn who they are first and last name." She told him, "Yes, sir." Robert requested them to gather the whole department outside this room so that he could talk to them. His supervisors got up and went and gathered everyone.

It was a big department, and they all crowded around, and he spoke. He explained what he expected from everyone and added, "If anyone of you has an idea, send it to both your supervisor and me." His employees were focused on him when he mentioned, I hated when other people took credit for my work, and I have no doubt it happens here, so I also will award ideas that help production and sales or anything that helps this company with what is known as a time of the award." The employees smiled when he explained it was a free paid day off and dismissed everyone to return to work. People were talking as he headed to the elevator and got in. The door closed, and he took a deep breath. In a few seconds, the door opened, and he went and talked to Veronica and his father-in-law.

As time passed, Thomas was impressed by how Robert ran his department. The employees talked highly of Robert on how he treated his entire staff. The Time off idea went business-wide, and all the good ideas used helped make the company more efficient and better run.

Robert Jr. grew, and Robert and Veronica ran more of the company, with Robert taking some of the burdens off Veronica. She told her dad, "Robert was her Rock, and people saw the way the winds were going and were listening to what he said." Thomas was always the final say on the big things and was impressed with how those two worked together.

After two years, Thomas promoted Robert to VP of the company, which Robert resisted but finally gave in to when Veronica begged him to take it. Robert wanted her to be happy. Robert Jr. was walking, and Thomas spent most of his time taking his grandson to places when Veronica and Robert were busy with the business. Veronica slowly began to spend less time at work and more time during the day with her child. Robert was helping her dad run the business. She felt more enjoyment with her child than dealing with work. Veronica would be down in the childcare, which she extended into a bigger area. She also added a teacher to help with kids preparing for kindergarten.

Veronica had everything she wanted a good husband and a child she loved. She wanted more and decided she wanted another child. That night she told Robert she wanted more children. Robert laughed and replied, "Ok, no issue here." Robert Jr. already had his own room and was a sound sleeper. So, they began working on another baby.

One day she walked into her dad's and Robert's office and asked him, "Can you take Robert Jr. for a walk? Robert and I need to talk about some things." Thomas looked at Robert and commented, "Alright, come on, kiddo," as he took the child by his hand and headed to the door. Thomas asked, "How long?" She stated about 45 minutes. He said, "Mmmm, serious talking," and walked out with his grandson.

Robert stood up and asked, "What's up, honey?" Veronica turned around and walked to the door, and locked it. She turned around, took off her coat, slowly stripped naked, stood there, and asked, "What's taking you so long?" He stood there looking at her when she commented, "There is only one way to have a child, so what are you waiting on?" He smiled, took off his clothes, cleared his desk, and lifted her on his desk, and they made love.

Fifty minutes later, the door opened, and Veronica walked out, and she saw her dad and her child standing by the door. Thomas asked her, "Is everything alright?" as she took her child's little hand. Veronica smiled, saying, "Everything is great working out perfectly."

Thomas walked in and noticed Robert fixing his tie, picking up papers off the floor, and putting them back on his desk. Thomas realized what she meant and asked Robert, "Well, how's your day going, son?" Robert grinned and remarked, "Just fine. I guess you know now we want more kids." Thomas remarked, "Good more grandkids," and they went back to work.

Veronica headed home with her child and asked her son, would you like an ice cream cone he smiled and replied, "Yes, Mommy." She told the driver what she wanted, and they went to a Baskin Robbins. They drove in, and she and Robert Jr. went in. They got an ice cream cone, returned to the limo, and took off for the house. When they arrived, she went upstairs to take a shower while a maid got their lunch, and Robert Jr. sat on the couch, taking a nap. About 25 minutes later, Veronica came downstairs, and they ate lunch.

Robert and Thomas ate lunch at their desk while discussing work when Thomas got serious and asked, "Well, Robert, how are things going?" Robert replied, "Fine, still getting used to things." Thomas then asked, "How are Veronica and the child doing?" Robert smiled and informed him, "Well, she is spending more time with our son than here, so I guess this is what she wants besides another child." Thomas smiled and nodded his head. Thomas said, "I appreciate your help, and I know Veronica is extremely happy with how things are going." Robert nodded and agreed with his father-in-law. Before he was asked, Robert told Thomas, "No, I don't have no regrets." Thomas commented, "I am glad," as he went back to work.

Two days later, Veronica and Robert Jr. headed to the tower after picking up lunch for Robert and her dad. She wanted to have a picnic, pick them up, and take them to the beach since the weather was perfect. While the limousine was waiting to turn, a large man jumped out, ran, and fired an automatic weapon at the driver and bodyguard in the front seat, killing them before they could do anything. He then turned it towards the vehicle behind them, with the bodyguards shooting numerous rounds into the Escalate, killing them before they could get completely out of the vehicle. The bodyguard behind the driver got out wounded but was shot in the head before he could return fire.

The big man broke the window to the back seat of the driver's side when a man jumped out of his car and fired at the big man—a random law-bidding citizen who was armed and trying to help. The big man turned and shot him twice, and he fell to the ground, wounded. The big man reached in, grabbed the door latch, and opened the door, grabbing Veronica by the hair, and Robert Jr. tried to hit him as they were dragged out of the vehicle. Veronica tried to resist, but he was too big and strong. Robert Jr. was carried to the vehicle in front and thrown into the back seat, and the driver took off after the big man squeezed himself into the back seat. Drivers were astonished at what they just witnessed.

Veronica covered up her son, demanding, "Who are you, and what do you want from us." The female driver informed her,

"Your husband killed one of my sons, and now we are going to deal with him through you." Veronica asked, "Who was your son?" The lady driver said, "He was chased by your husband, hit by a truck, and killed." Veronica realized they were involved in killing all those women. She yelled at the old woman and told her, "Too bad my husband didn't kill the both of you also." The old lady's son smacked her blooding her mouth. Robert Jr. was crying and stood to try and stop the man, and he was pushed back into the seat. The lady driver responded, "Both sons dealt with those sluts who would not take care of my boys." She breathed and continued, "They were evil and had to be taken care of because they refused to marry my sons. Her son wrapped Veronica s wrist with zip ties and the little boys. They stopped in an old run-down parking lot, and Robert Jr. grabbed Veronica, and Robert put them in another vehicle. The older lady smiled at Veronica and advised her, "I will get my revenge by either killing you and the boy or your husband," and they drove off with Veronica and Robert Jr.

Chapter 37

Retaliation

Robert was in his office when he received a phone call from his cell. Seeing it was Veronica, he answered it, asking, "What's up honey?" Someone on the phone claimed, "You killed my son. Now I have your son and wife." Robert clenched his fist as the lady informed him, "All I want is your life for theirs and no police, and we will be watching your every move," and she hung up. Robert was quiet and slammed his fist on his desk. Thomas was on his phone, saw what was happening, and told the person on the other side, "I will call you back," and he hung up.

Robert stood up and walked to Thomas's desk, and told him, "My wife and son have been kidnapped by a woman and others." Thomas went pale and suggested, "We need to call the police." Robert said, "No, not that way because they are watching, so I will make some calls." I will make some phone calls. Thomas looked at Robert and asked, "How much money do they want?" Robert said, "None. They want my life for theirs."

Thomas looked at Robert, who added, The lady informed me, "I killed her son, and they will kill my wife and my son." Thomas was shaking and asked, "What are we going to do?" Robert told him, "We will get them back, I promise." Thomas asked, "Then what?" Robert looked out the window and back at his father-in-law and told him in a vicious tone, "I kill them. First thing is you need to get your security company and spread them out all over town looking for all clues". He paused for a moment and stated, "I will call some friends." Robert went and called Foster and told him what had happened.

Foster got quiet and told Robert, "We found the limo close to Star Island. The limo driver and the bodyguard in the front seat were killed before they could get out." Robert asked about the chase vehicle when Foster informed him, "The chase vehicle was made into Swiss cheese, and the men are all dead." Robert wanted to know, did any get any shots off? He was told, "One almost got out, but he was killed before he could do anything. Also, there was a wounded bystander who tried to help and was shot twice." Foster added, "He is on his way to the hospital, and I just got here five minutes ago and was getting ready to call you when you called." Robert remarked, "Mr. Jackson and I will be there in a few minutes," and he hung up.

Robert told Thomas, "Let's go. I will explain things on the way and have your limo ready and secure." Thomas called his driver and repeated what Robert had said. Five armed big men followed Mr. Jackson when they made it downstairs, and they all jumped into the limo.

When they arrived, they saw police cars everywhere and media vans. People were crowding around the sidewalks as Robert and Thomas drove up. They jumped out and ran to the crime scene. They were stopped by police officers, and Robert yelled out to Foster, who saw Robert, and he told the officers, "Let those two in." Robert looked at the crime scene and asked, "what do you have"? Foster informed him, "It's what I told you, and it's what you see." Foster pulled Robert away from Thomas and told him, "It was a large white man about 6ft 5, bald who did all this".

Witnesses claimed, "An older women were in a vehicle in front of the limo, and by the way, we found the vehicle five minutes from here." Foster asked Robert, "What do you need?" Robert informed him, "The FBI needs to be at his house to hook up in helping to trace." Five minutes later, the COP and Mayor showed up minutes later in a separate vehicle. Thomas went and talked to them as the media filmed. Robert told Foster the lady called me on Veronica's cell phone. Foster asked what did they want? Robert looked at Foster face to face and said, "They only want me for them."

Robert looked around and then said, "We were wrong on the beach murders. There were two men involved, not one and remember, there were a couple of pizzas delivered, one for each person." Foster replied, "Yea, we thought it was either a big man who ate a lot, or he spread it over a day or two." Foster looked at Robert, asking, "Well, what are you going to do?" Robert looked down and shuffled his feet and looked up and commented, "Kill them with extreme prejudice."

Foster looked at Robert and informed him, "I can't condone that, but we will help you get them back one way or the other." Robert told Foster, "You are my friend, but I will do everything in my power to get my family back and my 10 pounds of flesh." He then walked to where his father-in-law talked to the Mayor and Police chief. When Robert walked up, everyone shook hands, and he informed them, "Gentleman, let's get in the Mayor's vehicle so nobody hears what I am going to say." Thomas, the Mayor, Chief of Police Gomez and Foster went and got in the Mayor's vehicle.

The Police Chief stated, "Go ahead, Robert. What do you want to say?" Robert looked at the men and informed them, "I was partially wrong a couple of years ago on the beach murders." The Mayor looked puzzled and asked, "What do you mean?" Robert explained, "There were two men involved with a mother." He then went into what was missed and how lucky they were not to have any more homicides.

Robert discussed his phone call with them, what they wanted, and how they must have planned this. He was very insistent; this was not just a thrown-together plan. The Mayor asked, "What do they want, Robert?" Robert told everyone in the car, "They want me for them." as he looked at his father-in-law. Robert added, "He will go along with the plan if we can't find them." The Police Chief announced, "We will flood every place to see if we can catch them." Robert remarked, "No." The PC asked, "Why?"

Robert wanted it to look normal. He mentioned, "They will kill them if they see police, and I have no doubt they might be watching." Robert scratched his chin, saying, "I doubt it, but I do not want to risk it because there are only two of them." The Mayor asked, "How do you know this?" Robert replied, "Witnesses only saw the big man and an older lady driver."

Robert added that If more were involved, they would have been involved in the kidnapping, and witnesses would have seen them. The Mayor responded and said that makes sense. So, what do we do? Thomas was quiet and said Robert, what do you want me to do? Robert got quiet for a moment and told the men in the car, "I want you three to go and tell the press the truth, but not about the swap, so do the usual talking points about justice and not the town crap and Thomas stand in the background with me but do not say anything until after I speak." Thomas agreed.

When it was time for Thomas to speak, he mentioned: how distraught he was, and he agreed with his son-in-law on how they would do whatever was required to get his daughter and grandchild back. Robert told Thomas, "Let's get home," after the conference was over. The Mayor looked at Robert and asked him, "What are you going to do?" Robert looked at Thomas and informed him, "We will swap me for them, and I will kill them," as Robert walked away. The Mayor and Police Chief looked at each other in shock. Thomas followed Robert when Foster approached them and notified them, "We found Veronica's cell phone in a parking lot, and It was still on."

A few minutes later, two large vehicles drove up, and Thomas saw eight men get out, and he acknowledged them. Thomas informed Robert, "Our escort is here." Robert turned and saw the men, then looked at Thomas and asked, "Whose Defense and offense of line did you get those guys from? Did you get it? Robert was informed, those men are former players I hired for my security company?" Robert remarked, "I have no doubt." Robert suggested to Foster, "Please show me the area where the cell phone was found." Foster replied, "Let's go." Thomas informed Robert, "I will be at the house, and are you sure you will be ok?" Robert told him, "I will be fine." Thomas looked at one of the bodyguards and told him, "Take one vehicle and follow them." Robert said, "Fine, let's go."

Foster and Robert went and checked out the area. Robert saw two detectives walk up and show Foster the cell phone in an evidence bag. Robert looked at it and advised them, "That's hers." Robert looked around and told Foster, "Please take me home. The FBI should be there."

While driving up to the house, two armed guards were at the entrance, and they waved them in, and Robert and Foster looked around and saw about 12 armed men walking around the compound. Foster declared, "Well, nobody is breaking into this place." Robert commented by saying, "No shit." Once they drove up, they parked by a bunch of FBI vehicles and a couple of other state vehicles. They walked inside and observed 12 FBI agents and a couple of the Governor's assistants there talking to Thomas.

Robert went and sat down in the backyard by himself, thinking. Thomas saw him go sit down by himself with his cell phone, which was hooked up to a tracing system the FBI was using. Robert got up, and when everyone was ready, he picked it up, and the lady yelled at Robert telling him, "I said no police." Robert told her, "Listen, lady, you and your son shot up two vehicles and people. What the hell do you think was going to happen," with a scoff. The lady asked, "Are there cops there?" In a sarcastic tone, Robert said, "Yes, that part is out of my hands. Now what do you want?" The lady laughed and told him, "I want you, and just to make it interesting, 10 million in cash with a mix of 5, 10s and 20s."

She stuttered for a second and said, "You have to midnight tonight and don't give me this crap about needing more time because I will kill your wife first. You know she is nothing to me," and hung up. The tracer picked up a location, and phone calls were made, and the police went to that location with a SWAT team.

Fifteen minutes later, she called back and told Robert, "You need to get in your truck at 12:01 am with the money in the back of your truck and head south on Highway One. Do you understand?" Robert replied, "Yes, I do." She further informed him, "I will call back at 12:01 am, and if the money is not with you, I will kill your pregnant wife first," and she hung up. Everyone was quiet. Thomas was pale, and he looked at Robert and asked, "Did you know?" Robert notified him, "No, I didn't."

Robert looked at Thomas and advised him, "Get the money now." Thomas called the bank he owned and ordered 10 million dollars in the way the kidnappers wanted. The FBI notified Mr. Jackson, "They can't condone it, but we understand the situation, and we will send men to help pick it up in an armored truck." Thomas called the manager and told him, "The FBI with an armored truck will pick it up, make it happen." Thomas notified the Manager, "I will be there in 30 minutes to sign the paperwork." The bank manager agreed, and they each hung up. Thomas's bodyguard was called and escorted to one of the vehicles waiting. There were three vehicles, all full of armed men, and they took off for the bank. Two FBI agents in their vehicle followed after the escalades.

Robert was extremely pissed, and he was walking in the yard being watched by FBI agents and others in the house, including Foster, who went up to him and told him, "Robert, you are my friend and former partner. I know what you are going to do, but just be careful to do something to risk their lives". Robert asked Foster, "What would you do?" Foster looked down and around and stated, "Probably what you would do." Robert remarked, "I thought so. When I go, give me distance and follow with drones. No vehicles close." He walked away and went and sat down on a bench and thought about what he was going to do and how. He thought about all the possibilities and scenarios that could come up.

Thomas came back four hours later with the money. It was loaded up in the back of the truck as ordered, and he walked in when Robert's cell phone went off. He was asked, "Are you ready,

Robert?" He responded, "Your call is early, and yea, where do I go?" She told him, "Get in your truck and head south on highway one." Robert demanded, "I want to talk to my wife or no deal." The lady said, "Hang on." Veronica was heard being dragged to the cell phone and saying, "Hello." Robert informed her, "I am coming when she replied, I love you. Our son is scared and is being brave like his father." The lady came back on and advised him, "I will call you while you are driving," and hung up.

Robert looked at the FBI agent and shook his head no, meaning he had no idea of the exact location, only the general. Two minutes later, FBI agent Fox came in with a dropped phone which they had called from earlier. Foster proclaimed, "They are using another one, so we need to find out where this one was purchased." An FBI Agent took it and said, "They will follow it up."

Robert walked upstairs and said nothing to anyone as he entered his room. He went to the closet and pulled a black bag from the top shelf. He took it to the bed and opened it. He changed belts and put on his sidearm and his vest. He knew they would make him take it off, but he wanted them close. Once done, he walked down the stairs and looked around the room. Agent Fox told him, "This is a tracer. Swallow it when she calls back so we know where you are at. This can last up to 72 hours." Fox saw two agents step in from outside and give Fox a thumbs up. Fox informed Robert, "We hooked up a mike in your truck so we can hear you in the vehicle." He then pulled out a pen and explained, "This pen also has a mic. Put it in your shirt pocket because it also has a GPS-locating device in it." Robert followed the instructions. He looked at Thomas, who was pale and had a scared look, so he walked up to him and told him, "I will do whatever I have to do to save them. I want you to know that no matter what happens." Thomas shook his head up and down and replied, "I know. Please save them." Robert shook his head. He understood and left and headed to highway one.

While driving on highway one, he was thinking about his family and everything that had happened over the last few years. He was mad, but he kept his cool, knowing what he does will help or hurt the ones he loved. Once he hit HWY One bridge to Key West, he received a phone call from her and was told, "Drive to Key Largo. There is a boat waiting for you, big enough for you and the cash." She informed him, "The boat is at the end of Buccaneer Drive on the water, and don't let the cash fall overboard." He asked, "Where to?" She stated, "Pelican Key," and she hung up. Robert announced, "I was told to go to Pelican Key Island on a boat." The agents listening called and had a chopper ready to head that way with armed coast guard divers who are trained to assault and rescue.

The agents and Detective Foster jumped in choppers that landed on the yard and took off for Pelican key island. As time went by, the chopper lights went out, and the team of specialized divers worked their way close to the island and waited. This team was highly trained and knew what they were doing. The nine men hid out on the reef and waited. They checked in every 15 minutes while the choppers landed at Key Largo airport and waited. One medic was on each chopper, waiting for the signal to head to the island.

Robert was driving, and as he drove through Key Largo, she called back and told him, "Pull off on Dove Road and drive to the end, and you will see a white and blue boat with a preset GPS. I am sure the captain on board will tell you our resolve." Robert asked, "Will the captain be coming also?" He was told, "Take the boat to Dove Key Island, and you better hurry. The storm is getting worse, and we wouldn't want you to sink," and she hung up. Robert announced, "Big change, it's Dove Island. I am turning onto Dove Road right now." Robert drove to the end, jumped out, and ran to the boat described. He jumped on board and saw the Captain dead in his seat. He dragged him off the boat and laid him on the pier. He ran to his truck and loaded up the boat with the money. He swallowed the tracer and checked his pen to activate it.

Robert headed to the island, and in a few minutes, he docked, and it was extremely dark, and he could feel it started raining slowly. Dove key was about 1000 feet in length and approximately 500 feet in width. He pulled the bags of cash off the boat and stacked them on the beach. Then he saw a fire start, and he headed towards it. He then saw two more fires start as it continued sprinkling. He pulled his gun, chambered around, and started walking towards the fires. He knew what they would do, but he wanted them to show all their cards before he made his final move.

When he got close, Robert was told, "Drop the weapon." He stated, "Not until I see my wife and son." The old lady laughed and told her son, "Bring them over." Her son dragged Veronica and the child, threw them on the ground, and sat them on their knees. The big man took their blindfolds off, and Robert saw the two people he loved more than anything scared, in tears and afraid. He asked, "Ok, lady, what do you want?" She stood between his son and wife and informed him, "I want your life there because you killed my son. Now I will kill one of them or you."

Robert asked her, "How did you get away, lady?" She explained, "When my son you chased ran, we went in the opposite direction, nice and simple." Robert asked, "So you sacrificed one of your sons?" She remarked, "He volunteered to save his family. Sound familiar, and we thought he would get away, but you wouldn't quit, and he got hit by that truck."

Foster was listening as they flew to pick up the divers and get to Dove Key Island as quickly as they could. He called Miami to ask if they were picking up what was being said. They informed him, "Yes, clear as day, and they sent a patrol to the dock and found the dead boat captain."

Robert told her, "Let them go. The money is off the boat and stacked on the beach, just waiting for you." The lady laughed and commented, "I guess the rescue people are not here, no choppers or police, just us." She looked at her son, who was smiling, when she suggested, "I guess they went to the wrong place." Robert replied, "It doesn't matter, I am here. Let them go," as he looked at his wife, who was watching. Robert was told, "So will you sacrifice your life for her and your son?" He looked at Veronica and his son, who was crying and scared, and stated, "I would die for them." The women stepped over and cut the ropes from Veronica and the child. She demanded him to "Drop the gun, or I will kill her," as she put the Glock against Veronica's head. Veronica looked at her child and told him, "Baby look at the ground. Whatever you hear, do not look up, baby. Look down."

The child cried and said, "Mommy," through his tears. Veronica said, "Baby look at the sand and close your eyes and do not open them." Her child crying, said, "Mommy, I am scared." Through her tears, Veronica says, "Baby, close your eyes. Please close your eyes." Then Robert said loudly, "Robert, listen to Mommy and close your eyes." His son looked at his dad and closed his eyes.

Veronica looked at Robert and told him, "I love you through her tears." Robert smiled and whispered, "I love you," as the rain turned into a drizzle. Robert looked at the old woman telling her, "Fine, don't hurt her," and tossed his gun to the ground. The woman told him, "Take off the vest you have on." Robert took off his shirt, laid it down with the pen facing up, took off his vest, and tossed it aside. He was told, "First, you have to deal with my son," he stepped up and knocked Robert to the ground. He was told, "If you fight back, I will blow her brains out." Robert got up, was hit again, punched in the ribs, and fell to the ground, spitting up blood. Little Robert opened his eyes and watched his dad get beat up by the big man.

The child ran to help his dad, and the big man, grabbed him and threw him five feet away. Veronica yelled, "No, don't hurt my baby." Robert was grabbed and thrown to the ground, still not fighting back, trying to get closer to Veronica. Veronica ran to her child and covered his face so he could not see when the old lady's son struck her. A moment later, Robert was struck in the face again, and he fell by his wife, and he slipped her a small knife he had palmed from his vest, and she felt it and palmed it how Robert taught her in self-defense in the backyard.

The woman grabbed Veronica's hair and said, "No-no-no," and she was pulled away from Robert, who shook his head no. The big man grabbed him by his hair and knocked him to the ground again. When Robert pulled his knife out and stabbed the man in the throat as blood poured out onto Robert. He kept stabbing him in the throat repeatedly, and then Robert stood up and kicked him in the stomach after the old women's son fell to the ground. The man's mother screamed, pointed her gun at Robert, shot him in his left side, piercing his left lower rib cage, and fell to the ground. Veronica screamed in anger, then jumped up and stabbed the old woman twice, and she fell to the ground in pain as she was bleeding out.

Robert crawled to his gun a few feet away and grabbed it, and turned as the old bitch suddenly sat up to shoot Veronica when. Robert squeezed the trigger and sent three rounds into her chest. As she fell back, words dead. Veronica turned as she ran to her child.

Veronica and her child ran to Robert as he lay there, looking at them. He told them, "Get my shirt." Once it was brought to Robert, he grabbed the pen and handed it to Veronica, who was told, "They can hear you. Tell them where we are and need help." She grabbed the pen and informed them, "Robert has been shot, and we need help." Veronica pressed the shirt down on the bullet wound. He told her, "Help will be here soon enough," as his eyes closed. Veronica yelled, "Robert, keep your eyes open, baby, don't close them. Please don't close them, and we need you."

Robert suddenly saw the big man standing wobbling towards him and his family when Veronica grabbed Robert's gun and stood up and shot him, squeezing the trigger four times until he fell to the ground dead. She turned to Robert and her son and began pressing the shirt against Robert's wound again. Their son asked, "Mommy is daddy going to be ok?" She told him, "Yes," as she kissed her husband. When she saw the choppers coming as Robert closed his eyes, unconscious, Veronica yelled, "Stay with me, please stay with me," with tears flowing.

Chapter 38

Family

Once the choppers arrived, the medics responded and initiated medical treatment on Robert. When they were done hooking fluid and blood IVs, they put him on a stretcher, loaded him up with Veronica and their child, and headed to Miami Hospital. Robert flatlined on the chopper, but they were able to revive him. The FBI arrived on the island with three other choppers to retrieve the money and process the crime scene.

They landed on the rooftop of Miami General, and Robert was taken to the emergency surgery department. Foster escorted Veronica and her child to a treatment room, and not long after, Thomas arrived with a bunch of bodyguards. Robert Jr. ran to his grandpa, and Thomas lifted him and held him tight. He asked Veronica if she ok and he grabbed her and held her. She held on to him and started crying.

Thomas informed her, "I am so sorry this will never happen again," when Veronica told him, "Robert saved us." Thomas asked Foster, "Where is Robert?" Foster looked down and said, "He is in emergency surgery. He is in very bad shape. Robert took a beating and getting shot didn't help". Veronica was informed by the doctors her husband was still in surgery and being worked on. Thomas looked at the doctor and nurse and told them his daughter was pregnant and to take care of her and his grandchild. The doctor said, "he will." Thomas looked at Veronica and remarked, "I will go with him."

She put her hands to her son's face and said, "Baby grandpa is going with you to be checked, ok?" The child smiled for the first time since the ordeal began and said, "Grandpa will take care of me as daddy does," and they left the room. Four bodyguards stayed outside while Veronica was being checked to see if the three-week child in her body was ok. Foster had two more officers stand outside with the bodyguards as the PC and Mayor came down the corridor. Foster told them what had happened and how serious Robert was. One police officer came around the corner and notified them, "The press is here and downstairs."

Foster looked around and back at the officers, told them, "Keep them downstairs," and went back to talking to the PC and Mayor. He was informed, "Robert is in bad shape and being worked on." The Mayor went and found Thomas with his grandson, and it was not hard to find him. There were Six big bodyguards outside the room. The Mayor knocked on the door and heard, "Come in." He stepped in and saw Thomas Jackson sitting with his grandson while a doctor and nurse examined the child.

Thomas stood up and shook hands with the Mayor as the Mayor asked, "How is the child?" Robert Jr. looked up and smiled at his grandpa, and Thomas asked him, "How are you doing, kiddo?" The child smiled and said, "I am doing good," then he wanted to know about his daddy and mentioned how his daddy fought the bad man. Thomas looked down and remarked, "We pray he will be ok. In fact, let's go see your mommy." The doctor stated, "Your grandchild is a little dehydrated. Besides that, he is fine physically, if you know what I mean."

Thomas knew his grandson would need psychological help for a long time due to the traumatic situation he was involved with and what he saw. He would make sure it happened. They then headed back to Veronica's room to see how she was doing.

The doctors were done, and she was allowed to be released. She had bumps and bruises and was dehydrated, but she could be released despite those injuries. Veronica said, "Dad, I want to go to the waiting room." Thomas helped his daughter up, and he lifted up his grandson, and they went to the waiting room and waited for the results of the surgery.

A couple of hours later, more police who knew Robert and his family arrived. Thomas sent his Jet to pick them up and bring them down when Robert left the Mansion. Robert didn't know he did that. His parents arrived, ran to Veronica and the child, and hugged and kissed them. Veronica informed them, "Robert saved us, but he was beaten up badly and shot." Robert's mom began crying, and his dad went quiet.

Thomas stepped over and shook hands with Robert's parents when the surgeon came out. He stepped up to Veronica and told her, "We almost lost him, but he fought back. Your husband had a strong will to survive." The doctor shook his head and remarked, "Something in him would not quit." Veronica, through her tears, asked, "Can she see him?" The doctor said, "Yes, you and your son only."

The doctor showed them the way to the room he was in. Thomas asked a nurse to get the hospital administrator when she told him, "The administrator is not here this late." Thomas requested, "Could you please get the shift supervisor, ma'am?" The nurse replied, "Sure." About 10 minutes later, the shift supervisor came over to Thomas and introduced herself. He asked, "Could you please call the hospital administrator and give her this message please as soon as possible." The shift supervisor informed him, "We don't do that, sir." Thomas advised her, "Look at the paper. I believe you will want to." She looked at it and responded back, "Sorry, I didn't know. I will call her immediately."

Five minutes later, Thomas's cell phone went off, and he answered it. The hospital administrator said, "Yes, Mr. Jackson, what can I do for you?" He explained, "His son-in-law is in recovery, and I want a single room for him and my Doctor full access to follow up on what is being done." The Hospital administrator informed him, "I will make it happen." Thomas hung up. He was the main donor to the hospital for years, and now he is collecting.

When Veronica and her son arrived in the recovery room, she saw Robert in an induced coma. She grabbed his hand, leaned over, and whispered, "I love you, and I will always be there for you." The doctor and nurse came in and informed her, "We will be moving him to his room in a couple of hours as long as there are no effects from the surgery."

She sat in a chair and held her son, who asked, "Will daddy be ok?" She looked at him and said, "Yes, he will be, but he is going to need your help to get better." Little Robert smiled, saying, "I will help Daddy." She kissed him and announced, "Soon, baby, you will have a brother or sister." Her son asked, "When?" Veronica replied, "In about eight months," as they watched Robert sleep. A couple of hours later, they moved Robert to a private room, and Veronica and Robert Jr., with Thomas and bodyguards, were following. They watched the medical staff do their jobs when they entered the room. Veronica and her son sat down and watched Robert sleep after the medical staff left.

After a few minutes, Thomas arrived and informed Veronica, "My doctor will be checking and ensuring Robert is treated properly." She told her dad, "Thanks." Veronica looked at her dad, stood up, and hugged him, saying, "Dad, I truly love him, and you are going to have another grandchild." Thomas replied, "I know I heard over the mike." He saw his grandson sleeping on the chair and told her, "Honey, let's go home to get needed sleep and you two some good food and rest."

Veronica looked at her sleeping son, shook her head and stated, "No," and notified him, "I am not leaving Robert." Thomas told her, "He is going to recover, and he is sleeping, and I told the doctor they will be keeping him in an induced coma until tomorrow." Veronica looked at her dad and replied, "Ok," she got up, walked over to Robert, kissed his forehead, and whispered, "I love you." She wiped her tears and told her son, "Come here and kiss your daddy." Robert Jr. walked over, and Veronica lifted him up to kiss his dad. Then they left as Two bodyguards stayed at the door outside.

While heading home, Thomas looked at his daughter, who looked run down and exhausted. He felt lucky they were alive and what Robert did. He made up his mind, but he will wait until Robert gets better. He watched his grandson sleep when Veronica leaned on her dad and told him, "I love you, Dad, and I am so sorry this happened." Thomas said, "It's not your fault. I'm just thank full Robert got you two back alive."

Before they made it home, Thomas looked at Veronica and declared, "I want to tell you something, this will never happen again. I swear I will do everything I can". She smiled and closed her eyes. Thomas meant what he said. Everyone in the future would notice the change in his being overly protective of his family, but he would tell those who questioned him that he did not care. It was his family who went through it, not theirs.

EPILOGUE

Two years later, Thomas is at home with his grandkids playing in the backyard, where he loves spending time with his grandson and granddaughter. Bodyguards are always on the premises to protect his family 24 hours daily. He knew where Veronica and the kids went, and the six bodyguards were always with them. One technical team used drones to follow them when they left the house, and the vehicles had cameras and bugs that always traced them. Without knowing, the children had a tracker on their shoes or clothes.

Thomas handed over full control of the business to his daughter, who appointed Robert as President. Robert's recovery was quick, and after the second child was born, Veronica told her dad she planned to put Robert as the President, which she had planned on doing years earlier. Thomas laughed and asked, "Did Robert know?" She responded back and stated, "No, and she will never tell him." She looked at her dad and said, "Some men, you have to let them make the decision without the women telling him it's what he really wants to do."

Her plan allowed her to work on her charity work with Robert and spend time with the kids. She owned it, and Robert ran it once Thomas helped him in the beginning. Once Thomas was satisfied with Robert running it, he would always be an advisor when needed. Robert and Veronica were the unofficial Southern Florida royalty by the press. They were involved in many charities, businesses, and politics. The business and political communities respected them.

One early afternoon, Veronica was walking towards her husband's office, and the staff said, "Good afternoon, ma'am." She stopped and looked on the wall at the pictures of her and her family with the title The Royalty of Miami. She smiled and went to Robert's office. The staff watched her, and they knew her husband ran the business, but the business was all hers. They were well aware of the love between them and what they had gone through in the past. Veronica walked into Robert's office, looked back at the chief secretary, and stated, "My husband and I will be in conference all afternoon, so please cancel his schedule." The secretary replied, "Yes, ma'am." When she walked into Robert's office, she saw Robert putting on some golf balls, talking with Foster and Gomez.

Robert hired his friends because he needed people he could trust and relate to on the job. Foster was chief security over all areas of the business, and Gomez was over business and purchasing. Foster and Gomez were taking notes as Veronica walked in. Robert looked up after telling Foster to ensure the new security system at the house was done by the end of the month. Robert looked at Veronica and said, "Hey honey," as he walked over to her, and they kissed.

Veronica looked at Foster and Gomez and asked, "How were they doing and if their families are happy?" She was told just to find them by both men. They were offered huge salary increases and benefits to leave the police department. Gomez told her, "We have all the items to add to the workers' elementary school on the first floor, and the construction will be done before July 30th." Veronica smiled and said, "Outstanding." She commented, "Gentlemen, Robert and I have some things to discuss, and we will be in conference all afternoon." Foster and Gomez got up and smiled and told her, "Nice seeing you again, Veronica." They walked out and shut the door.

Robert looked at Veronica and remarked, "What's going on, honey?" She asked him, "Do you miss being a Detective?" Robert grinned and informed her, "No, I enjoy my job, and I get to sleep with the boss." She smiled, saying, "I am glad," as she slowly walked over to the door and locked it. She continued to smile, turned around, looked at Robert, and told him, "I want another child," and she unbuttoned her dress as it fell to the floor, standing there naked with her hands on her hips.

Robert smiled, looking her up and down while dropping his putter on the floor and stated, "Sounds good to me, honey." She walked up to him and kissed him passionately, and whispered in his ear, "I think you need to use your driver for this job." He smiled and remarked, "It's good to be the king." Veronica bit his ear and whispered in a sexy tone, "And the queen," as he lifted her and carried her to the couch. Robert asked, "Boy or girl?" She said, "We have one of each so far. Let's just see what happens," as they kissed. Veronica looked at Robert as he held her and asked, "Are you happy?" He smiled and told her, "I have never been happier." She looked at Robert and replied, "Good," as they kissed passionately.

Glossary

Before noon- A.M

Chief of Police—COP

Chief of Detectives- COD

Federal Bureau of Investigations-FBI

Identification- I.D

Past noon- PM

United States- U.S

Very important person-VIP

Son of a bitch-SOB

911-Emergency number